The Hummingbird War

A Divine Comedy: Volume II

Also by Michael Simms

Poetry Collections

Jubal Rising
Strange Meadowlark
Nightjar
American Ash
Black Stone
The Happiness of Animals
The Fire-eater
Migration
Notes on Continuing Light

Novels

Bicycles of the Gods: A Divine Comedy
The Talon Trilogy:
The Green Mage, the First Chronicle
Windkeep, the Second Chronicle
The Blessed Isle, the Third Chronicle

Nonfiction

Longman Dictionary of Poetic Terms (with Jack Myers)
Longman Dictionary and Handbook of Poetry, (with Jack Myers)

Anthologies Edited

The Autumn House Anthology of Contemporary American Poetry
O. Henry's Texas Stories

The Hummingbird War

A Divine Comedy
Volume II

Michael Simms

Lake Dallas, Texas

FIRST EDITION

The characters and institutions in this novel are fictional and any resemblance to actual humans or institutions is entirely coincidental.

Requests for permission to reprint material from this work should be sent to:

Permissions
Madville Publishing
P.O. Box 358
Lake Dallas, TX 75065

Author Photograph: Eva-Marie Simms
Cover Design: Jacqui Davis
Cover Art: *The Great Red Dragon and the Woman Clothed with the Sun*, William Blake, 1810.

ISBN: 978-1-963695-45-8 paperback, 978-1-963695-46-5 ebook
Library of Congress Control Number: 2025947296

For Eva

Is there another world for this frail dust
To warm with life and be itself again?
Something about me daily speaks there must,
And why should instinct nourish hopes in vain?

—John Clare

Prologue: The White Tigress

Gaia stretched her long feline body and settled comfortably on the meadow grass. Maria noted the seven gray she-wolves who always attended Gaia, stationing themselves as sentries in a semi-circle behind her in the shadows at the edge of the forest. Against the blue and white sky, a red-tailed hawk perched in the top of a black walnut tree, alert.

"What did the council decide?" Maria asked her mother.

"After some debate about the efficacy of killing humans and demons, your petition for a waiver to kill them was granted. It's an open license to be used at your discretion."

"Debate?" Maria asked.

"Lilith the Disobedient One was in favor of killing as many men as possible, but she had some hesitancy about killing demons, not wanting to start a war with The Evil Presence."

Maria tried not to roll her eyes. "Lilith is always in favor of killing men, but when the time comes, she hesitates out of fear. I think she was traumatized by her divorce. Adam treated her so horribly."

"Lilith is an important voice for feminine anger," the White Tigress pointed out. "Without her, we'd just sink into blobs of self-pity blubbering into cartons of rocky road ice-cream."

"I suppose so, Mother," Maria conceded, laughing. "But Lilith's anger at men is hard to take."

"Yes, it is." The Tigress looked at her daughter, this beautiful Mexican woman who so loved humankind. "How is José?"

"He's great. He's started designing masks for the Day of

the Dead celebration this fall, and he's thinking of buying a new truck."

"You've got a good one. Hold onto him."

Maria wanted to know more about the Council's decision. "Was Singing Waters there?"

"Oh, yes, she spoke beautifully about the need to protect the wild places of the earth, but then abstained from voting. All she cares about is her music, and she hates politics."

"And Wind-in-the-Trees?"

"Wind was in favor of granting your waiver. She said she trusted your judgement."

Maria smiled at the praise. "And how did Where-Water-Meets-Land vote?"

"She voted in favor of the waiver. She's very angry at the way that humans are treating her. Dumping thousands of tons of garbage in the sea every day. What an insult to all of us."

"And what about the Spirit of Elegance? The Heron Queen? The Architect of Mitochondria? The Elderberry Witch? How did they vote?"

"Yes, yes, yes, and yes. Everyone is on board. The goddesses are willing to give you the freedom you request, but you have to understand that the goddesses are also very irritated with you. They are impatient for the Kali Yuga. They worry that you are procrastinating because of your love for humans. To the goddesses, all this dispensing of justice and saving women from the abuse of men seems trivial compared to what is truly needed."

"Mother, you and the council know that I am not responsible for starting the Kali Yuga."

"Don't be coy, Daughter. We know that Shiva is holding back because Jesse has asked him to. He is loyal to Jesse, and Jesse is loyal to you. You need to get out of the way, and let Shiva do what needs to be done."

"I understand, Mother. Are you irritated with me as well?"

"Never. I know that everything you do, even what may look

like mistakes, is motivated by your love for the silly hairless apes. Your error lies in loving too much."

The Tigress and her daughter sat in silence for a few moments, quietly enjoying their time together. The ancient mother asked about her grandson Jesse, and Maria said that the previous year, he had despoiled Hell and released the tormented souls to begin their redemption.

"I never saw the point of Hell," the tigress confessed. "I don't know what your first husband was thinking when he invented it. We were doing just fine with re-incarnation. Recycle the spiritual energy, I say. Don't trap it in one identity." The goddess shook her head in exasperation, smoothed her whiskers with a large paw, and looked at her daughter. "Are you in touch with Shiva and Kali?"

Maria nodded. "Shiva, who is calling himself Xavi now, is as you know, close friends with Jesse, so I talk to him often."

"Are he and his girlfriend ready to begin the Kali Yuga?"

"They're ready, but as you said, Jesse has convinced Xavi to wait. Jesse wants to save more souls before the carnage begins."

"Maria, again I have to emphasize that I think it's a mistake to wait. It is time for this fourth epoch to end, so the new one can begin. Humans are destroying creation. Can you imagine? We've given them a beautiful world and all they've done is to destroy it with their greed and selfishness."

"The time is coming soon, Mother. We now have a Chosen One."

"He's descended into the world?"

"Soon. He's the son of a poet and a wise woman."

"That sounds promising. In what community will he be raised?"

"The Yaqui."

"Good choice. The Yaqui have stayed close to the Old Ways." She thought for a moment, looking into the alternate paths of the future. Her eyes narrowed. "You must protect the Chosen One from the Evil Presence at all costs," the White Tiger said emphatically.

As her daughter rose to leave, the White Tigress said, "Remember, you have a waiver to kill humans and demons, but not gods. We've lost too many gods already. When I was a kitten, there were over 400 gods, now there are less than 20."

Maria nodded, said goodbye to her mother, turned and followed the worn path down the mountain to a narrow dirt road, where six old women and one young woman with a prosthetic hand sat on their Harleys waiting for her. "We have the waiver, Sisters," Maria said, answering their unspoken question. "Let's ride. We have women to save."

The Lakota girl woke on the ground next to a large man snoring loudly, her whole body in fierce pain from the rapes of the night before. The men had penetrated every orifice of her body. There were four of them, two white, one black and one brown, perhaps a Lakota, but she didn't know or care who they were. She just wanted to go home. Two days before they'd grabbed her and thrown her in a van as she walked down the road to her aunt's house. They'd driven for hours, and now she had no idea where she was, but she knew the only reason they'd taken her was that she was a young woman alone. They didn't know her name, nor did they care. She had no doubt that when they tired of raping her, they would kill her and leave her in the desert to be consumed by vultures. Hundreds of young women had disappeared from the reservation, and now she would be one more.

Dawn was gradually coming to the desert, the long shadows of the cacti spreading their fingers over the sand. She'd never seen a cactus until the day before when the men had forced her from the van after driving for hours and made her lie down on a blanket. She'd thought about running away, but she didn't know where they were, and she thought the men would easily catch her and punish her, so now she lay very still, not wanting to wake the men and start the abuse again. She heard motorcycles on the highway a few hundred yards away. Then silence.

Turning her head toward the east, she saw what she thought was a vision: eight women dressed in black walking toward her. The sun shone from behind them, creating an aura around their heads. The women made no sound as they moved across the sand. As they approached, the tall woman in the middle, who looked Mexican and seemed to be their leader, put her finger to her lips, signaling her to stay silent. Each of the women pulled out a pistol with a silencer and quietly walked toward the sleeping men. At a signal from the tall one, each woman fired a shot into the head of a sleeping man. A sound like ripe melons falling on a hard floor filled the desert air.

"Kimimela," the Mexican woman said, using her spirit name which means Butterfly, a name known only to the girl herself. "My name is Maria, and this is Sister Delphina. Delphina is a medical doctor. May she take a look at your injuries?"

The girl nodded her head. "Who are you? Are you gods?"

"We are the Sisters of the Piston. The grandmothers of your tribe asked for our help. We're taking you home."

Chapter 1

It happened that Emperor Huitzilopochtli had taken up residence in a meadow on the edge of a housing development in Conroe, Texas, an ideal spot for nesting. Nearby, many of the homeowners had flowering bushes in their yards, and a few had put out feeders. There was a commercial rose farm not far away, and the meadow next to the oak tree where he was building a new nest had a wide variety of flowering weeds.

"I don't know what the big deal is about hummingbirds," Xavi was saying to Jesse as they pulled into the parking lot next to the meadow. "I mean how badass can they be? Huitzilopochtli is the size of my little finger. I could flick him off my sleeve like a dead leaf."

"I wouldn't suggest doing that," Jesse said, shaking his head. "Male hummers have been known to chase eagles out of their nests. An eagle has a wingspan of seven or eight feet while a hummer weighs less than a nickel. Hummers can fly 60 miles per hour. They can hover, fly backwards, even fly upside down. It's easier to swat a fly than a hummer. They use their beaks like daggers to go for the eyes or the throat. Hummingbirds are the fiercest warriors on the planet."

"And Huitzilopochtli?" Xavi asked, beginning to see what Jesse was getting at.

"Huitzilopochtli is the god of the hummingbirds." Jesse looked at this friend. "Xavi, haven't you ever wondered why there aren't more gods? There used to be many gods, and now there are less than 20. Don't you wonder what happened to all the gods?"

"I just figured that they got tired of living. Immortality is a bitch. I thought they just offed themselves, you know, evaporated and came down as rain or something."

"Well, perhaps some of them did," Jesse said, looking off into the distant red horizon. He'd always liked the Texas sky. "But most of the gods were killed by Huitzilopochtli."

"Really? What happened?"

"The story is that Coatlicue once picked up a bundle of hummingbird feathers that had fallen from the sky. Putting them inside her dress for warmth, she became pregnant. This angered Coatlicue's other 400 children, so they conspired to kill their mother—but no sooner was the plot formed, than a fully grown, heavily armed, and mad as hell Huitzilopochtli, sprang from her womb and started cutting off heads. This, of course, created job openings, so he became the god of the sun and of war."

"And Coatlicue is one of the names of…"

"That's right," Jesse said, "My mother."

"Huitzilopochtli is your brother?"

"My half-brother," Jesse said. "But we've never been close."

"When did all this happen?"

"I'm not sure. Thousands of years ago. Before I was born."

"So how come I never heard about it?"

"It's kind of a family secret. Would you want everyone to know that your half-brother killed 400 of your siblings?"

"Yeah, I get it. Every family has a few skeletons in the closet. I could tell you stories about my family…" Xavi's voice trailed off. "But you feel safe around him, right? I mean he is family."

Jesse laughed ruefully, "No one is safe around Huitzi. He's killed more gods than you and I have ever known."

"And you brought me along as your bodyguard?"

"Let's hope it doesn't come to that. Ah, there's the giant oak. Huitzi's nest should be about forty feet in the air."

As Jesse and Xavi approached the tree, they heard a slight humming directly behind them. They turned to see a ruby-throated hummingbird a dozen feet away, hovering in the air. The bright afternoon light caused the red, blue, and green colors to radiate. Jesse had always liked the fact that the colors of hummingbird feathers are not the result of pigment, but of refracted light, so as the bird rose to a height of about eight feet, the colors altered, creating an aura around the vibrating wings. Surely, Jesse thought, these small birds are among the most beautiful of all living things.

"Tell me one reason why I should not kill the two of you where you stand," said a huge booming voice which Jesse knew was not a physical voice, but one which occupied the celestial plane.

"Older brother," Jesse said, bowing his head. "We have come on a mission to ask for your help."

The hummingbird turned slightly toward Xavi. "You are the one known as Shiva Destroyer of Worlds?"

"I am," Xavi said. Jesse could see that Xavi had subtly lowered his body into a crouch, ready to spring at the hummingbird at any moment.

"I have destroyed many gods and many creatures, but I have yet to destroy an entire world," the deep voice boomed. Jesse detected a slightly sardonic tone, implying but not quite saying that Xavi's reputation for violence was exaggerated.

Xavi didn't respond, but continued facing the hummingbird in a ready position, his feet planted parallel on the ground, his knees slightly bent, his hands wide and flat at his side. Jesse knew that at any moment, Xavi could raise a hand, palm forward, and a wave of energy would emanate in front of him. Jesse had seen the power of the open palm of Shiva, and he wanted to avoid a conflict between these two gods if possible.

"Hey guys, loosen up," Jesse said, sounding more relaxed than he felt. "Xavi and I are here to ask a favor from you, Huitzi. If you can't do it, we're cool with that, but just let us explain why we're here, okay?"

The hummingbird waited a full minute before answering.

Jesse thought the long pause was a purposeful ploy to make his visitors nervous. Then the tiny god of war said, "Very well, let us move to the shade of my oak tree where we can talk."

Once Jesse and Xavi had settled on the grass beneath the oak, a yellow gourd appeared on the ground in front of them. "Spring water sweetened with nectar," Huitzi said, sounding less portentous than before. "Please drink. It is believed among my kind that nectar encourages truth and wisdom."

Jesse lifted the gourd and took a long draught and passed it to Xavi who hesitated a moment, then took a small sip. Jesse was aware that in Xavi's line of work, one had to be careful with the truth. War, after all, depends on deceit.

The hummingbird had settled on a branch above them. It was quite clear he wanted the strategic advantage in case the negotiations didn't go well. And indeed, Jesse thought, this is a negotiation. We're trying to recruit the world's greatest warrior to join us.

Jesse began by saying that a huge battle of the gods is coming. He and his friends and followers needed allies. Since hummingbirds are known as the greatest warriors on Earth, Jesse was here to ask his older brother Huitzi to join them. At this point, Jesse fell silent to give Huitzi a chance to think about the request, allowing Jesse a chance to think about this place a hundred miles north of Houston. Shortly after Easter, male Ruby-throated hummers migrate to the woods north from Mexico and Central America. The males stake out territory and defend it from the other males. Those who are weaker are killed or forced to move further north to stake out other territories. The females and youngsters follow once the boundaries are firm. Here in Texas where the fiercest hummingbirds established their territories, Jesse hoped to recruit allies to stand beside him in the coming war. The first step was winning his half-brother's confidence.

However, Jesse was also aware that hummingbirds are notoriously independent. Unlike, say, wolves or dolphins which have well-established social hierarchies, each hummer is a nation unto himself. He defends not only his territory, but also his mate and offspring. Jesse knew that ounce for ounce hummers are the fiercest fighters in the universe. Even demons are afraid of them. And Huitzilopochtli is the only god that hummingbirds recognize. They would follow him anywhere.

"Tell me about this war that's coming," Huitzi said. "The other gods hate me, so no one tells me anything."

"Okay, you may have been aware that the Second Coming was scheduled for last year?"

"No, I didn't know. As I said, no one tells me anything," Huitzi said, a hint of anger in his voice.

"Well, it was scheduled, so Xavi and I came to earth to start the fires to consume the cities, but we had a change of heart." Jesse glanced at his friend beside him, grateful he was staying silent. Xavi had been in favor of starting the Apocalypse, but out of friendship had gone along with Jesse's revised plan of giving the humans a chance to reform.

"What did the Old Man think of your changing the timetable?" asked Huitzi, amused. He and the Old Man who was not his natural father, had never gotten along.

"He didn't like it, of course, so we had words. But the larger issue is that because the Apocalypse didn't happen on schedule, the temporal plane was torn, allowing my uncle, Lucifer, to try to take over the world."

"So, you and your angels fought Lucifer and his demons for control of the world?"

"That's right. You didn't hear about any of this?" It seemed strange to him that Huitzi was so out of touch that he wouldn't be aware of the most recent war between Heaven and Hell.

"Well, I heard rumors from some of my subjects in the west, but I don't pay a lot of attention to what the other gods do. They leave me alone and I leave them alone." Huitzi cocked his small head and looked at his half-brother. "I'm wondering though why you would want to save the humans, or, for that matter, why you would want to destroy them? They're doing a pretty good job of destroying themselves. I'm looking forward to a world without humans."

"If it were that simple, I would agree with you, brother. But Lucifer is playing havoc with human society. If we let him have his way, then the forests will be cut down and the wetlands will be filled in and paved over, and many more species will be lost before humans wipe themselves out. I want to work with the best of the humans to save the world." Jesse looked into the deep black eyes of Huitzi who was hovering in front of him now, and said, "My dear brother, your isolationist strategy has worked brilliantly for a long time, but in this coming war, the Hummingbird Nation will not be able to remain neutral."

"And why is that?" Huitzi asked.

"Because this region, the northern range of your beautiful species, is going to be the center of the war."

Chapter 2

Stefan hadn't slept in weeks. It was just too damn hot. He was trying to sleep between Christina, who was, in her own words, "the size of a pregnant orca," and Dharma who had perfected the art of placing all four paws on Stefan's back and gently pushing until she was pressed against Christina's warm body. The air conditioner in the window was blasting out warm air, no doubt due to its motor over-heating. Stefan found himself missing the small cave under the bridge where he and Dharma used to live. It was dirty and primitive, but at least it had been cool.

He climbed over Dharma, tiptoed through the dark apartment to the kitchen, and turned on the radio, keeping the volume low. Stefan was worried. On any given day, it seemed like half of California was on fire, and here in southern California, they were especially vulnerable. He hoped to hear the news, but it was too early for the first reports of the day. He had a habit of putting a pitcher of filtered water in the refrigerator before he went to bed, and as he poured himself a tall glass of the cool water, he heard Dharma come padding across the linoleum. He poured cool water into her bowl, and she lapped it up greedily. Stefan loved this kelpie. She had been his only friend and companion during the three years he was homeless, and they'd helped each other to survive. And now, making a home in what had been Christina's apartment, life was comfortable. He loved his wife and was excited—and scared—about becoming a father. He worried about his son someday finding out that his father was a convicted felon and had been homeless, but perhaps Stefan could sustain this normal life long enough that his past would no longer matter. He had a job working for a non-profit in Watts, and Christina was a therapist at the Veteran's Hospital nearby, so they had healthcare. They were solid citizens, a fact he marveled at every day.

Stefan sat on the couch, sipping his water, Dharma comfortably beside him. He stroked her ears and thought about the previous year when the three of them participated in the skirmish on the Otay Bridge in Arizona. Thirty thousand migrants from Central America who had been camped out at the US-Mexico border had broken through the fence and marched northward. At the same time, a group of North Americans, led by civil rights activists, had peacefully but stubbornly confronted State Troopers backed by right-wing anti-immigrant groups who had tried to stop the migrants at the bridge. Stefan, Christina, and others had been beaten with truncheons, but the migrants managed to push through and enter the country where they scattered and found refuge with families and supporters. Stefan had suffered a broken arm and a concussion, but he'd recovered. He was proud of the part he played in that march, and he believed it may have been the first useful thing he'd done in his life. Now, working for the Pearl Box in Watts, he'd found a method for continuing to be useful to others. He stroked Dharma's ear. She had also played an important part in the skirmish on the bridge by joining a pack of coydogs who attacked the right-wing groups from behind. Without the help of the canines, the activists on the front line like Stefan and Christina, would have been beaten to death by the racists.

As the light from the window began to grow in the living room, he realized that Christina would be awake soon. He went into the kitchen and heated up water for coffee and laid out the box of oatmeal and the bananas and oranges they usually ate for breakfast. He ground coffee beans and put them into a filter before pouring the hot water and watching dark liquid drip into the pot.

Christina came out of the bedroom, her nightgown soaking wet from sweat. Stefan felt so sorry for her. The heat was wearing him down. He couldn't imagine what it was doing to her at the end of her pregnancy.

"I smell coffee," she said, still half asleep.

Stefan poured the coffee, doled out a small amount of cream and sugar, and handed the steaming cup to her.

"You want me to run you a cool bath?" Stefan asked.

When she nodded, he went into the bathroom and started filling the tub. Then he fed Dharma, made oatmeal, and set the table. After about ten minutes in the cool water, Christina seemed to be feeling better. She dried herself with a towel, put on her bathrobe, and the two of them sat at the kitchen table and ate breakfast. "I'm calling in sick today," she said after a few bites of her cereal. Stefan nodded his head and touched her arm in what he hoped showed his agreement with her decision.

Jesse and Xavi were wandering around the parking lot looking for their car.

"I thought it was right here," Xavi said, pointing at the second row beyond the meadow where they'd left Huitzi to consider their request to join them in the war. "This parking lot was empty when we got here at daybreak. Where did all these cars come from?"

"I guess people showed up for work at those buildings over there." Jesse scanned the second row, then the third row, then the fourth. "I've forgotten what our car looks like."

"It was blue. No, it was green," Xavi answered. "And it was named after an animal."

"A blue or green automobile named after an animal," Jesse muttered helplessly. There were more than a thousand cars in this parking lot.

"A green Cougar?" Xavi walked down the row of cars which were virtually identical. "A blue Kestrel? A Beetle, a Mustang, a Viper?" Xavi felt rage starting to boil inside him. "Why were we issued a car this time, anyway? Those bicycles with the retrieval app were cool last time. It would be nice if we could whistle and make the car come to us like that. Why can't we have a retrieval app this time?"

"I don't know," Jesse answered. "I guess the shop steward thought a self-driving car would be too dangerous. Wait a minute, this is it!" Jesse nodded toward a sleek blue car, remembering how a few hours before, the shop steward had handed Xavi the keys and told them, obviously proud of his creation, that it was a 1960 Shelby Cobra. Xavi who loved motorcycles, knew nothing about race cars and was unimpressed.

"It's an exact replica of the famous machine manufactured by the British company AC Cars. It was designed by the racing legend Carroll Shelby," the shop steward had said, amazed at the two gods' indifference to this mechanical work of art. "It has a Ford V-8 engine, and at the time was preferred by many professional drivers to the Corvette."

Xavi had started the engine, revved it up, exited the garage, made a few quick turns, and drove down the long ramp to earth, hitting I-45 north of Houston going 140 mph .

Jesse had seen the excitement in his friend's eyes.

And now, Xavi was again behind the wheel of the Cobra, and they were in the far-left lane heading for Houston with traffic parting before them like a mechanized sea.

"Do you think Huitzi will join us?" Xavi asked.

"I don't know. He's hard to read. At least, he didn't try to kill us."

"Yeah, that was a plus," Xavi said, sardonically. "You know I could have taken him, right?"

Jesse looked out the window at the Houston suburbs flashing by.

"All I would have had to do," Xavi asserted. "Was to hold up the palm of my hand, and the force would have knocked him backwards like a wasp caught in a hurricane."

Jesse said nothing. He didn't like the way that Xavi saw Huitzi as a competitor, not as an ally. He was sure that Huitzi had sensed Xavi's hostility. Jesse wondered if he should keep the two gods apart. A fight between them would be catastrophic for their cause, and it might get Xavi killed.

"I'm really starting to like driving this baby," Xavi said, changing the subject and pressing the accelerator. "I wonder how fast it will go?"

Jesse could feel the car speeding up, the cars ahead of them moved out of their way.

"Slow down, Xavi," Jesse said urgently. "I don't want to get pulled over."

No sooner had Jesse said this, then he saw a flashing red light behind them.

"Pull over, Xavi!" Jesse said.

"What? Why? I can outrun that cop."

"No, no!" Jesse felt a lump of fear rising in his throat. "We've been here for only a few hours, and you're already going to turn us into fugitives? Pull over now!"

"Okay, okay…" Xavi slowed down, moved into the far-right lane, exited down the ramp onto the feeder road, pulled over, and parked.

In the rear-view mirror, Jesse watched a tall state trooper with a ruddy complexion approach their car. The trooper glanced at the two boys, then looked at the car. "Are you the owner of this car?" he asked Xavi.

"No, it belongs to his father," Xavi said, inclining his head toward Jesse.

"I need to see your driver's license," the trooper said, his eyes narrowing.

Xavi gave a small shrug of this shoulder, "Don't have one."

Oh no, Jesse thought. It would have been so easy for Xavi to ask a scribe for a driver's license before they left the kingdom, but Xavi of course hadn't bothered.

"Sir, I have a driver's license, let me get it for you," Jesse said, trying to be helpful. He reached behind him to pull out his wallet from his back pocket.

“PUT YOUR HANDS WHERE I CAN SEE THEM!” The trooper yelled, pulling his pistol from its holster, and pointing it at Jesse. “GET OUT OF THE CAR SLOWLY.”

As Jesse got out of the car and put both hands on the top of the car. The hot metal made him quickly pull his hands back. The trooper opened the front door, pulled Xavi roughly out of the car, and handcuffed him. He then aimed the gun at Jesse. “KEEP YOUR HANDS WHERE I CAN SEE THEM!” The trooper walked around the car and handcuffed Jesse.

After the trooper had Jesse and Xavi in the back seat of the patrol car, he contacted the station by radio and was instructed to bring the two suspects in for questioning.

Chapter 3

Christina went into the bedroom and lay down, and Stefan finished getting dressed. He had a meeting with foundation representatives today, so he had to put on what he thought of as his Executive Director uniform. New jeans, tweed jacket, button down shirt, and a dark green tie. Green for money, he thought sardonically.

As he stood in front of the mirror, tying his tie, he looked at himself. A thin, pleasant looking white man with a well-trimmed beard and short hair stared back. He was a far cry from the dirty shaggy homeless veteran of a year ago. He owed his re-integration into society to Christina and a small group of friends who believed in him. Patrick, the young black man who had founded the Pearl Box, hired Stefan because who better to run a nonprofit that helps the homeless than a man who had lived on the street himself? Reverend Sheffield, the pastor of the Ebenezer Revival Church had recommended Stefan for the job, and Patrick's mother, Angelina "Birdie" Hawkins, had inspired all of them with her selfless devotion to children and to justice. Birdie had been killed by a state trooper at the Otay Bridge. Stefan thought about Birdie every day. It wasn't lost on him that three of the four people who'd saved him were Black. They'd gone out of their way to help a white homeless veteran, an ex-con, a man convicted of aiding and abetting a gang of rapists and murderers in Iraq.

The doorbell rang, startling Stefan, and Dharma barked furiously. *Who could be dropping by at 7:30 in the morning?* Stefan wondered. He looked through the peephole and saw a middle-aged man wearing a billed cap with the name *LF Plumbing* stitched across the front. The man wore a green shirt with the same logo on the left side of his chest. He held a toolbox in his right hand. Stefan grasped Dharma by the collar, took her into the bedroom. Christina was sitting up in bed.

"Sorry to wake you, darling," Stefan apologized. "There's a maintenance guy at the door, and Dharma is afraid of him. I'll come back and get her in a moment."

When Stefan opened the front door, the man smiled at him. "I'm the plumber. There's been a report of a gas leak in the building, so we're checking all the appliances to see where it's coming from." He glanced over Stefan's shoulder. "I need to ask how many people live here?"

"Just two. My wife and me," Stefan answered.

"May I come in? Like I said, we're checking all the apartments in the building. It should take only a few minutes unless I find a leak, and then I may have to do some repairs."

Stefan opened the door and let the plumber walk past him. Christina came out of the bedroom where Dharma was still barking furiously. "Who was at the front door?" His wife asked.

"Just the plumber, darling. He says he needs to check the appliances for gas leaks. Evidently, someone smelled gas in the building. You can go back to bed."

Stefan turned back to the plumber and saw him staring at Christina with narrow eyes. Christina must have noticed the man's look as well because she clutched the top of her robe and hurried back into the bedroom, quickly closing the door behind her. Stefan was about to say something to the man asking him not to look at his wife that way when the doorbell rang again. *What the hell?* he thought. *Why are people dropping by at this hour? I don't have time for all this nonsense. I need to leave for work.*

He opened the door and saw a tall, fit, middle-aged Black woman with a pleasant smile. She looked at a slip of paper in her hand, and asked, "Mr. O'Malley?"

"No, O'Malley is my wife's name. My name is József. Stefan József. What can I do for you?"

"I'm here about the baby-sitting job," the woman said.

Stefan was puzzled. This was the first he'd heard about hiring a baby-sitter. He felt a little irritated that Christina would recruit a sitter without discussing it with him. And isn't it a little early to be recruiting a sitter? The baby's not due for weeks. He opened the door wider and stepped back so the woman could enter the apartment.

No sooner was Stefan out of her line of sight, than the woman locked eyes with the plumber. Her eyes shone blue, his red. She hissed. He growled. She took two long strides and leaped at the plumber and the two of them fought in a fierce ball of fury, tumbling over the cabinets and falling on the floor. His talons tore at her chest while her powerful hands grasped his throat. She suddenly had large white wings which flapped wildly, knocking dishes off the counter. Finally, she was able to pin the scaly monster down with her knees, and she reached up to the kitchen counter and grabbed the toaster-oven, hitting him in the head with it again and again until he lay still.

As the woman stood up, Stefan backed away from her. He wondered whether he should run into the bedroom and lock the door and make a stand with his wife and dog beside him, or race to the knife drawer beside the woman and arm himself? The woman held up her open hands and spoke gently. "Stefan, there's nothing to be afraid of. I've been sent to protect you and Christina and the baby. My name is Evangelina Peregrine. People call me Birdie."

"Birdie?" Stefan asked.

"Yes, that's what they call me. Why?"

"I used to know a woman named Birdie. She's dead now, but she was the best person I've ever known."

"Well, then, Stefan, I'm sorry I never had a chance to meet her. Step over here, please. I want to show you something."

Stefan took a few reluctant steps toward the woman and

peered at the body lying on his kitchen floor, blood pooling on the linoleum around his caved-in head. Stefan noticed that his fingers were now sharp talons and claws had also sprung from the toes of his work boots. Behind him, he could hear Christina opening the bedroom door cautiously. He turned to his beloved and saw she was holding a pair of sharp scissors like a dagger. *That's my girl,* Stefan thought. *She's not going down without a fight.* Dharma slipped between Christina's legs and trotted to the kitchen where she sniffed the bloody head of the body on the floor, then looked up at the woman and wagged her tail twice. Birdie leaned down, scratched behind the dog's ears, and asked, "How are you, girl?"

"Okay, Birdie, if that's really your name, who sent you and why are you here?" Stefan asked levelly, but he already knew the answer.

"Maria sent me. She figured you could use a babysitter."

Chapter 4

Jesse and Xavi were sitting in separate interrogation rooms at the Texas state trooper station. Xavi had been charged with speeding, driving without a license and suspected auto theft. Jesse was being held as a material witness.

"Name?" asked the burly sergeant sitting across from him.

"Jesse Nazarene." The sergeant wrote the information on a detainee form.

"Middle name?"

"I don't have one."

"Date of birth?"

"Whatever it says on my driver's license," Jesse answered. He hadn't expected to be questioned about his cover, so he'd barely looked at the license and didn't remember what it said.

The sergeant looked at him suspiciously. "Place of birth?"

"Whatever it says on my license," Jesse repeated.

"Sir, I need for you to confirm the information on the license."

"Sorry, Sergeant, I don't remember what it says."

The sergeant leaned back in his chair and crossed his arms. "You don't know when or where you were born?"

Jesse realized that his thin cover had already been blown. He hadn't foreseen he would need a deeper cover. He thought he would be able to show up, talk to a few people, and then leave. He hadn't expected to be interrogated.

"Occupation?"

"Carpenter."

"Religion?"

"Jewish."

The sergeant attached a photocopy of Jesse's driver's license to the form and had Jesse sign it. Then the sergeant went into the next room where Xavi was handcuffed to a pipe bolted to a side of the table in front of him. The sergeant sat down opposite him with a fresh detainee form and asked, "Name?"

Xavi, who'd never had much patience with trying to maintain a cover story, especially a thin one, said, "Shiva Destroyer of Worlds."

The sergeant dutifully wrote down the information.

"Date of birth?"

"Approximately half a million years ago."

"I'll need an exact date, sir."

"April 26, 432061 BCE."

"Place of birth?"

"The Indus Valley."

"In what country would that be located, sir?"

"What is now Pakistan."

"Occupation?"

"Celestial warrior."

"Religion?"

"Hindu. No wait, I'm a pantheist. No, I'm an animist-pantheist."

"Are you a Muslim?"

"Yeah, I guess. But I'm not a very good Muslim."

The sergeant asked a few more questions which Xavi couldn't answer, asked him to sign the bottom of the sheet and walked down the hall where he stood in the doorway of his captain's office.

"Okay, Fred, what you got?" the captain drawled.

"A couple of weird ones, sir. They were stopped on the interstate going over 100 miles an hour. The driver has no license. The passenger's license is obviously fake—he can't even remember the date or place of birth. The driver claims he is a celestial warrior from Pakistan whose job is to destroy the world."

"It sounds like we've caught us a couple of terrorists."

"That's what I was thinking, sir."

The captain walked down the hall and looked through the one-way mirrors at the two suspects. They were both dark-skinned, smooth-faced, seventeen or eighteen years old. Usually suspects handcuffed to a table awaiting interrogation were frightened and agitated. These two seemed strangely calm.

"A couple of cool customers," the captain said.

"Way too cool in my opinion, sir," the sergeant agreed. "Like they know something we don't know. You think we should call the Feds and let them handle this?"

"I guess we have to. I have no idea how to investigate suspected terrorists or what we could charge them with other than speeding and driving without a license."

The captain heard his phone ringing, so he went to his office and picked it up. "Captain, there are two Federal officers at the front desk asking to talk to you."

"Send them back," the captain said. "This can't be a coincidence," he said to the sergeant.

The two Federal officers were tall women in business suits with salt and pepper hair pulled into buns. They flashed their badges and the taller one said, "Captain Hochstetler, we're from Homeland Security. We're not allowed to give you our names. But we've given our clearance numbers to the people at your front desk. I trust that will be sufficient to establish our identities?"

The captain nodded. He'd dealt with HS before. He didn't like their secrecy or their arrogance, but he understood they had a difficult job to do hunting terrorists.

"We understand that one of your patrolmen picked up two suspects today."

The captain nodded.

"May we see them?"

The captain walked with them to the viewing room. The two women glanced at the suspects. The tall one said, "We've been tracking these two men since they arrived in this country. We need to take them into custody."

"How did you know they were here?"

"As I said, we've been tracking them."

The Captain nodded. He knew that with satellite surveillance, the Feds could track anyone anywhere. He nodded to his sergeant, and they took the two officers into the interrogation rooms. When the one who called himself Shiva Destroyer of Worlds, obviously a code name, saw the two women he gave a broad grin and started to say something, but the tall woman said, "I advise you to remain silent. Say nothing. Nothing, you hear?"

The tall agent then turned to the captain and said, "This is a highly confidential action. You will need to destroy all records of this arrest and of any involvement by Homeland Security. Failure to do so could subject you and your staff to serious legal penalties. This arrest and Homeland Security's involvement never happened. Do you understand, Captain?" And the Feds goosestepped the two handcuffed suspects out of the building and into the back seat of a large black Suburban and drove off.

"Damn Feds," the captain muttered, shaking his head as he watched them disappear down the highway.

"Well, that was fun," Xavi said, smiling and slipping out of his handcuffs.

"Xavi, we screwed up," Jesse said.

"You certainly did," said Maria, turning to glare at them from the front seat. "Oh, how I hate dressing like this." She grabbed her tie and gave it a good yank. The whole outfit—shirt, jacket, slacks, shoes and socks—came off as one piece. Underneath she was wearing her usual cotton dress with embroidered flowers across the front. "That's better," she said. "If you want to change clothes, Sister Theodora, we can pull over."

"Thanks, Mother Superior. I'm fine, and we're on a tight schedule."

Maria nodded and turned to give her full attention to the

two young men in the back seat. "What were you thinking driving a hundred miles an hour down the highway? You nearly compromised the entire mission."

"I'm sorry, Mom. I guess we just weren't thinking," Jesse said, looking at his hands, so he didn't have to meet her flashing eyes.

"It was my fault, Maria," Xavi said. "I got carried away with the thrill of that car. Are we going to go back to the place on the highway where we left it?"

"Absolutely not, Xavi. That Cobra is way too much machine for you. I've given it to someone else who can handle it more responsibly."

"What? You're taking our ride away? You can't do that. How are we going to get around?"

"I'm assigning two Sisters to you. They'll be your chauffeurs."

"You mean our babysitters, don't you?"

Maria laughed. "Well, babysitting is why we're here, no?"

As Birdie covered the demon's body in extra-wide cellophane wrap so it wouldn't spoil before the clean-up team arrived, Stefan's phone rang. It was his boss Patrick.

"Hi Patrick, I'm glad you called. I'm going to be a little late this morning."

"It's okay, Stefan. I had to lock up the Pearl Box. We're going to have to close it for a few days," Patrick shouted into the phone to be heard over the roar in the background.

"Really? What's going on?"

"I can't explain right now, but do you remember the Sisters of the Holy Piston?"

"Of course." The sisters were Maria's minions, a.k.a. Nuns with Guns, the strike force Maria recruited to fight demons.

"I'm with one of the sisters," Patrick shouted. "Weird shit is starting again. You and Christina need to get out of your apartment and get down to José's place in Mexico."

"Yeah, I know. Weird shit is happening here too. We'll meet you at the Presidio."

"Okay, I gotta go. You take care of yourself, brother poet."

As Patrick ended the call, Christina appeared beside Stefan, holding the small suitcase they'd put together for when the baby was coming.

"It's starting again?" She asked.

Stefan nodded. "Yes, love, it's starting again."

Her eyes narrowed with ferocity, and one hand rested on her belly protectively. "I will murder them all before I allow them to hurt my baby." Stefan remembered Christina coming out of the bedroom earlier holding a pair of scissors and thought, not for the first time, that there is nothing in the world more dangerous than a mother protecting her child.

Stefan glanced at Birdie who was mopping up blood from the kitchen floor. He grabbed a paper grocery bag from the kitchen, threw a toothbrush and a change of underwear and socks in, and said, "How are we traveling, Birdie?"

"There are two sisters outside with their choppers and sidecars."

"And Dharma?"

"She travels with you of course. She's declared her allegiance, so we can't leave her behind for the demons to torment."

"And you?"

"I've got a few things to do here in L.A. I'll meet you at the Presidio."

Stefan, Christina, and Dharma hurried to the parking lot where two women wearing black leather jackets sat on their rumbling motorcycles. Across the back of their jackets was the logo *Sisters of the Holy Piston* in a white arc below a blue cross. One of the women had gray hair falling from under her helmet. The other woman had a prosthetic right hand, and Christina, when she saw who it was, gave the woman a hug and a smile.

"Hey Marta, how you doing?" she asked, giving her former client a hug. "You seem to have adjusted well." She glanced at Marta's prosthetic hand.

"I'm fine. You know I'm a novice with the Sisters now? How are *you* doing?" Marta responded looking at Christina's belly.

"Good. I'm really good considering I've been pregnant for 75 months." They both laughed.

"You two remember Sister Inez, right?" Marta asked nodding toward the other sister on the motorbike beside her.

"How could I forget?" Stefan said, and he meant it. How often do you meet a former CIA operative who's now a leftist revolutionary nun?

With Marta's help, Christina climbed into the sidecar, and Stefan climbed into Inez's sidecar. In front of him, a steel basket was bolted to the frame. In it was a pillow, a seat belt, a red scarf, and a pair of goggles designed for a dog Dharma's size. Stefan helped his pooch with the scarf and goggles. After Marta and Inez had checked that everyone was safely buckled in, they pulled the Fat Boys onto the highway and headed south to Mexico.

Dharma, in the way of all dogs, understood what was going on better than her master. She had smelled the cloud of evil that surrounded the demon disguised as a man, and she'd tried to warn Stefan, but sometimes he was so dense. How could he not smell the stench of evil? She was well aware that what you see with your eyes can fool you, but the nose never lies. When she and Stefan were living on the street, how often had she smelled a threat and warned him? Sometimes he listened and they hurried off, but sometimes he was fooled because he was hungry to talk with other humans. More than once, she had had to save him from someone who wanted to rob him, not that he had anything anyone would want other than those army boots he always wore. She was sure when Armageddon came and blew them both away, those boots would still be standing like stone monuments.

How dare Stefan lock her in the bedroom where she had to

keep barking and barking, warning him of the evil he'd invited into their home! At least, Christina had understood and armed herself with scissors. Dharma liked Christina and was happy to have her as the leader of their tribe. She was smarter and tougher than Stefan, but Stefan was the great love of both their lives. His sweetness, his imagination, his generosity. He had plenty of love for the two females in his life, and he'd be a good father for the baby when it came. But Dharma knew that first the three of them needed to survive the next few weeks.

Patrick was in a sidecar beside Sister Genevieve. They were driving east along the border wall, a tall steel edifice constructed of vertical slats. Eventually they pulled over beside the road in a place which looked like any other, desert stretching as far as the eye could see. Sister Genevieve checked her watch and cut the engine.

"What are we doing here?" Patrick asked. The sun was bright, and even though he was wearing a hat and sunglasses, he worried about the sun damaging the flawless black skin of his face. He was, after all, a professional performer, a *drag queen* as they used to say, and he couldn't afford to have damaged skin.

"Here, spread this on your face, neck and arms," Sister Genevieve said in her barely detectable French accent, handing him a tube of sun block. He took the tube and began lathering his exposed skin. The fact that she seemed to have read his mind didn't surprise him in the least. He'd seen the Sisters perform some amazing feats. A little mind-reading was nothing for them, he imagined. He liked Sister Genevieve a great deal. She was a large powerful good-natured woman who liked to laugh. She was also a gifted mechanic, a genius with motorcycle repair.

"We wait," she said, answering his question.

"Wait for what?" he asked.

"The border is surveilled by a satellite, but there's a four-minute blind spot here every day."

They sat in silence for a while, and finally Patrick tried to make conversation. It wasn't as if there was nothing to talk about. He suspected that the Apocalypse, which had been scheduled for the previous year but was delayed by the intervention of Mother Maria and her son, was about to happen. "So can I ask you a question?"

"Of course, go ahead," Sister Genevieve said, checking her watch again.

"Why is the world as we know it about to end?"

Genevieve, besides being a motorcycle mechanic, was also a martial artist, and, as all the Sisters were, an expert in the use of firearms—thus the tag "Nuns with Guns"—said carefully, "I certainly don't have all the answers, but as I understand it, God requires that the world come to an end every ten thousand years. This is, you might say, a cleansing of the earth. The last time was a huge flood when the glaciers melted. You know the story of Noah, right?"

"Oh sure, I was raised in the Ebenezer Baptist Church, so I went to Sunday school every week. But what I'm wondering about was why the Apocalypse didn't happen last year when it was planned. Maria said that Jesse and Xavi stopped it from happening?"

Before Genevieve could answer him, she checked her watch. "It's time," she said and kick-started her Fat Boy. Patrick climbed into the sidecar and strapped himself in. Sister drove the motorcycle directly at the slats of the border wall, but instead of crashing as Patrick expected, they passed through it as if it were made of air.

As they roared over the desert on the Mexican side, Genevieve laughed and yelled over her shoulder, "We took out a five-by-five section of the wall and substituted an image projected from the Mexican side. It's an invisible hole we can pass through four minutes a day without being recorded by the satellite. So far, Homeland Security hasn't discovered it."

Chapter 5

Jesse and Xavi sat in the back seat of the suburban as it barreled down the highway, Sister Theodora keeping her eyes on the road, staying slightly under the speed limit.

"Where are we going?" Xavi asked.

Maria sat in the front passenger seat, staring straight ahead. Jesse turned to Xavi and shook his head, trying to keep Xavi silent. This was not the time to be engaging his mother in conversation. He could see she was furious.

"Maria, where are we going?" Xavi repeated. He had never been someone who picked up hints.

Jesse rolled his eyes, waiting for the inevitable response from Maria who turned around and looked at the two boys.

She knew she should be patient with them because in their current form as 17-year-old human males, they would have many of the characteristics typical of human males—namely, impulsiveness, poor judgement, and selfishness. "You realize you almost jeopardized the entire campaign, don't you?" she asked, trying to maintain a level tone when what she wanted to do was scream at the two fools in the back seat.

"I'm sorry, Mom," Jesse quickly said, always wanting to placate.

"Hey, it wasn't my fault," Xavi insisted. "Why were we issued an automobile that can go 150 miles an hour if we weren't supposed to use it? Hey, come to think of it, we left the Cobra beside the road. Shouldn't we go back and pick it up?"

"Oh, you'll never drive that automobile again," Maria said, her eyes narrowing at Xavi. "As I said, it's been given to someone who can drive more responsibly."

"What? That car was issued to me. You can't just take it away from me."

"Yes, I can. I'm in charge of this campaign, so I get to decide everything, and I'm certainly not going to let an immature brat drive a race car," Maria said, turning to face forward.

"A b-b-brat?" Xavi spluttered. "I'm half a million years old. How can I be an immature brat?"

"That's a very good question," Maria muttered under her breath.

They drove in silence for a while, Maria and Xavi looking at the fields flying by, simmering in their resentments. The land was changing from the pine forests of east Texas to the dry cedar and prickly pear expanses of central Texas. When Jesse could see that the mood in the car was calmer, he asked, in the most pleasant tone he could muster, "Mom, what's next? Where are we going?"

Maria turned to look at Jesse, pointedly ignoring Xavi. "We're paying a visit to the Queen of the Yellowjackets. She's an old friend and we could use her help. Jesse, I want you to come with me. Xavi and Theodora can stay here in the car."

About 75 miles west of San Antonio, the long sloping hills of the Balcones Escarpment mark the transition between the alluvial soils of the east and the Edwards Plateau in the west, a place of hundreds of sweet springs and picturesque waterfalls. These hills have a rich diversity of fauna, including about 340 species of birds, 140 species of butterflies, and 75 species of dragonflies and damselflies. There are also billions of wasps and hornets who prey on the insects. The queen of these meat-bees is Zahra whose castle lies hidden in a narrow cave.

Maria and Jesse left the Suburban and hiked the last half mile. When they were about 100 feet from the cave, a swarm of hundreds of yellowjackets surrounded them.

"Stay absolutely still, Jesse," Maria said softly. "They're just checking us out."

"And if they don't like what they see?" Jesse whispered.

"Then we are going to have a soul-changing experience."

The yellowjackets were crawling over the two visitors, checking out every wet spot, every crevice and cavity in these human bodies. The worst part of the ordeal occurred when the winged insects crawled up Jesse's nose. He tried to restrain himself, but he couldn't stop himself from exploding in a huge sneeze, blowing the insects from his nose, and causing hundreds of others to fly around his head, agitated. Finally, the insects seemed satisfied and flew toward the cave entrance. Maria and Jesse followed them.

They had to turn sideways to fit through the entrance. Inside, the cave widened into a room the size of a small house, and it was almost filled by a mud castle with hundreds of holes in its walls where yellowjackets flew in and out. Jesse imagined the long tunnels and great halls of the interior, and somewhere deep inside the castle, the queen's chambers where she gave birth to eggs that lay in small mud cups and eventually turned into larvae to be tended by nurse-wasps.

Maria and Jesse stood in front of the castle, waiting for the queen to come out to see them. "Zahra is the queen of this hive?" Jesse asked.

"She is the queen not only of this hive, but of all the hives in the Balcones," Maria answered. "She is very old, perhaps thousands of years. She is the incarnation of the hive itself which continually renews itself."

Eventually a wasp the size of a human hand emerged from a hole in the castle and flew toward them. The wasp was so large, her wings could barely carry her. Yellow and black stripes covered her distended abdomen. As she flew close to Jesse's face, he could see her eyes peering into his, and he sensed a great wisdom in this insect.

The large wasp settled on Maria's extended palm. Six smaller wasps landed beside her, each carrying a small rose petal with a drop of liquid on it. Maria nodded to Jesse, and he extended his hand as well. When Maria picked up a petal and lapped up the drop of liquid, then another, Jesse did the same. Suddenly, the buzzing of the insects became a language he could understand.

"Zzzz...Hello, Zizter," the queen buzzed, lighting on the top of a mud tower, her retainers flying around her.

"Thank you for coming out of your chambers to talk with us, Your Majesty," Maria bowing her head slightly.

"I have heard you are recruiting alliezzzz for the coming war."

"Yes, the forces of darkness wish to end the world as we know it," Maria responded.

"And zzzzz... why should we not let them? Humans have been a curse in the world for thousands of years. Zzzzzz why not end their so-called civilization and let them go back to hunting and gathering? Were they not happier then? And wasn't the world a better place?"

"Perhaps it was," Maria conceded. "And the humans have certainly become a threat to all living things. But the forces of darkness do not wish to simply end human civilization, they intend to end creation as a whole and put in its place a barren world, Hell on Earth. If we allow this to happen, your civilization which is much older than the human one would be wiped out as well."

"Very well.... zzzzz. Zuppose the wasps join you in your war, and together we defeat the evil ones. What then? What will you do about the threat to creation from the humans? Their poisons are killing all the winged ones, even the honeybees which the humans depend on for their very Zzzurvival . The wasps are not alone in thinking the humans should be wiped out."

"Yes, it is a shame what the humans are doing to the honeybees and other species, but the answer is not to wipe out the humans," Maria answered gently. "After all, they are part of creation as well, and all creation is holy."

"Then what izzzz the answer to their excesses?"

Jesse took a step forward toward the wasp-queen. "The answer is education, Your Majesty. We must teach the humans how to live on the earth in balance with the rest of creation."

"What makes you zzzzzink they are willing to learn?"

"They are remarkably intelligent," Jesse said. "After elephants and dolphins, they are the most intelligent of creatures, and they are by far the most creative. Look at what they've done with music."

"Yes, well, *The Flight of the Bumblebee* is a favorite among my subjects. zzzzz And Cherokee flute music has been shown to bring enlightenment to many creatures. zzzzz Perhaps there is hope for humans after all." Queen Zahra considered the issue. "Very well then, we will send our warriors to join you. I have heard the battle will take place in the eastern forest four days flight from here?" Maria nodded. "I will instruct my generals zzzz to prepare our warriors to leave tonight." Maria bowed to her, and in a gesture of gratitude let the petals fall from her cupped palm. Jessie followed suit, watching the Queen return to her hive.

As Maria and Jesse were hiking back to the highway, she asked, "Do you really think we can train an army of teachers to educate eight billion humans on their responsibility to creation?"

"What choice do we have, Mother? If the humans cannot learn to live in harmony with nature, then all of creation will turn against them and wipe them out."

Maria knew he was right. Humans needed to learn to live on the earth responsibly, or the earth would be rid of them once and for all. "You realize you're talking about deploying millions of teachers, right? Recruiting, training, and coordinating them is going to be a huge task. The last time something like this was tried was in the seventh century when the blessed final prophet was recruited by our friend Gabe to bring the Koran to millions of people."

When her son didn't respond, but just looked out over the lush spring-fed landscape, admiring the beauty of the bluebonnets and Indian paintbrushes, Maria asked, "Are you up for the job?"

Jesse looked at his feet on the white limestone path and shook his head, "I'm a really good teacher, Mother, but I've never been much good as a manager."

"My darling gentle boy," Maria said softly, "You have so much love and forgiveness in your heart, you can't compel others to do what they need to do. I think you need to hire a manager to build the organization. It needs to be someone pure in heart, but tough in attitude, well-educated, but with a gift for connecting to common people, and fluent in at least six languages. He—or she—needs to be a true leader who attracts followers who grow to love him, and to stay confident when millions are criticizing him, he needs to have a touch, just a touch, of narcissism. Do you really want to go ahead with this teaching business, even though there is only a small chance that it will work?"

"Yes, it's the only way I can see to save the humans. But where am I going to find someone like that?"

"It happens that I know someone who would be perfect for the job," Maria said. "And it also happens that he lives in Houston. Would you like to meet him?"

Father Alejandro Miguel Beltran, Alex to his friends, was the most brilliant scholar and teacher anyone had ever met. He was also the coolest. As he strode through the campus of St. Anthony University, his cassock flying behind him like a cape, co-eds were known to drop their books in shock at his sheer awesomeness. With broad shoulders, narrow waist and thick black hair pulled back in a ponytail, he had the bearing of a nobleman. There were rumors that talent agencies had tried to recruit him as a model because his classical profile was so perfect. On the squash court, he was like a hawk swooping down on a sparrow. At a recent charity event, he'd faced off with two champions simultaneously, flying through the air to make impossible returns. His Jesuit training gave him the skills of a logician, and his gift for mathematics had served him well as a physicist. He had gotten tenure in the philosophy department based on his publications arguing that the Big Bang Theory supported the principle of Divine Providence, the event which constituted The First Cause. Picking up where Aquinas left off, Professor Beltran argued that God caused the world and everything else to exist through The Big Bang, and Christian theologians should embrace the theory as evidence that God has His Hand in everything.

His homilies brought a packed chapel, and there were petitions circulating on campus that on the Sundays when he was delivering mass, the divine sacrament should be moved to the main auditorium on campus to accommodate the huge turnout.

However, Father Alex had a serious flaw in his character. With his striking looks, intellectual acuity, and physical prowess, he struggled at times with a certain lack of humility. As a faculty wag put it, Professor Beltran resembled not so much a humble supplicant as a Greek God, and the eponym The Apollo of St. Anthony's was sometimes bandied about. When this failing of the professor had been brought to the attention of the university leadership when he had been considered for the office of dean of the humanities college, the bishop had argued that perhaps Father Alex could be forgiven his arrogance since he used his extraordinary gifts to serve God. The Bishop went on to point out that despite his mastery of science, Father Alex also carried a Spanish language copy of St. John of the Cross's visionary long poem *Cántico Espiritual*, and in a recent faculty senate debate about the uncertain financial future of the university, Father Alex had quoted St John's imprecation, "If a man wishes to be sure of the road he treads on, he must close his eyes and walk in the dark." Father Alex, the Bishop implored, is a rare alloy, a man who uses both poetry and science to serve God. Nevertheless, Alex was not appointed dean, but in keeping with his character, he took this small defeat in stride.

The first day of the fall semester, Father Alex pulled up to the faculty parking lot in a blue 1960 Shelby Cobra donated by an anonymous benefactor. When it was delivered to the rectory the night before, he had, of course, refused to accept it for himself, but only on behalf of his order.

"That is one cool ride," a male student said.

"That is one cool teacher," a female student said.

Father Alex smiled at the two of them and hurried off to his undergraduate class *Faith and Science*, the most popular course on campus. When he walked into the classroom, the students grew silent. After checking roll, passing out the syllabus and answering questions about the requirements of the course. He turned to the whiteboard and wrote the word *FAITH*.

"Do you have faith?" he asked the class and waited for the answer.

A bright young man on the front row raised his hand. "Pardon me, Professor, but faith in what? Don't you have to have faith *in* something. Faith doesn't exist by itself, does it? There must be an idea we believe. So, an idea is a necessary precondition of faith, right?"

Father Alex rewarded the young man with a broad smile, showing his perfect teeth. "Exactly, Tristram. I'm glad to see that you were paying attention in my Intro to Religion class last year." He paused for a moment, then explained for the benefit of the other students. "There needs to be an object, that is an idea we believe in before there can be faith. For example, I believe in gravity, as I'm sure you do as well. I have faith that the earth will hold me on the ground. We believe in gravity because we have been informed that it exists, and the explanation fits our experience, so we come to think of it as fact.

"Take another example... We've been informed that the internet exists. We cannot see it as a whole, no one can, but we see it in bits and pieces, and we learn to use it to benefit us. We communicate with our friends through email. We store our poems and art in the cloud. We consult authoritative sources to support our arguments. We educate ourselves and expand our world by using the internet. However, none of us has ever actually seen the internet, have we? We see only tiny parts of it, and we assume that the rest of it exists because we're told that it is there and because what we experience seems to fit the explanation. But if we think about it and use our imaginations, there are other possible explanations for our experience with the internet, isn't there?"

Father Alex paused, letting the students catch up to the direction of his argument. "What other possible explanations are there for what we experience as *the internet*?"

A blonde girl at the back of the room, raised her hand. "Yes, Alice," Father Alex said, recalling her name from rollcall and gesturing toward her.

"Could everything in our lives actually be a dream someone is having?" she asked.

"Thank you, yes, that is a possibility, a *trope* that story tellers often use, and we've all had the feeling that our lives are not real. What other explanation might there be?"

"Maybe we're in a book, a story someone is writing right now?" a young black woman wearing glasses offered.

"Possibly. Thank you, Dinusha."

"Or a television series?" someone volunteered from the back.

"Or that movie..." Dinusha fished for the title...

"*The Truman Show*!" Another young woman blurted out.

"Tell us about that movie, Monica," Father Alex asked.

"Jim Carrey lives his whole life on a tv show thinking it's his real life. But actually everything... the town, his house, his job are just part of the script, and everyone he knows, even his wife and his best friend are actors tricking him into thinking his life is real when it's just a tv show directed by people interested only in ratings."

"And what happens when Truman discovers his life is a fiction, a lie?"

"He gets in a boat and sails to the end of the world as he knows it."

The room went quiet as the students began to see where their exploration had taken them.

Father Alex broke the silence. "Let's digress for a moment to ask *what is the difference between a lie and a fiction?*"

Tristram raised his hand and the teacher smiled at him, knowing they'd explored this idea in the last class Tristram had taken with him. "A fiction is a story told to entertain or educate someone. The reader or listener knows it is not factual, but agrees to a *willing suspension of disbelief*, in Coleridge's words. A lie, on the other hand, is an intentional misrepresentation of the truth with the intention to deceive."

The teacher suppressed a smile. The sentences were verbatim from one of his own lectures. "Can a factual story be a lie?"

"Yes," Tristram answered emphatically. "If the intention to deceive is present, then the facts are being used dishonestly."

"So, you are saying that a fiction can be a way of revealing the truth and that a factual report can be a way of deceiving? Can you give an example of a fact being used to tell a lie?"

"Our elections here in Texas are reported factually, but they are being used to support a lie."

Yikes, Alex thought, this kid has started thinking for himself. Although he agreed with Tristram's political point, he never would have said this in class. Most of his students were white kids who came from very conservative families. Even now, he could see some of them shifting uncomfortably. He decided to let Tristram prove his point.

"Our elections are a lie? What do you mean?"

"Black and brown people are systematically excluded from the political process, and the news media do not report this accurately for fear of offending their advertisers."

A dozen hands shot up. The teacher called on a few of the conservative students and let them spill out their patriotic clichés about America the land of the free and the ingratitude of Latinos and African Americans before the teacher brought the discussion back to the issue of faith and its relationship to perceived reality.

"Do you ever have the feeling," Father Alex said almost

wistfully, "that there's a different reality behind the reality we know? If we could somehow pull back the curtain, then we'd see the mechanics of how things really work?"

He noticed some of the students looking slightly disturbed, uncomfortable with the idea that the reality they knew couldn't be counted on. Other students nodded excitedly, perhaps because they had had this feeling before, that life was empty and fraudulent, and it was comforting to hear the feelings expressed in public.

"What do these other possible explanations for the internet tell us about faith?"

The teacher let the silence hang in the air as the students tried to work through the paradox that had been revealed. Finally, Monica raised her hand, and Father Alex nodded to her.

"We have to be careful where we put our faith because the ideas we believe could be wrong? And putting our faith in ideas that are wrong may lead to other mistakes? And we might even discover our entire lives are based on a lie?"

"Well put, Monica. This semester we'll be exploring these very questions of faith and certainty. I'm glad to see we have such a bright and imaginative group of companions on this journey. Your homework assignment is on the syllabus. Show up prepared or be prepared to look foolish in the eyes of your peers. Class dismissed."

Several students came up to his desk with questions which he dealt with by suggesting books or articles they might read. As Alex was conversing with them, he noticed two figures standing in the hall outside the classroom. He smiled and nodded to the woman who was an old friend and benefactor, but Alex had never met the young man although he did seem somewhat familiar to the priest.

"Are you enjoying the Cobra?" Maria asked Alex as the three of them walked beneath the tall live oaks on campus. They stopped in front of the obelisk celebrating the spirit of Martin Luther King. Nearby was the Rothko Chapel which contained the great artist's series of black paintings in which a person could fall through the dark layers until he encountered himself. Even Jesse, who had a strong sense of his identity, had experienced this feeling of falling as he meditated in front of the paintings. They sat on a bench beneath an ancient oak in front of the obelisk. This place was one of the holiest on this benighted continent, Jesse believed.

"I certainly am," Alex answered. "Of course, it is not mine, but the Jesuits are letting me drive it for a while until they find a better use for it. You realize they may sell it?"

Maria waved her hand, dismissively. "Of course, the order can do what they want. I imagine it will fetch enough money for a small library in Guatemala."

"Indeed." Alex turned to Jesse. He was curious about this handsome young man. "Are you here for long?" He let the vagueness of the word "here" stand, hoping the young man's response would confirm Alex's suspicion.

"Probably not long," the young man answered. "My mom and I are here to recruit talent for a campaign that's coming up." He wondered whether Alex was aware he was talking to celestial beings and not just a wealthy donor and her son.

"Campaign?" Alex asked, looking from Jesse to Maria.

Maria admired her son's graceful segue into the topic they needed to discuss.

"Alex," Maria began. "There's something about me I've never revealed…"

"And what is that?" Alex asked courteously, peering into her eyes.

"I am…" She didn't know how to say it. Usually, people kind of figured it out by themselves.

"You are the Blessed Virgin, Star of the Sea, Queen of Heaven, Mother of Mercy, as well as Our Lady of Loreto, Our Lady of Guadalupe, and Our Lady of Sorrows?" Alex could spill out the epithets easily, but did he believe he was talking to the Blessed Virgin at this moment? He wasn't sure.

"Yes, well, those names are accurate of course, but I never like 'Our Lady of Sorrows.' It makes me sound so grim. And 'Virgin' is just a metaphor..."

Jesse rolled eyes. He hated it when his mother talked, or even hinted at, her sexuality.

Alex smiled. "I practice celibacy, as you know. So, I hope you won't mind if I say that I'm glad you are not a virgin because, even though you are a celestial being, you are a very sensual woman."

Maria fluttered her eye lashes at him and looked down demurely. "*Gracias, Padre*, you are being very kind. And may I say..."

"Mother," Jesse said, "stop flirting with him. He's already told you he's celibate."

"I wasn't flirting..." Maria said, crossing her legs and smoothing her skirt.

Alex suppressed a smile. He was aware of how his good looks affected women, and the fact that they believed he was celibate seemed to make them want him even more. Having a crush on a priest was a yearning for forbidden fruit, he thought, not for the first time amused at the multiple meanings of *fruit*.

He turned to Jesse, bowed his head, and said, "So you must be the Savior? The one who died to save us from our sins? I guess I should say *Thank you, Lord*." Again, he wasn't sure he believed in the divinity of these two people in front of him, but it was obvious that they believed it, so he was willing to humor them, but it was difficult for Alex to keep his tone from becoming sardonic.

"You're welcome. But let's don't get carried away with gratitude. There were a lot of politics involved. My father..." Jesse cut himself off, seeing his mother behind Alex, her brown eyes were narrowed in anger, and she was shaking her head, signaling her son not to involve mortals in the back-office maneuverings and dysfunctional family dynamics that had resulted in many bad decisions. Best to leave well enough alone, as Pete the Fisherman often said.

"What can I do to help?" Alex generously asked.

"I'm glad you asked that," Maria said, catching her son's eye.

Jesse nodded, letting her know that Alex seemed the right man for the job.

"We need you to lead an army of teachers who will bring light and truth to the world."

Alex tapped his forefinger to his lips, then nervously stroked his mustache while he thought about the enormity of the job. "What do you want me to do?"

"We want you to go on a lecture tour across the country—college auditoriums, tv talk shows, radio and print interviews, however you can get the truth out," Jesse explained.

"The truth?" Alex felt his inner relativist, his distrust of easy claims of righteousness, rearing its head. "The truth is a slippery thing... I'm not sure I'm the best person to be claiming to know The Truth."

Maria smiled. "This is exactly why you are the perfect person for the job. You understand that people need to discover the truth for themselves, and what is true for one person may not be true for another, especially in matters of faith."

"And what would be the purpose of this public dialogue?"

"To prepare people for the Second Coming," Jesse declared simply.

"And you believe you know when the promised Second Coming is... coming," Alex said with a bemused smile.

"It was scheduled for last year, but it's been re-scheduled," Jesse said, noticing the skeptical look in Alex's eyes.

"I'm afraid that I'm not the right person to be doing this tour, but I'm honored that you asked..." Alex said, starting to rise.

Maria turned toward Jesse and gave a slight nod. Jesse stood and extended his hand as if to shake Alex's hand in reluctant farewell.

The moment Alex's palm touch Jesse's, the priest felt a warm glow spreading up his arm and into his chest, spreading through his whole body. He saw that both Jesse and Maria had golden halos over their heads, and the sky was swirling in shades of deep blue and the oak tree seemed to be holding out its arms to him.

After a minute had passed, he said, "Would I have your help in this Herculean task?"

"Absolutely," Jesse said. "We'll help you any way we can."

"Didn't you try this two thousand years ago, and the results were, shall we say, mixed?" Alex suddenly remembered who he was speaking to and what they possibly were, and he added hastily and unconvincingly, "I didn't mean… uh… You know I worship you and the failures… if there were failures… were the fault of human frailty, not because the truths you brought were not… uh… perfect."

Jesse held up his hand. "Don't worry, Alex, I've spent the last two thousand years watching my teachings used to justify murder, torture, bigotry, racism, sexism, colonialism, and capitalism… Obviously, I was not an effective teacher."

Maria stepped in to stop these two males from stumbling over themselves any longer. "Alex," she said. "We need you to do what you do in your classroom, except on a much larger scale."

"I would need to get permission from the bishop and the dean to take a leave of absence."

"Already taken care of," Maria said.

"May I hire my own assistant?"

"Of course."

"Alright," Alex said. "When do we start?"

"Tomorrow, we leave for Mexico," Maria said. "So, pack your undies, recruit your assistant, fuel up your Cobra, and I'll meet you at the rectory to give you directions."

"Are you riding with me?"

"No," Maria said. "I'll be traveling in the Suburban with Xavi and Theodora."

"What about me?" Jesse said.

"You'll be taking the bus to Mexico," she said with a slight smile.

"The bus? Mother, you can't be serious. You want me to take a bus all the way to Sonora, Mexico?"

"Yes, my dear. There are people on the bus you need to meet."

With a wave Alex hurried off to pack and make his arrangements. Maria and Jesse continued to sit on the bench, enjoying the birdsong coming from the oak trees.

"Is that a cardinal?" Maria asked.

"Actually, I believe it is a mockingbird imitating a cardinal. We're lucky. I've heard them imitate car alarms. Cardinal song is much more beautiful."

"I imagine so," Maria said wryly. "Which vision did you give him?"

"The watercolor that Liz Lemon painted a few years ago."

"The painting where we're embracing?"

"That's the one."

"Couldn't you have chosen another one? I look so old in that one."

"I wanted an understated vision. I was afraid that if I went all quattrocento on Alex, he would have thought it was a hallucination."

They listened to the mockingbird for a while, then Jesse, said, "Mother, I couldn't help but notice that you are attracted to Alex."

"Jesse, *mi cariño*, I know my sexuality embarrasses you, but it is part of who I am, and you are going to have to learn to live with it. Besides, that business of priests staying celibate is a ridiculous rule invented a thousand years ago by envious prelates who wanted to break up the family dynasties that had arisen in the church by delegitimizing the inheritance of the princes of the church."

"Oh, I agree completely, Mother. There's no reason why clergy shouldn't have sex or get married, but..."

"What?"

"You do realize that Alex is gay, right?"

"No, he's not." Maria was embarrassed by the defensiveness in her voice.

"Actually, he is, Mother. I could feel his desire when he spoke with me."

"Well, then, he must swing both ways because I felt the same thing."

"Have it your way, Mother, I just don't want your feelings getting hurt if he rejects you."

"Darling boy," Maria laughed in a way she hoped sounded light-hearted. "No one rejects me."

Jesse looked away and said nothing, thinking *why am I having to take the bus a thousand miles to El Presidio?*

Chapter 6

Stefan liked El Presidio. *It feels safe here*, he thought as he helped Dharma take off her scarf and goggles. He glanced at Marta helping Christina climb out of the sidecar next to her. The Presidio was an old mission which had been abandoned generations before. Maria's husband José had found the place and fallen in love with it. A skilled craftsman, he had completely renovated it, not only restoring the beautiful chapel with its stained-glass windows and carved oak altar and plaster creches, but he'd also rebuilt the high stone walls that surrounded the grounds. It was now the Convent of the Sisters of the Holy Piston, the warrior order Maria had founded on the model of the medieval Knights Templar. Each nun had a chosen profession (schoolteacher, attorney, computer programmer) and also was on call as a special ops warrior. The sisters were, as Maria often called them, "the tip of the spear" in fighting evil in North America.

Stefan was, by contrast, a pacifist who had served in Iraq, gotten caught up in a politically sensitive slaughter of civilians, and spent two years in Leavenworth and three years as a homeless veteran living under a bridge. He was one of tens of thousands of ex-service men and women whom America had used and thrown away. But looking back on his struggles, he now realized that his suffering had been for a purpose. The poetry he'd written in prison and on the street was now appearing in online magazines, and he was developing a modest but respectable reputation among readers. He was grateful to Christina for encouraging him to submit his poems for publication. Now he gently held Christina's arm as they walked through the front gate. Although they'd spent only a few days in the mission the previous year, they both felt comfortable here.

José came out to greet them. His short wide body moved with surprising grace. "*Hola, mis amigos,*" he said with a broad grin. He shook Stefan's hand and hugged Christina. "I hope the journey here was not too tiring."

"Well, the passage through the invisible hole in the border wall was weird," Christina said, massaging her lower back. "But I've missed the wonderful weirdness of Maria and the sisters."

"I'm a simple carpenter who would have been content just to practice my craft. Maria and her minions have certainly made my life more interesting," José said. "Please come inside. You must be tired. Let's get you something to drink. We prepared your room, the same one where you stayed last time. You can get cleaned up, eat some beans and vegetables from our garden, and we'll talk about everything."

The room was exactly the way Stefan remembered it: the double bed where he and Christina had first made love, the small writing desk and chair in front of the window that looked out to the long line of poplars beside the road and the mountains blue in the distance. For Stefan, this room, more than the cookie-cutter apartment they shared in the outskirts of LA, or the narrow cave under the bridge where he and Dharma had slept for three years, was home. He'd wished for some time that he and Christina could move here, but he'd never mentioned it to her. She seemed to love her work as a psychotherapist at the Veteran's Hospital, and he didn't want to take her away from it. As for him, his job as the executive director of The Pearl Box, by day a counseling center for street people and by night a drag show theater, was not a good fit for him. He believed in the mission of The Pearl Box, but he was not cut out for the fund-raising which occupied most of his time. He was terrible at schmoozing with funders, and he was sick of churning out boilerplate clichés for the reports and grant applications. The only good thing about the job was working with Patrick, the young founder of The Pearl Box, who was dynamic, funny, talented, and inspired. Patrick, who performed five evenings a week at The Pearl Box under the name Cossette, did nightly performances of sultry Marilyn Monroe and dynamic Aretha Franklin, as well as Cossette's own sweet love ballads. It was these inspired performances that had made The Pearl Box a popular place.

Dinner at El Presidio was always something of a miracle. This evening it was Sister Zenobia's turn to cook. She fused her Cameroon heritage with local ingredients to create Ndole with fried plantains, Jollof Rice, Hot Pot Potatoes and for dessert mango-coconut ice cream. As she brought out each dish, everyone at the table gave an involuntary *ahhhh* of anticipation.

"Where's Maria?" Christina asked, watching Stefan ladle corn mush and chicken gizzards into a bowl for Dharma who consumed the victuals with gusto.

"She's in Texas with Jesse, Theodora and Xavi," Sister Genevieve said, her mouth full of Ndole. The national dish of Cameroon is traditionally made of stewed nuts and bitter leaves indigenous to West Africa, but Zenobia had adapted the recipe to include peanuts, pecans, spinach, and collard greens spiced with cloves. It was so delicious no one wanted to speak until dessert was served.

"Maria and the others are in Texas recruiting warriors," Genevieve added after polishing off a second helping of mango-coconut ice cream.

"Warriors?" Christina prompted.

"Yeah, there's a war coming," Genevieve said, matter-of-factly as if she were talking about a thunderstorm. "Is there any of that Ndole left?"

"Sorry," Zenobia said smiling. "No more Ndole, Sister, but I set aside some extra Jollof Rice for you. You work so hard, Sister, you deserve a second helping."

"More like a fourth helping," Marta quipped. And everyone laughed good naturedly. Genevieve's appetite was something of a legend among the sisters. Along with her best friend Marta, Genevieve kept all the vehicles in good repair. She was almost twice the size of the other nuns, so she needed a lot of food to fuel her large frame as well as her heavy work schedule.

"Girl's gotta eat," Genevieve said, which sounded funny in her French accent.

"Hey, Genevieve," Marta said. "I thought French women were petite. How'd you get to be so big and strong?"

"My mother was French, but my father was a mountain," Genevieve said, laughing.

Stefan liked the way Genevieve guffawed with her mouth full of food. There was nothing dainty about this woman.

"Can you tell us more about this war that's coming?" Patrick asked. Christina was grateful that Patrick had asked. She didn't want to seem like she was pestering the sisters for information.

Sister Inez, the former CIA operative who now taught children in the convent school, said carefully, "Maria believes that the dark forces are gathering for an attack on the American Empire."

"Why the American Empire and not another place?" Stefan asked.

"Oh, Beelzebub and Leviathan have been grooming American society for a long time," said Sister Adelaide, the specialist in holy visions, throwing out the information as if it were obvious.

"Beelzebub is one of the seven princes of Hell, right?" Stefan said, vaguely recalling a few lines from the Testament of Solomon. Am I right in assuming that he was known as *Baal* in the Canaanite religion?"

"Very good, Stefan," Adelaide said. "He was also known as "Lord of the Flies" from which William Golding derived the title of his novel. And Leviathan?" She looked around the table like a schoolmarm expecting someone to raise her hand with the answer. "Leviathan is often used to refer to any monster, especially one from the sea, but the actual Leviathan is a fire-breathing serpent who brings chaos and destruction to humankind. Many cultures include this creature in their mythologies. The Chinese dragon, for instance, is a representation of Leviathan, as is the Ophites in the Gnostic sect."

"Ophites?" Stefan was fascinated by mythological creatures.

"Yes," Adelaide said. "The Gnostics venerated the serpent of the Garden of Eden. In their belief the Leviathan appears as Ouroboros, separating the divine realm from humanity by enveloping and permeating the material world."

"But this is just a story, right?" said Patrick, obviously uncomfortable with the turn of the conversation.

"All stories are descriptions of reality, Patrick," Adelaide said. "Myths are stories which describe the reality of the unseen world."

"I don't get it," Patrick said. "Are these creatures Beelzebub and Leviathan real or not?"

"They are real, Patrick, but sometimes they don't take the appearance of a man with the head of a frog as Beelzebub is sometimes portrayed, or as a fire-breathing serpent as Leviathan is often pictured, but they become manifest in the principles they represent. Beelzebub lives in America as greed. The fact that wealth is held in the hands of a relatively few people who allow children to starve is a result of extreme greed, and the fact that many people believe that the wealthy have the right to rule the country, making laws that benefit only themselves, is also a manifestation of the frog-headed demon."

"What about Leviathan? Is he present in America?" Stefan asked.

"Oh, most certainly," Adelaide replied. "Leviathan represents chaos and destruction. Tell me, Stefan, where have you seen wanton destruction for no purpose?"

"I was stationed in Iraq," Stefan said.

"What did you see there?"

"A lot of destruction."

"Was there a purpose to the destruction?"

"Supposedly we were there to help the Iraqis build a new

nation, but actually we were just blowing up shit, killing people, and arresting supposed terrorists based on accusations from their neighbors."

"Did you feel you were doing God's work there?"

Stefan didn't answer. The whole conversation was bringing up painful memories.

"Oh!" Christina blurted out.

"What is it?" Zenobia asked quickly.

"Nothing," Christina smiled. "Just the baby gave a strong kick. It surprised me."

Stefan was grateful to his wife for causing a distraction. The talk of America doing Satan's work in Iraq disturbed him. He suspected that Christina had diverted the conversation on purpose to save him any more discomfort.

"When are you due?" Marta asked. She had served as a helicopter mechanic in Iraq and had lost her hand in a crash of a routine flight. Although she wasn't on the front line as Stefan had been, she was proud of her military service and didn't like to think she was doing Satan's work by serving the American Empire. She usually avoided political discussions with the Sisters who sounded like Marxists to her.

"Officially, my due date is next week, but the baby could come anytime."

"Do you know whether it's a boy or a girl?" Sister Delphina, the medical doctor, asked.

"A boy. We've chosen the name Francisco Stefan József," Christina said, looking at her husband who proudly sat up straight in his chair.

Everyone at the table nodded and murmured their approval of the name.

"They're back," José said, rising from the table and hurrying to the door, Dharma following behind him.

Maria, Theodora, and Xavi got out of the Suburban and stretched their arms and legs. It had been a long drive from Houston to this place in rural Sonora close to the Arizona border.

José gave Maria a hug. "How was the trip?"

"Long. We left yesterday morning and drove all night. We need to eat and sleep."

"I have Ndole for you, Mother Maria," Zenobia said. When Genevieve looked at her resentfully, Zenobia added. "I made a separate pot of Ndole for them, Sister. I couldn't let you eat all the food and leave nothing for them."

Genevieve shrugged and nodded, accepting the fact that other people needed to eat as well.

A place was set for Maria, Theodora, and Xavi, and they tucked in, not having had a proper meal since they left Houston.

"Where's Jesse?" José asked. He had been concerned about his stepson ever since the planning for this campaign had started.

"He's on a bus traveling from Houston to Mexico," Maria answered.

"A bus? Why is he taking a bus?" José asked.

"There are a few people on the bus he needs to meet," Maria answered.

José was accustomed to his wife having secret plans, so he let the subject drop.

"When will he be here?" Zenobia asked.

"In a few days," Maria answered, helping herself to more Ndole. "Zenobia, I think you've outdone yourself with this version. You used pecans?"

"Yes, Mother. I had to make substitutions because the produce here is different than in Africa."

"Lovely job," Theodora said. "Thank you for saving some for us."

Xavi was silently shoveling the food away. José could tell he was angry about something, but he knew his friend wouldn't talk about it, guessing that there had been an argument between Maria and Xavi. It certainly wouldn't be the first time. They were exact opposites. Maria was the earth mother, Xavi the destroyer of worlds. He knew that once Xavi had finished eating, he'd want to find a woman to satisfy him. Since the women in the convent were off limits, he'd probably want to drive into town. No problem, José thought, he would loan Xavi his truck.

Dharma liked staying at El Presidio. The Sisters were great cooks, and they always set aside a generous portion for her. She was the only dog on the premises. Of course, there were cats, two large gray ones that lived in the garage and kept out of sight. Their job was catching mice, of which there was an abundance. Dharma didn't like cats, but she was even less fond of mice, so she was glad to have the cats skulk around the place. As the only watchdog, she slept under the front porch of the main building close to the steps where she could keep an eye on the front gate across the courtyard. When a car drove up, she would bark a few times to let the Sisters know there were visitors, then Dharma watched cautiously to see how the visitors were received. Friend or foe was always the question. So far only friends had arrived, but she never let down her guard.

On the second night after their arrival, long after everyone had gone to sleep and the lights had been turned out, Dharma lay with her head sticking out from under the porch, looking at an infinity of stars in the blackness of the sky. When someone came out of the building, she recognized Maria's footsteps on the porch. Maria descended the steps next to Dharma and walked through the front gate and into the desert. Dharma followed behind at a good distance, curious. Maria's hair was loose, and she wore a long blue robe. She stopped and looked up at the scimitar moon, stretched out her arms and began to rise into the air. Dharma could hear her singing, and she understood that this was a prayer, but not like the prayers Dharma had heard her friend Father Jack, make. It was more like a humming in the air, and Dharma felt that this was the original prayer, the song the earth made to the sky.

As anyone who has studied the issue knows, dogs have a much better sense of theology than humans. Whereas humans have to diminish everything to a scale they can visualize—Sky father, Earth mother, God-crucified-on-a tree, Darkness-where-death-abides, etc.—dogs know things as they really are, the basic core of reality that cannot be reduced further. The human world is constructed from visual images and ideas attached to those images, so humans are fond of stories about the gods which supposedly explain why things have happened a certain way. This is false for two reasons: first, the world is not made of stories because stories depend on a plot which exists on a timeline, and the universe is not bound by time. Instead, as physicists are beginning to understand, everything is happening at once. But humans use their imaginations to stretch out reality to accommodate the fiction of time, and in this way, stories are constructed.

Second, gods are not humans; in fact, they are not even gods as the term is usually used. Instead, what humans imagine as deities are actually forces of nature acting according to laws which humans don't understand. This idea of a hierarchy of beings in which Gods rule the lives of humans, and humans, wanting to be godlike, rule the lives of dogs, is, of course, nonsense. Dharma understood that Stefan provided food and a place for her to sleep, but she, in turn, watched over him. When they lived in a cave beneath a bridge and ate out of garbage cans, it was Dharma who protected them from rats and thieves and policemen. She was the one who knew when to fight and when to flee. Stefan was far too trusting. He needed her when they were on the street, and now with the baby coming into a dangerous world, Stefan and Christina needed Dharma more than ever.

Maria finished her prayer, and walking back to the Presidio, she saw Dharma. *Dear, dear Dharma* she thought. *The others will never understand your central role in the coming struggle.* Passing through the front gate of El Presidio, Maria walked to the front porch of the main building and sat on a bench, Dharma at her feet. She reached down and stroked the dog's ear.

Dharma looked up at Maria, and when their eyes met, an infinity of truth was exchanged between them. Maria remembered listening to a lecture by Alex Beltran, the wisest mortal she'd ever known, which he delivered to a group of theology graduate students a year before:

"Hold your hand in front of your face. What do you see? An appendage of a certain size and color, fingers that move at the will of their owner, nails that need to be cut, perhaps a ring of precious metal, lines on the palm which recall quaint concepts such as lifeline, fortune and love. But what if you were told that none of this business that you perceive as your hand is real? What is real is that your hand, in fact your whole body, is made up not of solid flesh and blood, but of atomic particles vibrating at a wavelength that makes our reality possible. The distance between atoms is proportionate to the distance between stars, and therefore, everything which seems solid to you, your body, the chair you're sitting on, the floor under your feet, is actually empty space. The amount of solid matter in your entire body is less than the head of a pin. The concepts which make up our reality such as cause-and-effect, object permanence, and sequential time are merely useful constructions.

"So, you may very well ask, what is real in all this emptiness?

"Love.

"Love is what holds the universe together. Now before you walk away from this lecture in disgust, thinking you've wandered unknowingly into a story of long-lost lovers finding each other, consider one of many strange facts discovered by quantum physicists.

"When two electrons pass each other in the vast emptiness between atoms, they sometimes cling to each other for a fraction of a millisecond before spinning off on their separate paths. However, the two electrons have changed each other during their encounter. They have become more alike, perhaps even identical. And no matter how far apart they travel, even to the other side of the earth, they influence each other. So if you interrupt one electron, changing its direction, the other is also interrupted in its path. This union between distant electrons, this shared destiny, is the basis of what we call love..."

Maria knew that dogs understand love in a way that humans do not. Someone who has never loved or been loved by a dog might look at Dharma's attachment to Stefan, and more recently her attachment to Christine and the unborn baby, as coming from a protective instinct arising from pack behavior. According to this thinking, Dharma is a subordinate member of the pack, and so she obeys Stefan as the lead male and Christine as the lead female. Dharma protects their offspring as she would a puppy that's been born into the tribe. And all of this animal behavior theory is true, at least as far as it goes. But where does this instinct for devotion come from if the dog is nothing more than empty space with a few quadrillion atoms vibrating in a certain pattern? Isn't there a principle operating in living things which has its roots in the behavior of the protons, electrons, neutrinos, and quarks following laws we cannot imagine? Is a dog's love less real than a human's? Is a mother's love for her child less real than the earth's love for its creatures? Is a man's love for a woman less real than the sky's love for the earth? What are stories of the gods but a way that poets make sense of the forces that hold together the earth?

But the need to harmonize science and religion, to explain one misunderstanding with another, is a human impulse, and a recent one at that. Dogs need no explanation. Nor do goddesses.

Chapter 7

Huitzilopochtli had enjoyed the recent centuries of peace, but he knew they were coming to an end. It was true that the humans cut down the forests and mowed the meadows, destroying the wildflowers that his kind had always depended on, but the humans also planted gardens and introduced exotic flora that made for a rich and interesting diet for hummingbirds. For a long time, the God of the Hummingbirds had had no problem with humans. The nearby greenhouses produced plentiful rose blooms all year long, and slipping through the air vents beneath the roof had never been a problem for the hummers, some even choosing to remain in the woodlands of east Texas all year long, food being plentiful, but he, like most of his subjects, enjoyed the long migration back to Central America each year.

But now, the humans had gone too far. They had broken the fragile truce between bird and man. In recent generations, humans had covered the vast meadowlands with asphalt to accommodate their monstrous automobiles, and now they had introduced poisons that kill literally everything—birds, insects, mammals, even humans themselves. Humans had committed sacrilege, spraying the remaining meadowlands with herbicides that turned the lush grasslands brown. They even sprayed their own food crops with *nicotinoids*—yes, he had had to learn that word. What were they thinking? Didn't they know that the web of life is sacred? You cannot wipe out one species and expect that other species will survive. Humans had gone rogue, destroying

Gaia for no reason but their own greed. He had heard that faraway the seas were rising, and the skies were roiling. It was clear that nature was restless and a revolt against the humans was coming.

Today, as the God of Hummingbirds flew over fields that should have been green and thriving with life but were now dry and brown, he grew angry. And when he got back to the nest, his mate, the beautiful Yaritza whose name means *You will always be loved*, the most favored of his ten thousand wives, lay weak among the fledglings. Like so many other of their kind, she had fallen ill from drinking nectar from a wildflower in a poisoned field and would not survive the night. Huitzilopochtli lifted his head and let out the high-pitched call of grief only hummingbirds can hear, bringing his adjunct flying to him. "Send a message through our Mexican network to the God who calls himself Jesse," Huitzilopochtli said, "Tell him we will join his war."

Queen Zahra spoke to her most brilliant general Zaberi, saying, "Gather a horde of a million wasps zzzz and fly four days east to the place where the God of Hummingbirds lives. Wait there for the Goddess of Heaven to arrive. You will serve her as you serve me. During this war she will be your ruler."

Zaberi raised his wings in a salute and flew off to gather his horde for the long flight to war.

And the wild animals of the fields and forest heard the news of the coming war from the mockingbirds who speak every language. The animals who do not love war as the wasps and hummingbirds do, moved away from the place where the battle would be. The groundhogs hid in their burrows, the squirrels in their nests, the sparrows began their southern migration early, not waiting for autumn. And men remarked how beautiful the herons were as they lifted their wings and flew down the rivers passing in front of the moon.

But the warlike animals knew it was incumbent on them to serve Gaia, and if the goddess needed them to fight the humans, and even to die fighting them, they were willing. And so it came to pass that the raptors—the mighty eagle, the fierce hawk, the swift peregrine flew to the place of battle and waited for orders. The blue jays and the crows, the owl and the nightjar, flew to the broad meadows of the hummingbird where they had never dared to fly before, being afraid of the hummingbirds. All the animals, even down to the worms in the earth, knew what was coming. And the dogs who live with humans heard the howls of their wolf-brothers and were afraid. In the great gathering place where the armies of Gaia gathered, the animals knew what was coming and had made their peace with death. The deer and the rabbit offered their flesh to feed the wolf and the eagle, for Gaia requested it of them.

And Gaia Herself walked among them as a white tiger. She did not speak but gave them courage and purpose for the animals knew She is the ancestral mother of the soil and the sea. She is the web of life itself.

Jesse had no idea why his mother had insisted he take the bus back to Mexico, but he trusted her instincts. There was evidently someone he was destined to meet and something he was supposed to do or to learn on the bus. He caught the bus in Houston, and they drove through the bright morning. The bus stopped a few times letting off passengers and taking on others. No one paid any attention to Jesse, but as they drove west, he heard more Spanish and the people seemed more subdued as if they didn't want to call attention to themselves. The highway was bordered by miles and miles of bluebonnets and Indian paintbrushes. Pine and oak forest gave way to grassland and then to the low brushland of cedar and mesquite. There was a holdover in San Antonio. Jesse got off the bus in the cavernous garage and entered the crowded bus station. He was reminded of the depot where souls depart for heaven after death. Lots of people standing in line to buy a ticket, families sitting together on wooden benches, babies crying, toddlers holding their mothers' hands while they waited for a family member to catch up to them, having tarried in this life longer than they should have. Here, though, instead of stepping into the blue to fly into the clouds, people stepped on a bus to go south to McAllen on the border, or north to Dallas, or west to El Paso, as Jesse planned to do. So far, the journey had been unremarkable. No one had spoken to him. No one seemed to need his help. He'd heard a few prayers from the passengers, but nothing that required his intercession.

The bus from San Antonio to El Paso ran roughly parallel to the Mexican border, miles and miles of desert where clumps of dry grass and jumbles of prickly pear punctuated the red sand. Every now and then they would see a trailer near the highway, and beside it a rusting truck and a few goats and chickens. And every fifty miles or so, there would be a diner and a filling station which constituted the center of a small town that wasn't much more than a bus stop where the passengers could get out, stretch their legs, and buy a soft drink and a taco. At one of these places, which was a town only because it had a name, Jesse noticed a white non-descript sedan parked in front of the door. There was wire mesh separating the front seat from the back seat. Two men in white shirts and blue slacks were inside the convenience store talking to the clerk who shrugged his shoulders and looked down at the counter.

As soon as the travelers saw the white sedan and the clerk being questioned, most of them got back on the bus, sat low in their seats and tried to be invisible. Some of the passengers held their hands up to their faces and turned to look out the window that faced the desert. Jesse was one of the few who left the bus and walked into the convenience store. He could feel the ICE agents' eyes following him to the glass case where the soft drinks were displayed.

"Show me your papers, sir," one of the agents said, approaching Jesse, who understood that speaking English to him was a test. With his dark hair and brown skin, the agent would assume he was Mexican, or perhaps Central American. If Jesse had blonde hair, blue eyes and freckles, the agent wouldn't have asked for his papers. And now seeing Jesse's hesitation, the agent said "*Muéstreme sus papeles, señor.*"

Jesse knew he could say to the agent, "I speak English," in the flat Midwestern dialect that was the acceptable patois of White America, but Jesse was offended at this agent's sneer. He obviously thought he had caught an illegal alien. So instead of sliding out of the situation with the least amount of friction, Jesse simply handed over his driver's license which after the last run in with the police, he had memorized.

The agent scrutinized the license, then asked in Spanish if the suspect had any other identification. As soon as Jesse shook his head, the agent ordered him to put his hands on the glass case, handcuffed him, and marched him out to the white sedan.

Birdie had one more task to do before she could rendezvous with Maria and the sisters. She took a taxi to the San Fernando Valley where she found the bar easily. If she had had any doubt that this was the right place, the large pick-up trucks with American flag bumper stickers would have confirmed the location. She walked into the bar and every face turned to look at her. She was the only person of color and one of the few women in the bar. She scanned the room and saw the man she was looking for, a middle-aged white man with a brush cut, chiseled features and tattooed biceps bulging from his leather vest which he wore without a shirt underneath. She locked eyes with him and strode past the pool game to the table where he sat with two of his friends.

"Well," he said. "It's not often we get a nigra lady coming in here." His eyes went up and down her tall muscular frame. "Is there something we can do for you?"

Birdie answered his question by snap-kicking him hard in the face, breaking his nose. As his two companions stood up, she used a round house kick to the side of one man's head and followed it with a quick punch to the other man's belly. Then she went back to the first man, grabbing his wrist with one hand and chopping the back of his elbow with the other, dislocating the joint. The man fell to his knees. She kicked him in the chest, breaking a few ribs. Then she stepped over to the other two men and bringing her right heel down hard on the right fibula of one man and the left tibia of the other, snapped the bones cleanly in two.

As much as Birdie would have like to finish off these three men, this mission was off the books, and she didn't have a death waiver from her boss Rafe, so she contented herself with only breaking a few bones.

With all three men immobilized, Birdie turned and looked at each of the dozen men in the bar. "My name is Birdie Hawkins. These men raped a 14-year-old girl. They got what was coming to them," she snarled. "If I hear any of you has hurt a woman, I'll be back." She changed her voice into a demur high-pitched whisper, barely loud enough for everyone to hear her. "Ya'll don't want me to come back here, do you?"

Several men, their beers halfway to their mouths, slowly shook their heads. Birdie walked out of the bar and every man watched her, completely silent.

Stefan was glad that Christina was still asleep. The heat had been difficult for her to tolerate, but the nights were cool. He looked at his wife, beautiful in her pregnancy, carrying their son who'd be born soon. She'd cut her red hair short on the sides, almost boyish, but left it full on the top. She lay on her back, her face turned toward him, freckles covering her cheeks and arms. Other than his parents who died when he was twelve, she was the only person he'd ever loved, and soon there would be another person, his son, whom he would also love.

He sat at the narrow desk in front of the window and Dharma curled up on the floor next to his feet. Stefan wrote, "The sun gives birth to the day…"

The poem came quickly, as the best ones tend to do, and Stefan looked out the window. Dawn was breaking on the wide dry plain of cactus and mesquite. Donkey dung shone like golden apples on the dirt road. In the distance, an expensive looking blue roadster, a classic from the 1960s Stefan guessed, was coming fast toward the convent, trailing a plume of dust. As the sleek automobile came closer, Stefan could see a handsome man with black hair at the wheel and beside him a young blonde man. Someone opened the front gate, and the roadster drove into the courtyard of El Presidio.

Alex and Tristram were greeted at the front door by José who gave them each a hearty hug and welcomed them to El Presidio . He showed them the men's quarters where they'd be staying and suggested that they freshen up for breakfast. When Alex and Tristram got back to the main room wearing fresh clothes, they saw eight women and two men sitting at a long table piled with platters of scrambled eggs, bacon, corn tortillas, refried beans, rice, *salada* and *salsa.* Sister Delphina, who like the other women was gray-haired and fit, stood next to the table with a spatula in hand, keeping a close eye on the supplies of food and ready to make more if needed. While Tristram stood nearby, trying to get his bearings after being in the car all night, Alex walked over to the counter against the wall and poured himself a cup of coffee from one of the decanters. The aroma of the coffee wafted up to him.

He smiled at Maria who had left the table and now stood next to him. "Is this decaffeinated?" he asked, lifting his cup.

"May God forbid," she said with feigned shock. "We don't

allow decaf in this establishment." She gave him a big smile which lit up the room. "Hello, Alex, how was the drive down?"

"Uneventful," he said, shrugging. "I have a sixth sense for where the speed traps are, so we made good time."

"I actually wasn't expecting you until tomorrow."

"You intrigued me with your offer, Maria."

Alex and Tristram joined the others at the table and helped themselves to the food. Once everyone was sated, Maria suggested that they move to the common area where there was more comfortable seating. As everyone settled in, she said, "First I want to introduce our two newest members of the team, Father Alejandro Miguel Beltran, who is a professor of theology and his assistant Tristram Tittle. They will be handling some of our educational outreach. Now, I'm going to ask each member of the team to introduce yourselves, but first I want to ask Father Alex whether he's familiar with The Holy Sisters of the Piston.

"Only by reputation, Maria," he said, tossing back his dark curly hair which he had forgotten to pull back into his customary ponytail.

"Holy cow," Christina said under her breath, as she took a seat the breakfast table. "That is the most gorgeous man I've ever seen." Then she caught herself, glanced at her wonderful husband who had obviously heard her. "Sorry, darling," she whispered, "My hormones are making me wacky."

"I know the sisters only by reputation," Alex said in his barely detectable Spanish accent. "They are the Knights Templar of the modern age."

"Yes, well, I'm sure you meant that epithet as praise," Maria responded, seeing that a few of the sisters seemed uncomfortable with the historical comparison. "Perhaps we are the Knights Templar but without the Crusades and the Inquisition. Right, ladies?" Theodora and Delphina, the most educated of the nuns, nodded their heads.

"To save time with introductions," Maria continued. "I'd

like to go around the room and each person will say his or her name, occupation and special skills. Please, this is not a time to be modest. Everybody needs to know your expertise. Let's start with you, Theodora," Maria said, turning to the woman on her right.

"Sister Theodora, formerly from the Dominican Order, a member of the bar specializing in immigration and criminal law. I'm also a black belt in Jujitsu and Kung Fu."

"Sister Adelaide, formerly a Carmelite, student of visions and miracles. I'm also a computer hacker."

"Sister Genevieve, from the French order The Little Sisters of Jesus where I counseled the homeless. Motorcycle mechanic." Alex noticed that even sitting down, Genevieve looked like a very powerful woman, almost twice as big as the other nuns.

"Novice Sister Marta. Former US Army. Motorcycle, automobile and helicopter maintenance." Alex noticed that Marta had a prosthetic right hand and wondered if she had been injured in the war.

"Sister Inez. Elementary school teacher and former CIA operative. Extraction and interrogation specialist."

"Sister Zenobia. I come from Cameroon. I am an elementary school teacher because I love children. I speak twelve languages and I'm an expert with explosives."

"Sister Delphina, medical doctor. Specialist in emergency medicine and interrogation."

"José, carpenter and mechanic."

"Alex Beltran. Jesuit priest and professor of philosophy."

"Tristram Jones," the young blonde man to Alex's right said. "I'm just a student."

"Patrick Hawkins, singer. I founded a nonprofit center for homeless people. I guess I'm just here for my own protection…" Patrick shrugged and looked around as if someone could tell him what his role here was supposed to be.

"Patrick, when Birdie gets here, you two will team up to do special outreach to marginalized communities," Maria said.

"Birdie?" Patrick said, reacting to his deceased mother's nickname.

Maria smiled at Patrick. "All will be revealed soon enough.... Please continue."

"Stefan József, poet and non-profit administrator. Also, I was trained as a medic by the army. And this is Dharma, war-dog for God." Everyone laughed and Dharma wagged her tail.

"Christina O'Malley. I'm a therapist at the VA."

"You will notice," Maria added. "That Christina is with child. It is this child, who is possibly the new messiah, who brings us all together."

Christina blanched and turned to Stefan who looked at her with his mouth open. It was obvious to everyone that until now this happily married couple had no idea their soon-to-be-born son was at the center of the looming war. Maria hoped that this meeting would clear up their role in the evolving situation.

Just then, Xavi walked through the front door. He was unshaven and wearing the same clothes he'd been wearing the day before. Maria looked at the floor as he walked past the silent Sisters. Only José met his eyes and nodded a greeting. José could feel the tension in the air, and he wondered what had happened between Maria and Xavi.

Maria began: "I'm going to explain a few things that are happening in the world right now. Some of you," she gave a quick smile to her husband. "Know the whole story. Others," she nodded to the Sisters. "Know bits and pieces. And a few of you," she glanced at Stefan, Christina, Alex and Tristram. "Are just now joining us. So please forgive me if I say things that you already know. If we are going to work together, then we all need to be on the same page, right?" Maria glanced around the room, and people nodded their acquiescence.

"All of you know that one of the principles of the universe is the struggle between good and evil, the basic distinction between these two opposites is that good creates and sustains life and evil diminishes and destroys life. However, this is an oversimplification because death is a necessary condition for life, and evil beings have a life of their own. So, a more accurate definition is that good and evil are aspects of the same process, a dialectic. Just as life and death cannot exist without each other, so good and evil cannot exist without each other. All life is part of the Great Cycle of rejuvenation and decay, and all goodness is part of the Great Wisdom which includes love and hate."

Maria let her listeners absorb what she'd said so far, then she continued. "And of course, if there is measurement then there is a Measurer, an Intelligence that is all-knowing and all-seeing. This is the G.O.D. that the gods believe in, Good Orderly Direction as it is sometimes called, a consciousness that holds the universe together and which is so large and so complex that even the gods themselves cannot comprehend it. Sometimes, this consciousness is called the Creator. Other times the Dreamer or the Author. This consciousness has created the earthly plane you are familiar with, as well as the celestial plane."

Maria paused and looked around the room at the expressions on the faces in front of her. José, having accepted this wisdom long ago, was serene. The sisters seemed calm and interested. Alex, by contrast, sat on the edge of his seat, his Jesuit mind racing with arguments and counterarguments, while Tristram's smooth pink face looked skeptical. Maria wondered about Tristram. Alex had introduced the young man as his assistant, but what purpose did he serve on the celestial plane? Maria turned to look at Stefan and Christina holding hands, clearly still in shock over the revelation about their unborn child. They probably felt as if they'd fallen down the rabbit hole where nothing was what they'd always thought it was. When Maria shifted her gaze toward Patrick, she found him staring straight at her, eyes wide, mouth open, apparently frightened by what he was hearing.

"I've told you about this Dreamer," she resumed, "so that you can accept that the gods in the dream are not all-powerful or all-knowing, but rather they are characters in a drama where they act out their own desires, and not out of a need to do good. Each of them—each of *us*—is a combination of good and evil. Each of us serves both life and death. Let's start, for example, with God the Father, the one you might call Jehovah, based on the Jewish god Yahweh, the Tetragram. He was discovered by a man named Abraham who saw that there was an intelligent being who sometimes took the form of a whirlwind, or a burning bush, or a voice in the desert. Abraham worshipped the Voice and taught his wife and children to worship it as well. And Abraham called this being the Word and attributed to it, with little evidence, the creation of the world. The Voice told Abraham that he was the only god, but this was obviously not true because there was another. Abraham experienced this other god as the presence of light. And sometimes the Word and the Light seemed to be working together and sometimes they seemed to be working against each other. Abraham continued to worship the Word and over time the Light became jealous and wanted to be worshipped as well."

Maria's audience followed the story with rapt attention, understanding that these were characters created to help them understand, real only in the sense that characters in a play are real. They were real only while the dream lasted, but the dream was the world they knew, and they knew no other.

"Abraham had a wife whose name was Sarai," Maria continued. "And Sarai was a good wife, obedient to her husband, wise in the management of their household, and more aware than she let on, wiser, in fact, than her husband. She understood that the Word was not the only god as Abraham wanted to believe. She understood that the Light was also a god. She knew the two gods were brothers of equal power, and she knew something that Abraham did not know, and that she did not tell him: there was another god much older than the two brothers. The name of that god was Gaia, and she was the mother of all things on earth because Gaia is the earth itself, separate from the sea and sky which are gods unto themselves."

Maria stopped again and looked around the room. "Any questions?" she prompted.

Patrick tentatively raised his hand. "So Gaia would be your mother?"

"Correct."

"And Jesse is your son?"

"Yes. Jesse is the product of my first marriage with the one you call Jehovah."

"Do you have other children?" Christina asked.

"I have had many children, but Jesse is one of the two who have survived."

The room was quiet while everyone wondered what kind of power could kill almost all of Maria's children, but no one wanted to ask her.

"And what relation to you is Xavi?" Stefan asked, breaking the silence. It seemed strange to be talking about Xavi when he was in the men's sleeping quarters on the other side of the wall, but Stefan felt this was the only opportunity any of the mortals would have to clear up the relationships between these strange beings known as gods.

"Xavi is the name he's using now, but he is known generally as Shiva, and he comes from a separate ancient lineage. His father was Rudra the Weeper, the god of storms and of the hunt. Shiva has a paradoxical nature. He is known both as *the Destroyer* and as *the Auspicious One*. He is part of a triad made up of Brahma the Creator and Vishnu the Preserver. Together they represent the cycle of the universe. Shiva is also the four-armed Lord of the Dance. Maybe you have seen the beautiful depiction where he moves beautifully inside a ring of flames holding a drum and a torch representing creation and destruction, as well as protection and salvation? He is simultaneously the celibate ascetic who holds a beggar's bowl made from a human skull and also the god of sexual energy who has both male and female parts. He destroys, and also he regenerates. He performs the dance of anger which can destroy the universe, and he also performs the dance of peace and love which brings blessings on households. Shiva, many believe, contains all opposites within him."

"He sounds like a very powerful god," Alex said softly, nodding his head and beginning to understand the reality that Maria was describing and wondering how all of this theogony fit into the Catholic faith he believed in.

"Shiva, who is currently in the form of Xavi, the young man you just saw walk past us, is indeed a powerful god. His worshippers believe he is the most powerful of the gods."

"Is this dude on our side?" Patrick asked, voicing the question they all had on their minds.

Maria shrugged, "In the celestial war that occurred last year and many of you participated in at the Otay Bridge, Xavi joined us to fight Lucifer. Without his help, we never could have won."

"I think that everyone has the necessary background. Let's take a break, okay?" Maria asked. "I need to talk with Xavi and also with Birdie, one of our operatives who should be here any moment. Let's meet back here in two hours to discuss our mission."

Jesse had spent the night sitting on the cement floor of an outdoor cage with two dozen other men. He hadn't slept because of the noise. It was so crowded he couldn't move in any direction without being jostled. Beside the gate was a bucket of water which smelled foul and had insects and bits of garbage floating in it. There was no toilet, so men relieved themselves in one corner of the cage. The guards never removed any filth. The cage had no roof, so the only shelter from the sun and rain was provided by the hats and coats the men might have brought with them. A couple of hours after daybreak, two buckets of food were put beside the door, but there were no bowls or utensils, so the men who were hungry had to dip both hands in the gray porridge and eat from the cup of their own flesh. Some of the men spat out the foul porridge and cursed in Spanish.

The other cage held the women. Unlike the men, they were silent, or they huddled in small groups of two or three whispering, crying, and trying to comfort each other. In one corner, they had hung a couple of blankets to shield their latrine area from the eyes of the men.

And beside the women's cage was a cage that held nine children, some of them no more than two years old. Jesse could see that the older girls and boys were trying to care for the younger children, but the small ones, separated from their mothers, cried constantly and could not be consoled. All the children were hungry, frightened, and ill.

None of the cages had soap or running water. No one was interrogated or given a chance to explain anything. Their papers, including Jesse's driver's license, were never returned to them. They had no chance to talk to an attorney or plead their cases for refugee status. They were treated as vermin, as animals who had wandered across the border and needed to be returned to where they belonged.

And knowing that there were hundreds of these facilities along America's southern border and tens of thousands of people detained, Jesse wept.

After three days in the cage, officers placed plastic wrist ties on Jesse and the other men, and they were marched to a bus. Jesse overheard one of the guards saying that there were new illegal aliens who were on their way to the detention center, so they were going to drive these men to the border and let them enter Mexico. The Mexican border police had already agreed to let them through.

As the prisoners walked past the women's cage, some of the men shouted to their wives or children that they would meet them on the other side of the wall, and the women waved goodbye, shouting "*Te quiero*" and "*Dios vaya con tigo, mi amor.*" The children screamed in terror as they saw their fathers and brothers taken away.

Jesse vowed he would return to help the children.

Birdie drove across the border and found El Presidio with no problem. In her previous life, which she remembered clearly, she'd spent several days at the convent. That time, she had taken the form of a Black church lady, Patrick's mother, a woman of uncommon faith and courage. She remembered being struck down by state troopers on the Otay Bridge as she led migrants from the Mexican border to the outskirts of San Diego. And now, here she was, a fit athletic woman who was something of a vigilante. Her mission now was to protect women and children by any means necessary. The terms of her assignment were that she was allowed to use violence and intimidation to achieve her mission, but she couldn't cause the death of a human unless, of course, she was awarded a waiver.

"So, you do remember who you are this time?" Maria asked from behind her desk in her office. Birdie was sitting in the hard metal folding chair in front her, feeling as if she were an errant student called into the principal's office.

"Yes, I do," Birdie said. "I'm an agent on special assignment. I'm not sure what caused me to forget my true identity last time. Perhaps it was just the length of the mission. I was on earth for over twenty years, and I adopted the life of a human. I raised Patrick. I helped Reverend Sheffield build and run the church. I guess I just submerged myself into the role so thoroughly that my celestial identity began to feel like a dream, a fantasy that I'd invented to feel my life was important."

"Well, your last life was important, Birdie. You accomplished so much. Patrick has emerged as a leader, and you helped Reverend Sheffield bring the light to so many lost souls. But I'm glad that now you know who you really are." Maria paused, looking at her old friend. "What can you tell me about your current mission? Or can you tell me?" Maria didn't like the way Rafe sometimes kept her in the dark.

"I don't have any secrets from you, Maria. Rafe sent me here to be your wing-woman. As you know, some of our most effective women are being killed or intimidated by men. Rafe thought you could use an enforcer to keep the fathers, husbands, and boyfriends in line."

"And random strangers as well?"

"If need be, but strangers usually don't act out their hatred against women. It's usually men who are close to the women who try to control them through intimidation. Sometimes, the process is subtle, taking place over a long period of time. Other times, the intimidation is brutal. In either case, we need to make it clear to these men that if they are going to be in the lives of these women, then they have to respect boundaries."

"What about women who hurt men? Women who abuse their sons or grandsons, for example? Are you involved in those situations?"

"I'm sure such things happen, but they are not part of my brief."

"Not your monkey, not your circus?" Maria asked with a wry grin.

"Exactly."

The Birdie that Maria remembered from before was a small thin church lady with a passion for caring for children while the woman now sitting across from Maria was grim and fierce. Maria missed her old friend.

"Birdie, I think we need to give Rafe's instructions to you a broader interpretation."

"What do you mean?"

"Well, I don't really need a "wing-woman." I have the Sisters here. What I need is for you to provide protection for Patrick."

"My son?" Birdie thought for a moment. "Oh, I see, you're sending him on a mission, and you need me to be his bodyguard."

"That's right. Are you willing to do it?"

"Of course. You know I would do anything for him. What's his mission?"

"We need him to do missionary work to underserved communities," Maria responded. "The established churches of all three Abrahamic religions have marginalized gay, lesbian, queer and trans people, often denying them participation in religious rites and pushing them out of the congregations."

"Yes," Birdie said sadly. "I saw this happen when I was raising Patrick. Our reverend was always kind and accepting, but most of the congregation was cold toward Patrick."

"Patrick has important work to do carrying the Word to the people, but he is vulnerable. There are many bigots who will want to silence him."

"Don't worry, Maria. I will do everything in my power to protect him."

Maria could see that Birdie wanted to ask her a question but was uncomfortable doing so. "What is it, Birdie?"

"Does Patrick know who I am?"

"I don't think so. This is a conversation the two of you need to have."

"Yes, it is," Birdie said, slowly. "He's still just a boy, barely twenty years old and we're putting so much responsibility on him."

"Well, now he has you to help him carry that responsibility."

After Birdie left Maria's office, Xavi came in. He looked at the hard metal chair in front of the desk, crossed his arms, and looked at her with a wry stare. With an apologetic shrug, Maria got up from her desk, grabbed the hard metal chair and moved it to the corner where she grabbed a larger, more comfortable wingback chair and put it in front of the desk. Xavi nodded his thanks, sat in the wingback and crossed his legs. Maria understood her show of respect was part of the necessary dance between them. Xavi was crucial to her mission, and he knew it, and if it took a little obsequiousness on her part to gain his cooperation, then she was willing to do it.

"Xavi," she began in her most gentle tone. "What's wrong? I'm sensing a certain reluctance on your part. You know we need you for this campaign. What can I do to make you feel more comfortable?"

Xavi stared at her levelly, his black eyes like onyxes beneath his dark brow.

She and Xavi had known each other for a long time, and she knew his vanity was vast, as were his powers. She sat across the desk from him, serenely waiting for him to speak. Although time was of the essence, she knew she would have to be patient with him.

"Maria," he said finally. "You should not be running this campaign."

Ah, she thought, *so this is what's bothering him. He feels his role has been usurped.*

Xavi said, "This whole campaign began last year when your boy Jesse and I were sent by The Old Man to destroy the world. Jesse changed his mind because, for some mysterious reason, he likes these little humans. I supported him in his decision to go against not only his father, but also his uncle Lucifer. Without my support, Jesse would never have prevailed in his desire to save this world."

"You're absolutely right, Xavi," Maria conceded. "Without you, we never could have won the campaign last year. Thank you for supporting Jesse and me." She felt like hugging him, but she refrained, fearing he would see affection as a ruse at this point. "Xavi, we still need your help. You know what's at stake."

Xavi shook his head slowly, still penetrating Maria with his dark gaze. "All of this organizing you are doing. This management, this business of inspiring and leading by example..." He gave a rueful laugh. "You should dispense with it all. I can destroy this world and then rebuild another one simply by dancing."

Maria nodded. "Of course, Xavi. You are the most powerful one of us, but the problem is that if you do all the work, then there's no place for the humans in their own salvation. They need to engage with the powers of light and dark themselves.

We cannot do their work for them." She waited, allowing him to consider what she'd said. "Xavi, I need to ask you. Are you with Jesse and me? Can we count on you in the coming war?"

Xavi shrugged. "I haven't decided yet." And just like that, he turned and walked out the door, leaving Maria with a sense of emptiness. *It's not time to panic yet*, she thought. *Let's see what he decides.*

"Does Maria know about us?" Tristram asked Alex as they walked down the road away from the convent.

"I don't know. I don't think so." Alex looked across the desert, noticing the long shadows cast by the poplar trees that lined the dirt road. *How strange*, he thought. *Poplars need a lot of water, but here they are tall and healthy in the desert.* He wondered whether there was an underground stream that followed the road, and the trees were bringing up the invisible life-giving water to make their beautiful white bark and broad green leaves. He was reminded, not for the first time, that sometimes what is essential for life is hidden to others.

"She actually thinks that she is the biblical Mary, mother of Jesus?" Tristram asked, shaking his head in disbelief. He looked at Alex. "Do you believe she's Mary?"

"I'm not sure," Alex said. He felt unsure of a lot of things right now. He didn't like the feeling of uncertainty. As a Jesuit, he'd been trained to think logically. Gather the known facts and proceed from there. His belief in God was the result of examining the evidence. He'd studied science which showed that the universe is ultimately unknowable, so the belief in a creator, a divine intelligence, was a reasonable, hypothesis supported by fact. The idea that a divine being could appear in front of him had never even occurred to him until he met Maria, but when he was with her, he had no trouble believing she was Mother Mary. As soon as he was away from her, his doubts returned.

"How do you know her?" Tristram asked.

"When I was an undergrad at St. John's, the dean called me into his office. I was an excellent student, but my scholarship covered only my tuition. I was having to work long hours in a restaurant as a busboy to pay my living expenses. I was exhausted and my studies were suffering. The dean told me that Maria had contacted him offering to establish a scholarship fund for a needy student. He had told her about me and offered to introduce us. The three of us went out to lunch, and she asked a lot of questions about my plans. Even back then, I knew I wanted to go to seminary and become a teacher. She offered to give me enough money to live on as long as I stayed in school. She told me very little about herself, just that she had come into some money and wanted to use it to help a worthy student."

"Did you see her again?"

"Yes. Every few years, I'd be working on a project, helping to found an elementary school in Honduras or helping disaster refugees in Louisiana, and Maria would show up with her checkbook. She was a Godsend." And right that minute, for the first time, Alex understood the meaning of the term.

"You know she's in love with you, right?"

Alex looked away from his lover. He knew that many people, men and women, were attracted to him, and he sometimes used that knowledge to get what he wanted. He tried to be ethical about his attractiveness, not asking anything for himself, but he had to admit he enjoyed the feeling that people appreciated his good looks. Once a week, he confessed his vanity, but he had never asked God to remove the character defect.

"How do you feel about her? Are you in love with her?"

Alex turned to the young man and saw the look on his face, not jealousy but fear. "Oh, no, Tristram," he said taking the young man in his arms. "You are my one and only. I love only you." And he leaned down and kissed the young man on the lips.

And looking out the window, Maria saw the two men embracing, and for the second time in one day, she felt an emptiness growing inside her. Then she remembered José, a good man who had stood beside her for so many years, a man who loved her and would do anything for her, and she resolved to put aside this desire for Alex, a passing yearning, the result of having a woman's body. She had always been faithful to José, and she would remain so.

Just then, José came into her office, and as she was turning toward him, he placed his hand on her shoulder and said, "I received a call from Jessie. He's been in ICE custody..."

José picked up Jesse at the bus station in town, and the two men, the middle-aged carpenter and the thin, almost effete, teenager drove to El Presidio in silence. José could see that his stepson was working something out in his mind, and didn't want to interrupt the process. José was glad to see Jesse. He'd always liked the boy and known he was special, but he also loved him as a father loves his son. Maria had been pregnant when he married her, and José had been glad to help the young woman who was younger than Jesse is now. José had known from the beginning that Maria was a remarkable young woman, intelligent and serene, with an inner light that brought peace to the people around her. It wasn't until much later, when Jesse was about six years old, that José had begun to sense that his beautiful young wife and their gifted son were not like the other people in their town of Nazareth. The boy had found a dead bird beside their front door and brought the corpse into the house. José was going to tell him to take the bird outside, but he saw the boy was weeping. Jesse put the bird on the floor and sat in front of it. He waved his small hand over the feathered lump, and the bird began to tremble, then it fluttered its wings and rolled over, lifting itself off the floor. Then the bird hopped a few times, spread its wings and flew around the room. The little boy ran to the front door and opened it, letting the bird fly outside. José looked out the window in amazement as the bird disappeared into the sky.

Ever since that day, José had understood that Maria and

Jesse were more than they appeared, and as the years passed, he'd seen more miracles, but the most remarkable one of all was that after Jesse had met his terrible fate at the hands of the soldiers, his parents never aged. José and Maria had remained the same age they'd been when Jesse had died. And now, José was over two thousand years old, but he still looked like a middle-aged man .

So now, if Jesse needed just to sit in the truck brooding, then José was glad to drive, silently following the dirt road back to the convent. As they sped through the dark, José remembered Jesse's youth all those years ago in Nazareth. After they'd celebrated the boy's bar mitzvah, José took him on as an apprentice, teaching Jesse how to measure and cut wood, to repair doors and windows, to lay a foundation and build a roof. By then he knew Jesse could have done these tasks simply by waving his hand, and yet he applied himself to learn the craft. His wife said, "He's destined for great things, but first he needs to learn how to be a good man. José, he's your son, teach him to be like you."

Chapter 8

"Alright, everyone," Maria said. "Let's get started again." Standing beside a desktop computer on a small table, she waited until the sisters had settled themselves into the kitchen chairs, leaving the more comfortable sofa and wing-back chairs for their guests Christina, Stefan, Alex, Tristram, Patrick, and Birdie, who had just arrived. Dharma settled herself on the sofa between Christina and Stefan and fell asleep.

"Oh, before I forget," Maria said. "Let me introduce Birdie Hawkins who just drove down from southern California where she was handling a special mission. Birdie will be accompanying Patrick as he travels across North America doing educational outreach."

Birdie raised her hand in a friendly greeting to everyone, and Maria noticed Sister Inez, a former CIA operative who was Maria's point person on Special Ops, looking at Birdie, sizing her up. Maria hoped the two of them could work together. There was no room in this campaign for professional rivalry. Maria also noticed Patrick who did a double take when he heard Birdie's name which was the same as his mother's. Maria decided to let Birdie explain her new incarnation to Patrick in her own way.

"Now," Maria said. "Good morning, everyone. I know you're all still confused about what we're doing here. Just suffice to say that the fate of humanity rests with us."

"No pressure there," Inez muttered under her breath.

"We are trying to save our world, and give humans another chance," Maria said. "Let's be perfectly clear about the fact that there are forces who currently wish to destroy the human race, forces who have given up on man's ability to be good...."

Maria could sense fear growing in the room, so she quickly added, "Let me assure you that the facility where we are now, El Presidio, is secure. We have an electronic shield that protects us from satellite surveillance, and we sweep the buildings for listening devices as well." Maria glanced at Inez who nodded.

"As I mentioned to you before," Maria went on. "Our ultimate aim is to protect Christina and Stefan's unborn baby and help the new mom to a healthy birth and a safe place to raise the child who, as most of you know, is the infant described in the King James version of *Revelation 12:1-6*." Maria recited:

> Now a great sign appeared in heaven: a woman clothed with the sun, with the moon under her feet, and on her head a garland of twelve stars. Then being with child, she cried out in labor and in pain to give birth. And another sign appeared in heaven: behold, a great, fiery red dragon having seven heads and ten horns, and seven diadems on his heads. His tail drew a third of the stars of heaven and threw them to the earth. And the dragon stood before the woman who was ready to give birth, to devour her Child as soon as it was born. She bore a male Child who was to rule all nations with a rod of iron. And her Child was caught up to God and His throne. Then the woman fled into the wilderness, where she has a place prepared by God, that they should feed her there one thousand two hundred and sixty days."

Maria paused and let everyone get used to the idea that the prophecy was coming true and that they were playing a role in it.

Sister Zenobia, the linguist, raised her hand. "Mother Maria, as you know, the King James Version is not the most accurate translation."

"Thank you, Sister," Maria said. "But it is the most beautiful, and right now I'm not sure that the prophecies are completely accurate. We threw some sand in the machinery last year, you might say, when we stopped the Apocalypse. To change the metaphor, we are now flying by the seat of our pants. And right now, poetry is the best way we have of understanding the current situation."

Everyone turned to look at Stefan, the poet, who gave a small shrug and nod.

"So, at the heart of the struggle, what we have is a woman, a dragon and a child." Maria said. "We now know that the woman is Christina, the child is the unborn boy in her womb, and the Dragon.... Who or what is the dragon?" Maria looked around and focused on Alex, the biblical scholar.

"The image of the dragon is used inconsistently through the sacred texts," Alex said, picking up the cue from Maria. "It first appears in the Old Testament to refer to Yahweh, probably a very old metaphor which found its way into the sacred text as a linguistic artifact. And later in the sacred text, Daniel kills a dragon worshipped by the Babylonians. So, in the Old Testament, the dragon is a symbol both of God the Father and of a blasphemous idol. In the New Testament a dragon appears only once: in the passage in *Revelations* that Maria quoted where the dragon embodies Satan the Evil One who attempts to vanquish the woman who has given birth to a new messiah."

As Alex was speaking, Maria clicked a mouse on the pad next to the computer, and an image of Blake's masterpiece *The Great Red Dragon and Woman Clothed in the Sun* appeared on the stucco wall behind Maria. Everyone in the room was transfixed by the beauty of the image. Sunlight bathes the woman sitting on a crescent sliver of moon. Darkness fills the sky above as the dragon's wings stir a great wind sweeping the woman's hair upward, flamelike. Below her feet, rising floodwaters overwhelm hapless souls. As Satan hovers over her, God grants her wings to carry her to safety.

Alex interpreted the scene for his new friends: "Notice the

outstretched arms of both the dragon and the woman arc toward each other in a mirror image suggesting the duality of good and evil which depend on each other for their existence. According to Revelation, the earth will open to swallow the water, and the thwarted dragon will fly away to wage war against the woman's progeny. For Blake, it is spiritual power—the purity and goodness represented by the woman—that always prevails."

Looking at the overpowering beauty of the image on the wall and thinking about the implications of what Alex had said, everyone in the room was silent as they absorbed the enormity of the task they were being charged with.

"And may I ask," Alex said. "What is our primary task, our ultimate goal in this endeavor?"

"Our primary goal, the task we need to always keep in mind, is the protection of Christina and her unborn child," Maria answered. "They hold the key to the long-term survival of all that is good in this world."

When Christina cocked her head, indicating puzzlement, Maria realized that the mortals in the room didn't understand the metaphysical importance of the unborn child in her womb. "The child is the Chosen One, he who is destined to establish a kingdom on earth that will align with the Kingdom of Heaven. It will be a just society where Creation is honored, not destroyed, where men and women will live in harmony with nature and with each other. We must protect this child at all costs, or Satan will rule the world in darkness."

Maria gave them a moment to gather themselves, then she said, "Now, let's talk about tactics."

The wall behind Maria that held Blake's image went dark, then lit up once more with a map of Texas. Maria used a poplar stick to point at an area north of Houston. "Our intelligence," she nodded at Sister Inez, the former CIA operative. "Tells us that the battle will take place here." She pointed at an area near Conroe, Texas, a heavily wooded region, now speckled with exurban bedroom communities. "For thousands of years, it's been one of the northern kingdoms of Huitzilopochtli, the Hummingbird God." Maria paused for a moment, wondering whether she should explain that Huitzi was her son and he'd murdered most of his brothers and sisters because they'd encouraged her to abort him in the womb. Finally, she decided not to distract her listeners with the tragedy of her own family, and she simply said, "Huitzilopochtli is an extremely violent, unpredictable, and beautiful god, but in this war, it's in his interest to fight the forces of darkness because if those forces take over, the hummers, his subjects, will certainly be wiped out for no reason other than evil hates beauty.

"We have other allies as well," Maria continued. "Queen of the Wasps, has sent one million warriors to aid us, and the White Tiger has been recruiting hawks, eagles, cougars, wolves, coyotes and foxes to join up—although their numbers are not large, they are fierce in defending their young."

Stefan leaned toward Alex who was sitting beside him. "The White Tiger?" he asked.

Alex gave a small shrug, as much in the dark as Stefan.

"The White Tiger…" Maria looked around the room, realizing that some people didn't know the pantheon as well as others, so she explained, "The White Tiger is the embodiment of Gaia, the mother of all living things. She was content to allow the apocalypse to happen as a cleansing, but things have gone far past cleansing and now we are looking at the triumph of darkness. Her power has been weakened in recent centuries with the rise of the humans and their destructive ways, but—"

Maria was interrupted by Jesse and José coming through the front door. Jesse ignored his mother and walked past the people sitting in front of her and went into the kitchen. José stopped and looked at his wife who nodded to him. José followed his stepson into the kitchen. It was obvious to Stefan that there was tension between Maria and Jesse.

"Now for the hard part," Maria continued. "The demons we'll be fighting have the appearance of humans, but animals can tell the difference."

"Excuse me, Maria," Alex said. "Why is it that humans can't see demons, but animals can?"

"Well, that's a long story, Alex," Maria answered. "But the short answer is that humans surrendered certain powers when they became aware of good and evil. Anyway, the important thing here is that we are going to be depending on the insects, birds, and mammals to fight the demons. The humans will provide logistical support. Got it?"

Everyone in the room nodded. Sister Inez, the attorney, raised her hand, "Logistical support? What might that be?"

"Whatever is needed to help the mortal species fight evil. Food and water certainly. Also, keeping other humans out of the area, so they don't become collateral damage. We'll need to invent a large-scale fictional emergency, such as a toxic chemical spill, to clear the area of civilians. We'll also need to stop or distract the military from moving into the area. Inez and Adelaide, perhaps you can work with our public relations team Stefan and Christina, to concoct some kind of fictional event to be released to the press?"

The two nuns looked at Stefan and Christina who nodded assent.

"Genevieve and Marta, perhaps you can figure out how to transport food and water to the non-human animals who will be doing the fighting? Theodora, I'll need you on standby to provide legal assistance because some of what we're doing will be considered illegal and the authorities will try to stop us. Zenobia, your mission is procurement of food and water for the animals and humans. And of course, Delphina, we'll be needing your medical skills."

"I'll brush up my veterinary chops, Mother Maria," Sister Delphina said.

Maria nodded her appreciation at the only physician in the room. "Thank you, Delphina, our primary mission is to protect Christina and her unborn child." Then she added, "Meanwhile, our celestial team, which consists of José, Jesse, and me, will be in the battlefield, fighting beside the White Tiger and her legions.

"To prepare the humans for what's coming," Maria continued. "We're sending out two teams of missionaries. Patrick, accompanied by Birdie, will be doing drag shows and making videos for the internet. He's tasked with reaching nontraditional and marginalized people."

Birdie stretched her long dark muscled arms and said, "Can't wait." Birdie looked around the room, then caught Maria's eye. The message was clear. *Where's Xavi? Where is the Destroyer of Worlds when we need him? Will he fight beside us?* Maria nodded at her friend. The two of them would speak with Xavi and see what he planned to do.

"And Alex," Maria said looking at the handsome priest and his young blonde companion. "You and Tristram have the essential task of carrying out a speaking tour."

"A speaking tour?" Alex asked puzzled.

"This is a war fought not only with violent confrontation with evil, but even more importantly, it is a war of ideas." Maria squinted at the two outreach teams—Patrick and Birdie, Alex and Tristram—bringing to mind their respective strengths. "Humankind has allowed itself to be misguided. Racism, sexism, xenophobia, homophobia have poisoned the minds of many people. When one believes that the other is inferior, then permission to mistreat them is implicit. Much of the evil in the world is caused by wrong ideas which lead to immoral actions. Patrick and Alex, you are great teachers. You will make parallel national tours, and with Birdie's and Tristram's help, you will explain, discuss, question and debate. Your goal is to undermine Satan by defeating the ideas he champions."

Alex nodded slowly, understanding the importance of the task and realizing that he had been training his whole life for this speaking tour. Tristram looked at him adoringly, the respect and admiration on the young man's face was obvious to everyone in the room, including Maria who realized she had to let go of the girlish crush she'd had on Alex for years. As Alex looked deeply into his young lover's eyes, Maria knew that these two men, the older wiser one and his young acolyte were meant for one another. Maria swallowed her pride, glanced at José who was watching her from the back of the room, aware of her struggle with her human desires, and she returned to the task at hand.

"Patrick," Maria said to the tall young Black man. "You have a gift for winning people over through song. Your Aretha impersonation on the Otay Bridge last year inspired our people to march into danger. You need to do the same thing with a wider audience. Use your gifts to teach and inspire people who feel they have no power. Show them the power within them."

Patrick looked at Birdie, tears in his eyes. She reached over and took his hand in hers.

"Now, my friends," Maria concluded. "Why don't you break into your respective teams and start strategizing. Delphina and Zenobia, how about the two of you, who are in charge of medical support and food procurement, work closely with Genevieve and Marta, the transportation team? There are lots of problems to solve with logistics."

Chapter 9

In the kitchen, Jesse sat at the table while José put plates of Zenobia's Ndole, Jollof Rice, and Hot Pot Potatoes in front of him. He had eaten only convenience store food since his release at the border, and he piled his plate high and started shoveling food into his mouth.

José watched him eat and when it seemed that the sharp edge of hunger had dulled, he said gently, "You didn't even look at your mother, Son. Perhaps when she's finished with the training session, you can give her a hug?"

Jesse said nothing but continued to eat. Ever since José had seen Jesse at the bus station an hour before, it had been obvious that the boy was angry, but he hadn't asked, understanding that Jesse would speak when he was ready. And now, having seen the way Jesse strode past his mother without acknowledging her, José decided not to intervene. This was a problem mother and son needed to work out between them, and if José tried to mitigate, then he wouldn't be available to them if they needed to talk.

As Jesse ate, José talked about the repairs he'd been doing to the outer wall which was almost three hundred years old and needed constant maintenance. Then, just to fill the silence, he talked about the Harleys and the work that Genevieve and Marta were doing to keep them in top condition. "Harleys are great machines, you know, but they are so temperamental. Almost like a racehorse. Things of great beauty need constant attention. I personally prefer the Ducati. It's fast and light, but we need the power of the Harleys for long distance hauls. Besides, we have only the one Ducati..."

José was relieved when Maria came into the kitchen. He was running out of things to talk about—babbling to fill the silence created by Jesse's resentment. As Maria slid into a chair at the table, José said he needed to talk with Genevieve about something and slipped out of the room.

Maria sat for a few moments looking at her son who refused to look at her.

"You're angry with me," she said. It wasn't a question.

Silence.

"I heard they arrested you and put you in one of those cages where they keep migrants who don't have papers."

Silence.

"When I told you to take the bus, I didn't know what was going to happen to you, so I'm sorry to have insisted. It must have been very hard for you."

Silence.

"Jesse, please talk to me. I'm sorry you've suffered, but I was not the one who hurt you."

Jesse turned his face toward this mother's. "You said I was supposed to meet someone on the bus. Who did you think I was going to meet?"

"I didn't know. I just had a feeling that it was an experience you needed to have. Here we are trying to save humanity, but the only humans you know are ones that are completely cut off from the rest of humanity. Christina, Stefan, Alex, the sisters... these are not ordinary people, but ones who have been chosen for a special purpose. I thought it would be good for you to meet ordinary people. Migrants, bus drivers, farmworkers, children..."

"Border agents, policemen, prison guards, torturers..." he said, imitating her voice. "Mother, do you have any idea what I've been through in the last four days? I was locked in a small cage with dozens of other men. We had nothing but polluted water and rancid food to sustain us. There was no latrine, so the men had to shit and piss in the corner of the cage. We all had diarrhea and who knows what other illnesses. There was no soap, no running water, no clean clothes. The smell in the cage was nauseating."

"I'm sorry you had to go through that, Jesse," Maria said, her eyes welling with tears.

"The point is, Mother, I didn't have to go through that. I chose it, or rather you chose it for me. But those other people did have to go through it. They were running from war, starvation, rape, threats to their children. The men I was imprisoned with were not angry. They were terrified and desperate. But the worst part was seeing the cage of children going through the same thing we were. The children were there through no fault of their own. Their parents brought them in order to escape lives that were even worse than what they found in the cages. Can you imagine?"

"And you are angry with me?"

"I am angry with you, Mother. You forced me to see what I needed to see. I'm exhausted and my heart is breaking." Jesse lowered his head to the table, hid his face in his arms. Maria could hear her son sobbing. She took him in her arms and comforted him. She understood now that his anger at her was small compared to his anguish at having witnessed the suffering of children.

Xavi was lying on his cot holding a notebook computer. Maria could see he was playing Grand Theft Auto. He was pretty good at it, navigating at high speeds through alleys, crashing through barricades and surviving machine gun fire from police. He made Maria and Birdie wait while he finished his turn, then set it aside, crossed his arms and looked at them levelly. Of course, he knew why they were here, but he wasn't going to give them any opening to begin the conversation. Maria knew that when a celestial being adopted a mortal form, he or she was subject to the emotions typical of that form. Xavi had the appearance of a seventeen-year-old boy, and he was acting like a kid who was in danger of failing his junior year in high school, but he didn't care and certainly wasn't going to work any harder to bring up his grades just because he'd been told to. Maria wondered what kind of persuasion would work with this obstreperous adolescent. Birdie stood beside her, silently waiting for Maria to start the conversation. They both knew they needed Xavi to join the cause. He was by far the best warrior in the universe, and they could not win against Satan without him, a fact he was well aware of.

"Xavi," Maria began. "I apologize for insulting you in the car on the drive here. I was angry that you and Jesse got arrested and Theodora and I had to waste time bailing you out. We have only a couple of days to prepare for the campaign."

"Okay," Xavi shrugged and went back to his computer game. Certainly not the response she was hoping for.

"I hope you'll come into the common room and talk with the mortals. They all know you are the most courageous and skilled warrior we have, and we cannot prevail without you."

"Oh, I can be persuaded, Maria," Xavi said, raising his eyes to focus on her ample breasts. His meaning was clear.

Maria felt her anger rising. It was like a dark bile coming up from her stomach. Her heart started racing. She was speechless. *The affrontery of this boy-god!*

Xavi shifted his gaze to Birdie. His eyes went from her dark face to her breasts, and then her hips. "What about you, Sweetie," he said. "Do you want to play?" He held out his tablet as if he were referring to Grand Theft Auto.

Birdie gave a fast right jab with the heel of her hand. If Xavi had been mortal, the blow would have hit him in the bridge of his nose, driving the bone into his frontal lobe, killing him instantly, but Xavi blocked the blow with his left hand and lifted his right hand, palm facing outward. Birdie was thrown back against the wall.

Maria hurried to Birdie who lay in an unconscious heap on the floor. She felt her pulse. "You could have killed her," she hissed at Xavi.

"Correction," Xavi said. "I could have ended her current mortal life. If I had, she would have found herself back in the kingdom."

"We need her here now," Maria said. "You know that."

Maria shouted for Delphina, the physician, to come quickly. Xavi smiled and went back to his game, crashing through barriers, killing civilians and police right and left, immune to bullets and other hazards.

Once Birdie was in the capable hands of Delphina, Maria went back into the common room where the mortals were still talking among themselves. They had followed her instructions and divided into task-groups. Christina and Stefan huddled with Inez and Adelaide, talking about hacking the federal and local governments' mass alert systems to keep civilians away from the battle-site. Maria listened to the discussion for a few minutes, and when the four people had settled on a strategy and each had his or her assigned duties, she said, "Christina and Stefan, could we talk in my office for a few minutes?"

Once the door was closed, Maria looked at the two lovely young people in front of her, the thin bearded poet and his pregnant wife with her glowing red hair, and said, "You need to know that there is a good chance we are not going to win the battle in east Texas."

Stefan shifted in his chair uncomfortably. Christina didn't move, but her eyes widened in shock, and Stefan gently took her hand. They had both assumed that the forces of good would prevail and that they and their baby would be safe.

"Don't get me wrong," Maria hastily added. "We have brave warriors fighting for us, and we will do everything possible to defend you and your baby, but Satan's warriors are fierce fighters, and they badly outnumber us."

Stefan cleared his throat and asked the question that needed to be asked, "What will happen to Christina and the baby if the battle doesn't go our way?"

Maria hesitated, then decided to say bluntly, "All three of you will be hunted down and killed. Your baby represents the salvation of humankind."

Stefan could feel his hands starting to shake, and he could feel, rather than hear, his wife's shallow quick breaths. The last time he felt this was when he was standing in a military court, having just been wrongfully convicted of aiding and abetting the rape and murder of an Iraqi girl. But this terror was worse because he was afraid not for his own life, but that of his wife and unborn son.

"What should we do?" He managed to ask, his voice a strange croak he didn't recognize.

As a mother who had watched her son die, Maria understood Christina's terror and dread, and she knew Stefan would do whatever he could to protect them, but she also knew that the power of the forces they faced far exceeded her own. These two humans needed to understand that they could not fight those forces but must hide until the storm of evil had passed.

"There is a cave that no one knows about but a handful of Yaqui. You should be safe there."

"My baby will be born in a cave?" Christina asked, turning to look at her husband in panic.

Stefan felt his anger rising. "This baby will not be born in a cave, Maria. Christina needs a qualified obstetrician and a sterile environment to give birth. I cannot allow her to be put in a burrow to have this baby. I will not allow it."

Maria was pleased. This protective instinct of Stefan's was exactly what was needed. "You are both going to have to trust me," she said. "Christina will have the best possible care, in fact, much better than any American hospital could provide. She will be under the care of a *patera*, a traditional midwife with decades of experience. Her name coincidentally is Maria. The cave is a traditional birthing place where women have given birth for thousands of years. Christina will be safe and in good hands."

"Can't I give birth here in El Presidio under Delphina's care?"

Maria shook her head. "You're not safe here. By now the dark forces know you're here. We need to hide you in a place they don't know about." Maria tried to sound confident, but the truth was that she didn't know whether Christina and the baby would be safe on the Yaqui reservation, but she knew that there was a better chance of their surviving there than here.

Stefan looked at his wife who was nodding slowly, thinking over what Maria had said. Finally, she turned to him and said, "Okay, Poet, let's do this thing."

As Stefan was throwing things into his knapsack, wondering what you pack for the apocalypse, he glanced at his wife sitting on the edge of the bed, staring blankly out the window at the darkness. "You've been very quiet, darling," he said. "What's going on? Are you frightened?" It seemed a reasonable question, since Stefan himself felt terror growing inside him, as if he was on the edge of a cliff that was crumbling under his feet.

"No," Christina said quietly. "I'm not frightened although I know I should be. I've just been listening."

"Yes, Maria does seem to have a good strategy in mind, doesn't she?" Stefan said more confidently than he felt. *Why did Maria change her mind? First, she assigned us communication duties and now we're going to hide in a cave for… how long?*

"Oh, I barely heard what she was saying," Christina confessed. "I was listening to…"

"Who?" Stefan remembered that Tristram had been sitting next to her. Had he said something to upset her?

"I've been listening to…" Her voice, already small, became so soft that Stefan couldn't make out what she said. He leaned toward her.

"I've been listening to my baby," Christina whispered.

"You mean his heartbeat?"

"No, his voice."

Stefan started to tell her that the baby couldn't possibly speak yet, and even if he did, you couldn't make out his voice through the amniotic fluid. But then, Stefan remembered where he was, who his companions were, and what lay in front of them, and he realized that anything, literally anything, was possible.

"It's like music," Christina said. "It doesn't mean just one thing. It means… everything."

Stefan, puzzled, was about to ask her to explain, but then he realized that there was no way he could ever understand what she was going through. His job was to provide and protect. The finer details of the metaphysical mess that he and his family were in the middle of were, as they used to say in the army, "above his pay grade." He reached under the bed and slid out the overnight bag Christina had brought and started packing her belongings in it. Then he slung his pack over his shoulder, picked up the overnight bag and helped Christina who seemed to have entered a fugue state, barely aware of where she was, out the door, across the common room, and into the courtyard where José sat in his truck with the engine running.

When Maria went back to the men's quarters, Xavi was gone. She sat down on his cot and started crying *Oh no no no no no no… everything is lost. We cannot win against the Darkness without Xavi's help.* She felt a rush of guilt and self-incrimination. She should have tried harder to get along with him. She should have held her tongue. Of course, he was selfish and intemperate and disrespectful, he was the Destroyer of Worlds, and she had ignored his nature and expected him to behave civilly? She felt a flash of shame course through her body. *I am a fool*, she thought, *a stupid fat old woman who… wait a minute… How old is this body? I'm fifty-two. I'm having a hot flash. I'm feeling horny for a handsome gay man. I get angry when others don't follow my orders.* She laughed to herself. Of course, she was experiencing Eve's curse.

Okay, she pulled her wits together. *Let's think this through. Assume Xavi isn't going to help us. What then? Without Xavi, we can't win on the battlefield, but we can diminish the enemy's forces, and distract them from Patrick and Alex who can win the war of ideas which is far more important in the long run. But the most important goal is to protect Christina and the baby. If Xavi changes his mind and comes back, then so much the better, but we can win this war without him... perhaps.*

"So why the sudden change of plans, José?" Stefan asked. He had to speak across Christina who sat in the middle of the front seat. It was crowded, but tolerable. "First, Maria wants us to be on the communications team, and then she changes her mind and tells us to go live in a cave that only the Yaqui know about. What's going on?"

José shrugged. "Hey, I'm just doing what I'm told. She said to drive you to the Yaqui Reservation and help you get settled there. So that's what I'm doing."

Stefan turned to look out the back window of the cab to check on Dharma who was curled up on blankets in a large basket between Christina's overnight bag and Stefan's rucksack. He had thought about leaving the dog at El Presidio, but she had looked up at him with such sad eyes, he hadn't the heart to abandon her.

"Let's see," Stefan said. "We're in the state of Sonora now. Where's the reservation?"

"It's in the southwest part of Sonora, a couple of hundred miles from here."

"You've been there before?"

José nodded. "Maria and I used to live there." He glanced at Stefan. "How's your Spanish?"

"I took a couple of Spanish language classes in college, and I can read it pretty well. I basically lived in the public library when I was homeless."

José nodded approvingly. "You'll probably want to learn some of the Yaqui language as well."

José's tone suddenly sounded sad. Stefan wondered how many languages José had learned in his long life, only to find that eventually he was the only one who still knew the language. With each language that died, a whole world died with it.

"It's a beautiful language, closely related to the ancient Aztecan," José said, musing. "It's pitch-accented, with the first or second syllable accented and all the syllables which follow high-pitched. It's very musical. It always reminded me of the wind moving through the high leaves of a tree."

Stefan surmised that he and Christina weren't just hiding in a cave for a few days. They would be living among the Yaqui for quite a while.

Stefan looked at his wife. She seemed to be dreaming with her eyes open, humming a high tune, and he wondered if she was listening to the baby inside her. He wasn't sure whether he should be worrying about her or feeling joyous at her new insight into the baby's consciousness. He had read somewhere that a mother relates to her baby in ways that no two other beings ever could. They were simultaneously one being and two.

When Birdie opened her eyes the next morning, the first thing she saw was Patrick's face looking at her with worry and concern.

"Hello, darling man," she said.

"How are you feeling?"

"Oh, I'm just fine." She lifted her palm to her forehead. I've got a slight headache though."

"Xavi hit you pretty hard, I guess."

"Well, it was my fault. I lost my temper when he insulted Maria. I should know better than to try to punch Xavi."

"Can I ask you a question?"

"Sure you can."

"Are you my momma? I mean, I know my momma died last year after getting beat down by a cop on the Otay Bridge, but are you her..." He searched for the right word.

"Am I your momma's reincarnation? Yes, Patrick I certainly am."

Patrick burst into tears and wrapped his arms around Birdie, being careful not to hug her too hard. Then he pulled back, a puzzled look on his face. "How does that work? Does everybody get reincarnated?"

"Of course, everybody gets reincarnated. Nothing in the universe goes to waste, no molecule, no breath of wind, no thought, no soul. Everything is recycled, you might say. But we usually don't retain our individual identity."

"You mean everything that's me will appear again, but not as Patrick. Part of me might go to someone in China, and another part of me might go to a blade of grass or to a drop of rain. Everything gets mixed together like a big soup."

"That's right."

"But how come you've come back as Birdie, except younger and..." he laughed. "More buff?"

"I guess Archangel Rafael, who's in charge of special operations, thought that you needed your momma to watch out for you a while longer."

"So, you're my guardian angel?"

"Not quite. I'm not an angel. My soul is human like yours. I've just been given a new life because these are unusual times and you, my boy, have a special mission."

"Yeah, tell me about my mission. I don't understand what I'm supposed to do."

"What you are supposed to do is to carry the message of the Lord in your own wonderful way."

"You mean I should wear my sequined dresses and my wigs to sing torch songs?"

"That's right. But you sing torch songs about your love for Jesus."

"And where do I perform?"

"Everywhere. In churches, bars, nightclubs, social clubs, schools… every place where there's an audience."

"I'm afraid, Momma. If I come out like that, singing everywhere, I'll be exactly what the haters want to destroy. Black boys like me have been killed for just whistling at a white lady. What do you think they're going to do to a black faggot dressed up like a movie star in public?"

"Don't worry, son. I'll be with you. And God will be with both of us."

Tristram sat at a table in the common room calling priests and religion professors across the United States, setting up a lecture tour for Alex based on a plan sketched out by Maria. No, he told them, Professor Beltran didn't require a speaker's fee, nor did he require travel expenses—it was all covered by a donor. All that the Professor needed was a podium and an audience. His topic was "The Struggle Between Good and Evil in the Post-Modern World." Yes, he would send a .pdf of Professor Beltran's *vitae* and a *précis* of his argument right away.

Tristram kept glancing at the door to Maria's office where she and Alex were sequestered talking strategy. Tristram had seen how Maria looked at Alex, and Tristram didn't like the idea of the two of them alone behind a closed door. He didn't buy all this hype about Maria being the mother of God, and he was amazed that Alex sometimes believed it. *For God's sake,* Tristram thought, *this is not the 12th century.* She may have other people fooled, but he knew she was just a rich bitch with the hots for Alex and an insatiable ego. He would go along with the program as long as it served his and Alex's interests—a speaking tour was good for building Alex's national reputation and may lead to a book deal, talk shows, radio interviews… but it wouldn't help his reputation to be thought of as a religious kook, someone who actually believes his chief supporter is the mother of God. After all, if she's the Virgin Mary, then that would make Jesse nothing less than Jesus. Tristram laughed to himself. Imagine this gawky seventeen-year-old Mexican kid with his sad eyes and long face as the embodiment of the SECOND COMING. How ridiculous! Tristram's plan was that he and Alex would go along with this charade for now, but as soon as Alex was on his lecture tour, they'd leave this cult behind—hopefully forever.

Meanwhile, Maria was listening to Alex as he spoke rapidly about how the ethical failures of America had brought about the current crises. "We have celebrated evil for so long. We have worshipped money, power, death. The failure of consumers to consider how the western lifestyle has brought about the cascading environmental collapse. The failure of the northern cultures to consider how their predation of African, Latin, and indigenous cultures has brought about the impoverishment of most of the world. American military power has destroyed entire cities and countries in the Middle East. And the emphasis on profit in medicine has brought about the destruction of traditional ways of thinking of health and disease."

Maria simply nodded as Alex spoke, understanding that he was using her as a sounding board for stream of consciousness ideas that he would later commit to paper, polish, and practice until his lectures and debates could come from his lips so smoothly that he seemed to be inventing the ideas as he spoke. He was truly brilliant, and his ability to explain and persuade was essential if they were going to save humanity from itself. Satan's powers, she understood, lay not in his armies of demons, but in the corrosion of human values. As long as greed, lust and violence were worshipped by mortals, Satan would have his way.

Maria understood the weakness of humans because she had occupied a human body most of the last two thousand years. She rarely returned to the Kingdom because she found humans fascinating. Their short lives made them pursue their desires furiously, afraid of running out of time. Alex, for example, was so hungry for the truth that it was hard to keep up with the quickness of his thought as he chased down every interesting possibility. He was relentless in his desire for wisdom. And Maria, having surrendered to the passions of her human body, felt a desire for him that was as intense as the soul's desire for God. On the other hand, Maria felt an even stronger bond to José. The two of them had been together for so long, they were like one soul. José was right to trust her. She would never betray him any more than she would betray Jesse. The desire she felt for Alex was merely a feeling, and feelings can never be wrong, but the sacrament of marriage was a promise to the fundamental Good of the universe, a living embodiment of Love. José was right to trust her although Tristram obviously didn't.

Meanwhile in the men's quarters, Jesse lay on his cot, tossing and turning in agony as he remembered the children in cages on the border. The little ones had looked at him with such innocent longing that he couldn't rid himself of the memory of their faces, nor did he want to stop thinking of them, as painful as it was to picture them. He needed to hold onto their suffering, accept it as his own, and let the power surge through him, giving him a purpose for his presence on this earth in this time.

"Excuse me, Maria," Theodora said after a quick knock on the office door. "I thought you would want to know that Jesse said he needs to save the children, so a few minutes ago, Marta drove off with Jesse riding in her sidecar."

"Why in Heaven's name would she agree to that?" Maria asked, trying to size up the situation.

"Marta's a novice. Jesse's your son," Theodora answered. "I'm sure Marta thought that Jesse was following your plan. Should I go after them?"

"No, I'll go," Maria said. "Please ask Genevieve to get the Ducati ready. It's light and fast, so I should be able to catch up to them before they get to the border." She wished that José was here. Jesse loved his stepfather, and José had always been able to get through to the boy whereas Maria and her son often butted heads. She turned to Alex, "I think your ideas are great. Keep developing and practicing them. I'd like to see you and Tristram on the road by daylight."

Maria caught up with Marta and Jesse just south of the border wall. She pulled her Ducati alongside Marta's Harley and signaled her to pull over.

"I'm sorry, Maria," Marta blurted out. "I thought…"

Maria shook her head and waved her hand dismissively. "It's not your fault, Marta. Jesse and I should have discussed this before you left. You couldn't have known."

Maria and Jesse walked a dozen feet into the desert, leaving Marta with the motorcycles. Maria looked at her son's face. Now seventeen, no longer a boy, not quite a man. The fact that he was born two thousand years ago was irrelevant to what he was feeling now—the blind beautiful idealism of youth.

"Jesse, cariño, where do you think you're going?"

"Back to the holding cells where ICE is holding children."

"And you want to save them?"

"Mother, they are keeping children in cages away from their parents. They are living in their own filth. No diapers. Only filthy water to drink. Oatmeal full of maggots to eat. The older children try to take care of the younger ones, but they can't…" Maria could see her son's cheeks glistening with tears, his body shaking with grief and anger.

"Jesse, you realize that there are thousands of children being held in cages along the border, don't you?" He nodded. "And there are children all over the world being held in prisons and camps. And there are others who are sold as sex slaves. And there are many who are recruited as child-soldiers? There are millions of suffering children. What good does it do to save a few?"

She watched her son double over in grief as he sobbed for the suffering children.

"Mother," he said between sobs. "I have to save at least a few. I cannot live with myself if I do nothing."

Maria stroked the back of her son's head and let him cry. She glanced at Marta who was looking away across the desert, obviously trying not to eavesdrop or to witness Jesse's emotional collapse.

"What do you plan to do, Jesse?" Maria asked softly. "How will you help them?"

"I don't know," Jesse responded, barely audible. "I just know that I have to get as many children as I can out of those cages."

"Very well, let me help you," Maria said. She handed him a slip of paper with two names and an address in northern California. "This couple has prayed every day for years to be blessed with a child. They will welcome the children and raise them as their own. They will also have the help of their community. They've been expecting you for quite a while. If the children's parents are able to make it to northern California to find their children, then the family will give the children back to their parents."

"Thank you, Mother," Jesse said, his voice no longer quavering.

"You're also going to need help in getting the children out of the cages and transporting them to northern California."

"Are you going to ask Xavi?" Jesse asked.

"Oh Heavens, no. Xavi would kill the guards and blow up the camp." Maria looked up at the stars. "I'll ask Mikey. He has a more subtle approach. Also, you'll need uniforms, official papers, and a vehicle. Mikey has friends in the wardrobe shop, documents department and the motor pool, so he'll be able to fast-track the requests."

"Yes, Mikey would be great." Jesse stood up. He understood now what he needed to do.

"Marta," Maria said. "Please take Jesse across the border to meet up with Mikey, then return to El Presidio." Marta nodded, waited for Jesse to climb into the sidecar, kickstarted her bike and rumbled north on the highway.

Maria watched the tail-lights of the motorcycle disappear

into the darkness, shaking her head at her brave beautiful impractical son.

Just across the border, Mikey caught up to them in a white van. When Jesse looked back over his shoulder, Mikey gave him a gentle salute behind the windshield, meaning he had the ICE uniforms and documents. Marta pulled the Harley to the side of the road. Jesse thanked her, got out of the sidecar and walked to the van parked closely behind.

"Thanks for coming, Mikey," Jesse said, opening the door.

"No problem, Boss," Mikey said, handing his friend a blue uniform with proper insignia, a billed hat, and an envelope of documents. Jesse quickly changed into the uniform and climbed into the seat, and they hit the highway, going north.

A few miles down the road, the guard at the gate of the detention camp inspected their papers and waved them through. The boys parked in front of the office and walked in. The captain came out of the back room, buttoning his shirt and rubbing the sleep from his eyes.

"What the hell are you assholes doing showing up at midnight with transfer orders?" He asked, opening the envelope and scanning the documents.

"Emergency orders," Jesse said, trying to sound submissive, urgent, respectful and apprehensive at the same time.

"These orders came from the top," Mikey added, glancing at the ceiling.

"You want all nine of the kids we got here?"

"Yessir," Jesse said, barely holding back his tears. "We need all nine."

The first stop for Patrick and Birdie was the Ebenezer Revival church in Watts where Patrick was raised by Birdie in her previous life. When the good Reverend Sheffield met this version of Birdie, he peered into her eyes, was startled for a moment, then regained his composure and welcomed her into the congregation. Birdie could see she didn't have to explain anything to this deeply spiritual man who had led hundreds of civil rights actions and given thousands of sermons. He understood the role of miracles in daily life.

"Of course, you can give a testimonial to the congregation at the Sunday service tomorrow," he said, enthusiastically welcoming Patrick back into the fold.

"I'm going to be dressed as Aretha," Patrick said, giving him fair warning.

The good reverend paused, looking from Patrick to Birdie, then said, "Very well, if that's where the Good Lord has led you, who am I to say you can't?"

The next morning Birdie sat in the pew she'd occupied for decades. Her fellow worshippers, of course, didn't recognize her, even when she greeted them by name although they did give a start when she introduced herself. They also wondered about the tall attractive woman named Aretha who had joined the choir and whose voice was like an angel's. After a few rousing hymns, the reverend took the pulpit and delivered a powerful sermon quoting *Matthew 10:23* in which Jesus prophesized his return and urged his disciples to go out into the world on the Great Commission to bring the news of his return.

"Jesus instructs us to be as shrewd as snakes and innocent as doves as we preach to the people and prepare them for the new world that is coming. He warned us that we will be rejected, persecuted, arrested, imprisoned, beaten and martyred, as we have been in our struggle for our rightful place in this country."

"Beaten and martyred," someone echoed.

"But this martyrdom our people have suffered is nothing compared to the coming battle preparing the world for our savior's return," the preacher intoned.

"Our savior's return!"

"The Great Commission makes disciples of us all. We who bear the name of Christians must get busy!"

"Get busy!"

"The Son of Man walks among us. He has arisen. We must spread the good news!"

The congregation was suddenly silent. People looked at each other, wondering whether they'd heard what their reverend, their spiritual leader, had just said. Jesus had risen? The Second Coming was happening? The Rapture was coming soon? The Faithful would be taken up in the arms of angels and reside forever in Heaven?

Patrick stepped forward and walked up to the reverend who stepped aside. And Patrick began singing acapella, "Behold the Lord is coming, His ransomed home to call, And we who watch all see Him, and crown him Lord of all..."

And the congregation began clapping their hands, swaying, and singing the old hymn they'd sung since childhood. And when Patrick finished the hymn, Reverend Sheffield stepped up to the podium and instructed the congregation to go out into the streets, knock on their neighbor's doors, call their friends and tell them the time had come to pray and to repent. Jesus had come to town.

Chapter 10

Xavi was winning big at the roulette table, and a lot of people had gathered to watch his winning streak. He shoved a huge pile of chips forward and shouted, "Thirty-two thousand, seven hundred and sixty-eight dollars on red!" and loved the murmur that went through the crowd at the table. Some of the seasoned players recognized he was employing the Fibonacci system of wagering in which the player bets on even money areas increasing the amount of the bet with each turn using the Fibonacci sequence where the next number equals the sum of the previous two:

> 1—1—2—3—5—8—13—21—34—55—89—144—233—377—610—987…

Xavi loved the Fibonacci system which he called the Pingala system after the second century BCE Indian poet who enumerated possible patterns of Sanskrit poetry formed from syllables of two lengths. Fourteen hundred years later, Fibonacci, whose real name was Leonardo Bonacci, learned of the mathematical formula and published a book claiming to have discovered it in nature. HA! Xavi thought, one more reason to burn down the world, all the thefts from the third world. The Pingala system described all kinds of things in nature, Xavi knew, from the rate at which sheep breed to the arrangement of florets on a dandelion blossom.

He could, of course, influence the path of the ball on the

wheel, but he loved the fact that he could win without cheating. And thus, he looked around at the crowd to impress the babes. He had more than eighty thousand dollars in chips in front of him when the croupier, at a signal from the manager, said that they would not be accepting any more bets from the young gentleman. The floor manager quickly moved to stand beside Xavi and said, "May I speak with you, sir? We would like to comp you a suite for the night." He held up a keycard which Xavi put in his shirt pocket. Xavi nodded, having expected to be shut off at the table at some point. He tipped the croupier a thousand dollars, shoveled his chips into a bag the croupier handed him and walked over to the cashier's window. Turning around, he caught the eyes of two beautiful young women, one blonde, one black, who followed him to the elevator. What a shame we have to burn this world down, Xavi thought, these creatures really know how to have a good time.

The suite was spacious and had a balcony with a nice view of the lights of the city. He asked the two women to take off their clothes, and he took his off as well. He always loved this moment when someone saw his huge member for the first time. He often thought of it as Mount Kangchenjunga, the highest peak in the world, Mount Everest being seven meters shorter by his measurement. He posed for a moment, this small Indian man with slender arms and legs and a huge penis which looked like it belonged on a rhino. Once they had gotten over the shock of his manliness, he asked the two women to lie side by side, and then working slowly, he simultaneously ran his hands up and down their thighs, then moving from one to the other, excited them until they were panting with anticipation.... At last, the three of them lay in each other's' arms, blonde hair spilling over Xavi's shoulder, dark hair spread across his torso. They were curled in a happy disk of contentment. What a shame, he thought, *these two beautiful young women will die soon.*

Stefan woke in a cave with Dharma on one side of him and Christina on the other. At first, he thought he was in the cave under the bridge where he and Dharma had lived for three years after he got out of prison and couldn't find a job. In those years, he spent the days at the public library and the nights in his cave, but what's Christina doing here? She had never seen, much less been inside his *poet's grotto*, as he liked to think of it. Then he remembered that José had driven them to the Yaqui homeland. It had been late at night, so after a quick introduction to Eduardo, who seemed to be the leader of the tribe, José had shown Stefan and Christina to the cave and helped them spread blankets. Exhausted, they'd fallen asleep immediately.

Now, bright light lit the entrance to the cave. He could see a cornfield which had been invisible when they arrived the night before. Men and women were working in the field, tossing green missiles of corn into baskets. Each cornstalk grew on a small hillock, and bean vines grew up the stalks. Between the hillocks were squash vines whose broad leaves covered the ground, casting shade and discouraging weeds. *The Three Sisters*, Stefan thought, remembering his reading. Corn, beans, and squash. Indians had grown these three crops together for hundreds, perhaps thousands of years because they perfectly complimented each other in both cultivation and nourishment. The cornstalk served as a trellis for the bean vines to climb, the beans fixed nitrogen in the soil, their twining vines stabilizing the maize in high winds, and the wide leaves of the squash plant shaded the ground, keeping the soil moist and discouraging weeds. The prickly hairs of the squash leaves also deterred deer and raccoons from eating the plants. In nutrition as well, the high protein of the beans complimented the protein of the corn, and the starchy yellow flesh of the squash was high in energy and vitamins. Not for the first time, Stefan thought that his ancestors' substitution of this kind of agricultural community life for the stressful high-tech life of modern Europe and America had been a bad bargain. If he and Christina needed to hide out in this community for a while, he couldn't have chosen a better life than this.

An old woman with long braided white hair walked up to him. "*Buenos días,*" she said nodding to him as she walked into the cave past Dharma who looked up at her and wagged her tail as if she recognized her. The old woman kneeled beside Christina and spoke softly to her. Christina, who spoke a little Spanish, responded quietly, and pushed the blanket off the hill of her belly. The old woman put her hand on Christina's belly and continued to speak softly to her. Stefan was grateful that the community had a midwife to help them. He walked out into the bright morning light. He could see in the distance a few houses and a small stone church with a bell tower above it. With Dharma beside him, he walked through the cornfield, following a well-trod path between the corn stalks, past the workers who smiled at him as they picked the corn.

As Stefan approached the church, he saw Eduardo, whom he'd met when they arrived the night before. Eduardo waved, lifted the brim of his baseball cap so the light could find his round brown face, and called him over. "*Buenos días*, Stefan," he said. "Have you eaten yet?" Stefan shrugged, not wanting to assume he was being invited to breakfast. Eduardo led him to a small house in a row of houses, each with a wooden cross in the front yard. The roof of each house was made of reeds covered with mud, and the walls were constructed of woven branches which, Stefan realized, would allow air to flow through the rooms, keeping the house cool. Before entering Eduardo's house, he and his host took off their shoes and left them beside the front door. Entering, he saw the house consisted of three rectangular sections: the bedroom, the kitchen, and a small living room, which Eduardo called *el portal*. Behind the house was a patio with cane chairs and mats for sitting in the evening. In the kitchen was a woman whom Eduardo introduced as *mi esposa Concepción*. She smiled at Stefan and went back to using a wooden spoon to stir a batter in a clay pot. Eduardo gestured to Stefan to sit in *el portal*. Concepción brought out a bowl filled with corn porridge sweetened with honey and cinnamon.

Stefan tasted it. "Delicioso," he said appreciatively nodding at her. Then he remembered Christina who must be hungry as well. "*Mi esposa,*" he said, gesturing in the direction of the cave.

"*No hay problema,*" Eduardo said. "She is in good hands with *la partera.*"

After eating the porridge and a sliced mango, Stefan thanked Eduardo and Concepción and looked out the front window at the people working in the fields. He saw Dharma with a pack of skinny dogs, smelling each other's butts, the universal canine greeting. "May I feed my dog?" Stefan asked.

"How is she at foraging?" Eduardo asked.

"She's great. She and I used to live on the street in LA."

"She'll be fine," Eduardo said. "All the dogs provide for themselves here, but sometimes we throw them a bone or leave some leftovers in the yard."

"I would like to work," Stefan offered to Eduardo, thinking that if he and Christina were going to live here for any length of time, then he would have to earn their keep.

"Today you rest, my friend," Eduardo said. "Perhaps tomorrow you can work."

They sat on mats on the floor in *el portal* talking quietly of the village and the Yaqui and how they lived and what they wanted out of life. "There are those among the Yaqui who transport people north and money and guns south across the border. Very dangerous work but profitable. Most of us though, we wish only a quiet life. We wish to see our children grow up healthy, get married, and have children. This is the way the Yaqui have lived for many thousands of years. Most of us are farmers or craftsmen. A few of us are warriors. The *Mexicanos* leave us alone nowadays although in the past there were wars when they took us as slaves to work on the plantations. They made our ancestors walk hundreds of miles, and if we died on the way they left our bodies beside the road. On the plantations, they worked the Yaqui men and women to death. And they made our girls concubines to the Chinese workers. So we revolted, killing a thousand *Mexicano* soldiers and losing five thousand of our own. It was not a fair fight. We had only machetes and they had rifles, but we refused to work anymore, and we freed our daughters from the whore houses."

"When did this happen?" Stefan asked.

Eduardo shrugged, "A hundred years ago perhaps. The Yaqui are free. We have our own laws, and we do not recognize the authority of the *Federales* here."

"Are the Yaqui Catholic?"

"Yes, but some of our ancient beliefs remain."

"I thought that the natives in Mexico had been largely wiped out."

"The Yaqui didn't suffer the decimation that other native peoples did because there was no gold or silver on our land. The Jesuits converted us, and the Yaqui lived with the Jesuits for 120 years."

"So the Jesuits treated the Yaqui well?"

José shrugged. "Compared to other native peoples, the Yaqui did well. The Jesuit rule over the Yaqui was stern but the Yaqui retained our land and our unity as a people. The Jesuits introduced cattle and horses. We prospered because the nearest Spanish settlement was 100 miles away and we were able to avoid interaction with everyone, Spanish settlers, soldiers, and miners."

"The Yaqui weren't affected by epidemics?"

"Not really. The reputation of the Yaqui as warriors, plus the protection afforded by the Jesuits, shielded us from Spanish slavers. The Jesuits were expelled from Mexico two hundred and fifty years ago, and the Franciscan priests who replaced them never gained the confidence of the Yaqui. An uneasy peace between the Spaniards, and later the Mexicans, and the Yaqui endured for many years after the revolt, with the Yaqui maintaining our tribal culture and most of our independence."

"And now?" Stefan whose only acquaintance with the Yaqui was through the novels of Carlos Castaneda , was beginning to understand that the survival of this culture had been dependent, in part, on being invisible to mainstream Euro-American culture.

"The Yaqui refuse to pay taxes to the Mexican government because we consider ourselves independent and self-governing. There have been revolts through the years against the Mexican government, but things are much better now. We are allowed to control our communal lands and are usually left alone."

"Your English is very good, Eduardo."

"Thank you. A lot of us speak English because we have relatives across the border in Arizona."

"Do people still speak the Yaqui language?"

"Some of us still speak the old Yaqui tongue. We call ourselves *Yoeme* which means *The People*. Most of the languages of the First Nation peoples have died out, especially in the United States, but the Yaqui have made a strong effort to keep our language and culture alive."

"I've read that the Yaqui have shamans..."

Eduardo looked down at his hands and said politely, "You are speaking, my friend, of the stories of Don Juan."

When Stefan nodded, Eduardo said, "Those are made-up stories, you know. There is no one here named Don Juan. However, we do have shamans who help people when they are ill and who ease people into the next life. They do not claim to have magical powers. Rather they know how to listen to nature. They act as guides or intermediaries between gods and people."

"May I meet one of these shamans?" Stefan asked, but immediately recognized that he was being rude. As a North American, he was used to asking for what he wanted, but if he was going to live with these gentle courteous people, he would have to learn to stay silent and be grateful for whatever came his way.

Before Stefan could backtrack from his request, Concepción came into *el porto*, leaned down and whispered in her husband's ear, then went back into the kitchen. "My wife says that your wife is now in labor." When Stefan started to get up to run back to the cave, Eduardo held up his hand. "No, my friend, you should stay here. The midwife will take care of her. You would just be in the way. Perhaps tomorrow you can see your child."

Huitzilopochtli was reviewing his troops. Ten thousand hummers were floating among the pine and oak trees, spilling over into the meadow next to the parking lot, their shimmering feathers almost blinding in their beauty as if the sun itself had lent its magnificence to this section of the Texas woods. His mother Maria had hired men to place ample supplies of sugar water fifty feet apart in the area, and the hummers, who always burned with a fierce fire in their hearts, kept coming back to dip their needle-like beaks in the vats. The battle would start soon, and Huitzilopochtli moved among his soldiers, offering a nod of recognition here, a word of encouragement there, an acknowledgement of brave reputation now and then. He was both the greatest warrior who ever lived and a general of undeniable genius.

He glanced across the asphalt parking lot to the housing development a few hundred meters away. He could feel, rather than hear, the army of a million wasps led by General Zaberi in the yards and gardens that lay between the suburban houses. Maria had told them that her sources had reported that the human agents of Lucifer were having a large rally in the parking lot that lay between the army of wasps and the hummers. At a signal from Huitzi, the wasps would attack from the north and east and the hummers would sweep in from the south, leaving the meadow and woods on the west of the asphalt the only escape for the humans. Once the humans were on foot away from their cars and trucks and among the underbrush of the forest, there was no escape for them, and they could be picked off easily.

Now Huitzi could see the caravan of six long semis led by José, a Sister at the wheel of each. Once the attack started, they would move the trucks into position, blocking the exits, trapping the enemy's vehicles, forcing them to try to flee on foot, and enabling the wasps and hummers to herd the men into the woods. Huitzi studied the empty shopping mall, closed on a Sunday, no shoppers to get in the way of the battle. He estimated the enemy's forces at less than a thousand, most of them human, probably a few dozen demons mixed with them. He hoped that Lucifer, or Luke Ferris as he preferred to be called these days, would show up late to make a grand entrance to the rally as he usually did. Otherwise, his presence on the battlefield would be problematic since Huitzi's forces of hummers and wasps would not be effective against a god. If Lucifer showed up before the battle was over, Huitzi himself would have to fight him, and Lucifer was known to be a fierce fighter, the equal of Xavi Destroyer of Worlds. On a different day, Huitzi would love to have fought the Prince of Darkness, but not today. Huitzi needed to lead his army and not be distracted by Lucifer.

The enemy humans were arriving, their trucks coming into the parking lot. They appeared to be the advance team, showing up early to prepare the stage and sound system. Huitzi watched the men lift a generator off the back of a truck and set it up next to the stage, then run cable up to a mic. As they worked, a dozen other men showed up with pistols strapped to their belts, each wearing a red tee-shirt with the word SECURITY in large letters on the back, four men stationing themselves next to the stage, the others scattered to strategic spots around the parking lot. Huitzi instructed one of his aides to fly to General Zaberi and tell him that the men in red were the chief warriors and should be taken out first, along with the demons. Their pistols were useless against wasps and hummers, but Huitzi didn't want anyone taking charge of the men once the battle started. He wanted the humans panicked and ready to stampede. As for the demons, they were easy to spot. Humans were the only ones who confused demons with mortal men.

The cars and trucks started arriving. It looked like caravans had been organized and driven here from Houston, as well as individuals driving what looked like work and farm trucks. Some of the cars and trucks looked new and expensive. Others looked like they had driven straight from farms and construction sites. The crowd was growing, almost all of them men with pink or tan faces, but there were a small number of women and men with brown or black faces. Huitzi took no interest in the politics of humans, but he understood that the divisions among the humans had developed along race, gender, and class lines. Lucifer had taken the form of Luke Ferris, a rich white man, and he was dividing the society along the fault-lines that had existed for hundreds of years. Huitzi also understood that this struggle was happening all over the world, but the key lay in this empire because its military, economic and cultural influence spread like tentacles into virtually every human society.

Now two lines of cars and trucks were snaking into the broad parking lot, one line on the north side of the mall and one line on the south. Once the parking lot was full, he would give the signal to José, and he and the Piston Sisters would park the semi-trucks across the entrance ways, two semis on the access road behind the mall and four trailers on the front of the mall where the parking lot narrowed between the mall and the woods. The security team in red shirts were flagging the cars and trucks into the parking areas in an orderly way, and men were walking the last hundred yards to the area in front of the dais.

Huitzi glanced at one of his aides whose job it was to count the enemy. "Over 1,100, General," the lieutenant reported.

"Fly to General Zaberi and tell him to stand by. When he sees we've started the attack, then he should charge as well," Huitzi ordered, and the lieutenant flew off across the green meadow and into the trees north of the parking lot.

"Fly to José and tell him to move the semitrucks into position," Huitzi said and watched his second aide fly east across the parking lot.

"Remind our hummers that they are under orders not to

kill any humans, but we may blind or maim them," he said to his three remaining aides who spread the word among the hummers who were nervously waiting for the order to attack. The no-kill order had come from Maria, but he agreed with this rule of engagement because as a matter of strategy Huitzi preferred to injure the enemy soldiers rather than kill them. A dead enemy soldier did no one any good, but an injured soldier required help from his mates who had to carry him off the battlefield and care for him. And nothing took the starch out of soldiers' resolve more than having to listen to the moans and screams of their friends.

After a few minutes, the semis pulled slowly into position, blocking the two bottlenecks north and south of the mall. Parked bumper to bumper, no cars or trucks could get into the target area although individual humans could easily crawl under the trailers, but the humans, who were slow and tired, were effectively trapped. He could see humans in the dais area looking over their shoulders at the confusion caused by the semis blocking access to the parking lot, and a few red-shirted security men started moving toward the trucks, their hands on their holstered pistols.

Huitzi quickly rose thirty feet in the air. He knew his distinctive feathers would shimmer in the bright morning light, signaling both the hummers and the wasps to attack. Then he hurtled forward, quickly reaching a speed of over 100 miles per hour on a level plane. Without looking, he knew his loyal hummers were in a wedge formation behind him. Once they reached the crowd of humans, the birds swooped down on them. Not expecting to be attacked from above, the humans panicked and started running north with the hummingbirds pecking at their eyes, throats, and hands. Men fell, screaming in terror and agony. Some of the men tried to run east toward the line of semis, but a horde of wasps intercepted them, turning them back. A special detail had been assigned to attack the red-shirted security men who were swarmed by birds and bees until they lay curled up on the ground, trying to protect their eyes and genitals. Another detail of hummers was assigned to the demons who were easy to spot by their furry snouts and long talons. They didn't fall as easily as the security guards, but within a few minutes the demons had been brought down as well.

All was going according to Huitzi's plan. Most of the men had been turned toward the green meadow to the west of the parking lot, and the birds and the wasps let them run into the woods unmolested. The men stopped there thinking they were safe. Meanwhile, Huitzi and Zaberi simultaneously moved their troops into the woods in an orderly way, surrounding the men on the north, south and east. On Huitzi's signal, they attacked again, making use of the cover of trees and bushes which made the birds and insects almost invisible in the woods. Again, they tried to refrain from killing men, but they did blind a few, and Huitzi guessed that a few would die from anaphylactic shock from the wasp stings. When all the men had run off into the woods in panic, and dozens of others lay on the forest floor in pain and terror, Huitzi gave the signal to retreat, and both birds and wasps flew off to their respective rendezvous points. General Huitzi sent a message of enthusiastic praise to his ally General Zaberi and made sure that the few wounded hummers were transported to safety. His troops had suffered no fatal casualties. He was aware, however, that this was the beginning of the war, not the end.

Luke Ferris was in the back seat of his limo listening to Elvis, his chauffeur, sing *Love Me Tender*, one of Luke's favorites when his cellphone rang, interrupting his ecstasy. The call was from a member of his forward team at the shopping mall parking lot.

"What?" he asked. "Wait. Slow down. Tell me what happened. Start at the beginning... I see... Hummingbirds, you say?... Wasps? Millions of them?... Why didn't you... Semi-trucks driven by old women?… Our guys ran into the woods? Where are they now?… You heard screams?"

Luke told Elvis to turn the limousine around. He didn't care about his followers who were wounded. Screw them. They were no use to him now. He thought about the incoherent report his lieutenant had just spilled out, and he began to understand. General Huitzilopochtli and Queen Zahra had thrown in with Maria and the Sisters. The war had begun.

Chapter 11

At three a.m., Xavi was having breakfast in the hotel restaurant with Tiffany and Keisha, amazed that they could manage to eat with those bejeweled fingers putting scrambled eggs into those lovely mouths thick with lipstick, when his phone rang. He listened for a few moments and said, "Thanks. I'll be at the convent tomorrow." Putting away his phone, he said, "Let's finish up breakfast and go upstairs, girls."

Upstairs, Xavi was standing in the middle of the hotel room, admiring the beauty of the two women, and thinking about how he wanted to spend the last day of his ribald vacation when there was a knock on the door.

"Who's there?" Tiffany asked, walking toward the door.

"Room service," a male voice answered from the hallway.

Despite Tiffany's innocent question, Xavi knew something wasn't right. They hadn't ordered room service, and Tiffany seemed a little too nonchalant as she walked toward the door and opened it.

A man wearing a black ski mask burst through the doorway brandishing a pistol. He slapped Tiffany and she fell on the floor, not moving, as if a single slap could have knocked her out. *Bullshit*, Xavi thought. *Tiffany set us up.*

When the masked man swiveled his gun toward Xavi, he flicked his finger as if brushing off a fly and the man flew backwards hitting the closed door behind him with a thud and lay on the floor, bleeding from the head. Keisha backed slowly to the wall and watched Xavi with wide eyes. Xavi walked over to the man, picked up the pistol, a Walther, removed the clip and ejected the round from the chamber. Then he turned to Tiffany who lay on the carpet, pretending to be passed out. When he lifted her by the arm, she struggled, trying to scratch him with her jeweled nails. He goose-walked her to the balcony and held her partly over the rail. A hundred feet below was the blue opal of a swimming pool.

"Who is he?" Xavi asked.

"What? I don't know what you mean," she said trying to wriggle free.

"Is he your boyfriend?" Xavi lifted her over the rail and held her by one arm in mid-air. She glanced down, immediately stopped struggling, and looked up at him with terror in her eyes.

"He's my brother," she croaked. Not able to control herself, she wet her sequined dress with yellow droplets falling a hundred feet into the pool.

"Don't pee in the pool," Xavi joked. "Who do you work for?"

"Nobody! I swear! We just work a few high-flyers, then we skip town! Please. Please. Please! Xavi!"

Xavi could see she was too frightened to lie anymore. He thought about letting her fall into the swimming pool a hundred feet below like he'd seen in a James Bond movie, but she was trying to climb up his arm back to the balcony and he was afraid if he let go, she might miss the pool and make a mess on the sidewalk, so he pulled her to safety on the balcony and she sat there, quivering. He walked back into the room in time to see Keisha leap over the man on the carpet and run into the hall. Xavi was confident that Keisha hadn't known about the scam, so he let her go. He turned the man over, pulled off his mask and looked at his face. There was a family resemblance to Tiffany. Brother and sister. A couple of small-time scrubbers playing the oldest game in the world. He laughed and thought of how coyote bitches in heat will howl upwind from a farm driving the male domestic dogs crazy. But when a dog runs into the field to mount the bitch, her brothers ambush him, and they have the poor dog for dinner. He laughed and shook his head. Some things haven't changed in the last million years.

If these two had known who he was, they never would have tried such a clumsy strategy. He knew that the next attempt on his life wouldn't be from small timers. It would be from a hit squad sent by Luke Ferris, and unlike Maria, Jesse, and Luke, Xavi wasn't immortal—just hard to kill. He knew the war was finally coming, and it was time to return to *El Presidio* and team up with Maria and the Sisters.

After Jesse and Mikey dropped off the immigrant families into the capable and loving hands of the Seventh Day Adventists who had promised to help them get settled as workers on the farms outside Modesto, Jesse and Mikey left one of the trucks with them and drove down highway 86 toward the border crossing at Mexicali.

"That was really a nice thing we did for those families, Boss," Mikey said, taking his eyes off the road to glance at Jesse who was looking out the window at the desert in the morning light.

Jesse shrugged, and Mikey knew his friend was thinking that there are thousands of families on the Mexican side of the border, and more were arriving every day, fleeing violence and starvation. It was no longer just Central Americans that were moving north. Haitians, some of whom had been living in camps in Columbia for years, were walking twenty-five hundred miles to the American border hoping to find a way across.

"Why are you here?" Jesse asked, turning to look at his friend who, like him, had taken the form of a young man with dark skin, possibly Latino or Middle Eastern.

"Your mom asked me to help you," Mikey said.

"I know, but *why* are you here?"

"What do you mean?"

"Are you here to save humans from the cruelty of other

humans? That is a bootless task, my friend. Humans seem to have an endless appetite for hurting each other."

"Look, Jesse, you know I'm not a philosopher. I'm just a soldier who got demoted because I helped you with your last escapade. The Old Man busted me back to herald after Xavi and I helped you derail his plan last year to destroy the world. I'd like to get my archangel commission restored, but if you need me to do something that's going to get me busted again, then count me in. But don't ask me to decide the future of this world. Those are decisions way above my paygrade. I'm not in charge here. You are. Well, you and your mom. The way I see it is that the Old Man wants this world destroyed, so he can start on the next phase of history, but he doesn't want the world to fall into the hands of his brother Lucifer. The two of them have been fighting over this world forever, and the Old Man doesn't want to lose. Lucifer, for his part, wants to take over this world and populate it with his minions, demons, rats, cockroaches, vultures, racists, torturers and other scum. And you and your mom want the world to be made safe for the best of the humans, since the two of you have an irrational love for these hairless primates... In other words, what we have is a three-way war between Lucifer, the Old Man, and Maria. Have I got this right?"

"Yes, I think you've described the situation very well. So, whose side are you on?"

"Well, all the angels are caught in the middle, you might say. On the one hand, we work for the Old Man and owe him our allegiance. On the other hand, you and your mom inspire us in ways the Old Man never did. So, each angel, including myself, is trying to help you without getting in trouble with the Old Man."

"Okay, slow down a little. We're going to make a short detour up here."

"A detour? Why?" Mikey wasn't sure if Jesse was talking about celestial strategy or their route through the desert, but as it turned out, Jesse was talking about both.

"There's somebody we need to pick up. He lives in the mountains near here."

Mikey nodded. "Abe, right?"

"Right. The old patriarch wants to join our little rebellion."

"With Tristram's help, I've arranged a book tour for you," Maria said, trying not to bat her eyelashes at Alex. She was sitting at her desk, and he was right in front of her, feeling, she knew, as if he had been called into the principal's office.

"A book tour?" Alex responded. "Well, my publisher will be pleased ." Thinking that the sales of his last book *What God Wants from Us* had been abysmal. "What's the itinerary?"

Maria handed him a few sheets of paper with a list of two dozen events. He skimmed over it. A couple of radio interviews, a college lecture, a tv talk show, half a dozen podcasts, and… a debate with Bill Sebastian. "Who is this Sebastian guy? I've never heard of him."

"All in good time, my friend," Maria said. "We need to talk about why you're on this team."

"I can't say I haven't wondered," Alex admitted. "I haven't been in a fight since I was twelve when Tommy O'Hara insulted my heritage."

"Did you win?" Maria asked, teasingly.

"No, he beat the crap out of me." He paused for effect, then deadpanned. "I've been a pacifist ever since."

Maria laughed, then turned serious. "The war with the dark powers takes many forms, Alex. On the temporal plane, the war between Good and Evil has already started. There was a skirmish at a parking lot in east Texas a few hours ago in which hummingbirds and wasps ambushed Luke Ferris's men. My husband José and the Sisters of the Holy Piston provided strategic support."

"How many casualties?" Alex asked.

"Two of Luke's men were killed, hundreds of others injured. We have a waiver to kill humans, but we try to refrain from killing them because it calls too much attention to us. The fatalities were the result of anaphylactic shock. I'll have to write a report about them."

"A waiver?" Alex said. "Who gives you a waiver for such things?" He peered at his friend. "Maria, there's a lot you are not telling me about who you are and why you are doing all this stuff."

Maria looked at Alex levelly thinking, *for such an intelligent man, you are certainly dense sometimes. Everyone else—Stefan, Christina, The Sisters—had twigged quickly as to who she was, who Jesse was, and what they were doing here.* But of course, Alex was a Jesuit, and Jesuits have always relied too much on logic to understand life, never realizing that the basis of life is not logic, but love, and love is, by its very nature, illogical. She had decided years ago not to explain to Alex who she was, but rather to let this gorgeous, intelligent, block-headed priest come to his own conclusions. He had always thought of her as nothing more than a rich patron, and he didn't want to give up that comfortable assumption and replace it with a leap into the mystery that underlay everything.

"Never mind all that, Alex. We need you for a different kind of task. As I was saying, there is a physical war going on, but there is also a war of ideas. In order to save this world, people need to reach an understanding of what Good and Evil are and how they manifest themselves in modern society. " She saw that Alex's interest was piqued. "Using mass media, you will explain and persuade people that they are involved in a struggle to save their souls."

"Are you sure I'm the right person for this job, Maria? My strengths are in logic, rhetoric and scholarship. Most people are not persuaded by these strategies. You need someone who will appeal to people's need for story and spectacle. Someone who will appeal to them emotionally."

"Not to worry," Maria said. "We have Patrick, accompanied

by Birdie, making a tour of America doing the very thing you suggest. Patrick has a gift for spectacle. He'll win people's hearts, and you'll win their minds."

Alex leaned back in his chair. The tips of his fingers formed a globe of his two hands. Maria had seen theologians make this gesture hundreds of times as they tried to force the limited tools of logic to embrace the ineffable. She knew he was a gifted rhetorician who could construct a linguistic reality guiding people in the right direction.

"Alex, it will do no good at all, and possibly a great deal of harm, if we win a victory against the racists, sexists, liars and thieves, but the rest of humanity doesn't reform their ways and embrace the true faith."

"The true faith being the Church?"

Maria laughed. "No, no, the Church, as you call it, is part of the problem. I'm talking about the *Truth*, not the *Church*."

"And what is the Truth?" Alex asked, revving up his dialectical engine.

Oh, for Heaven's sake, Maria thought. *A Jesuit would argue with a fencepost.*

"The truth, my friend," she said after a pause. "The truth is that love is the principle that binds the universe together."

"I'm not sure that I accept your thesis," Alex said. "According to Aquinas…"

Then he stopped and saw the exasperation on her face and conceded, "But it's a thesis we can work with for now…"

"Thank you, Alex." Maria said and added, trying to appear nonchalant. "Tristram will of course, be accompanying you. You'll need an assistant."

Alex looked her in the eye, then looked down at the floor and said, "Maria, there's something I need to tell you. I've not been entirely honest…"

She waved her hand dismissively, "There's no need to explain, Alex. Tristram is a beautiful, intelligent, charming young man. It's obvious that you are in love with him."

Alex nodded his gratitude at the woman he thought of as his patron. As he left, Maria sighed, relieved that her fantasy of an affair with Alex had not become reality. In this human form, she had committed the human fallacy of confusing love with sexual desire. José was the man she loved, and if she had an affair with Alex, it would break José's heart. She was grateful to spare her husband this pain.

Chapter 12

After Christina's water broke, she became very aware of her lower abdomen. She felt things shifting inside her, marshalling the forces of birth. It was like having an earthquake inside her, she thought. Her senses were heightened. Her newly discovered sense of smell was drawing her attention to the odor that hung in the cave, the scent of her own skin, the smell of the midwife's gray braided hair. And she suddenly understood… everything. The midwife had been speaking to her in Spanish which Christina just barely understood, but now she understood everything that was being said. She had instantaneously gained fluency in the language. *Now, sweetheart, la partera* was saying, *it's time to get up on your heels. It's going to feel like you need to take a giant shit. It's okay. Don't hold back. Push it out.* And Christina felt something like a bowling ball moving through her lower parts. She held onto the old woman's shoulders for balance as the baby finally passed through her into waiting hands, and Christina lowered herself to the blanket and gingerly stretched out, exhausted and bloody from the birth.

That was not poetry, she thought as she drifted into sleep. *Or maybe it was.* Then suddenly she was alert again, her senses heightened and focused on the baby in *la partera's* arms, and she felt the labor pains starting again, just not as fiercely. Embracing the baby with her left arm, la partera pulled the afterbirth out of Christina, and with a small sharp knife, separated the afterbirth from the child. Then she sponged the blood off the baby.

A voice filtered through the fog in her mind: *Say hello to your son*. Christina took the baby into her arms and helped him find the nipple which was already seeping a white fluid which was not milk but something else, something like the pure essence of life. And only then did Christina, exhausted, allow herself to sleep.

Christina awoke to *la partera* handing the baby to her again.

Later she woke to sharp pain in her perineum. She looked down across what seemed like an endless flat plain of her belly, shockingly white, glowing in the slant of afternoon light from the cave entrance, and saw *La partera* stitching her up. *I'm just fixing a little tear, Virgen. You'll be fine*. And as Christina drifted off to sleep, she wondered. *Why did she call me Virgen?*

In a few hours she woke up again, this time in the dark, feeling a hand gently stroking her cheek and she recognized Stefan's touch. She smiled and took his hand and kissed it and went back to sleep.

In the morning, when she opened her eyes, she realized that she'd been holding the baby to her breast all night. *The baby*, her son Francisco Estevan József, named after the patron saint of animals and nature, was sleeping soundly. He was such a beautiful baby, she thought, she had never seen such a beautiful being in her whole life, and a surge of joy came over her as she looked at the little boy with his tiny fists in front of his rosy squinched face.

When you are ready, the people of the village would like to see your baby. Christina knew *La Patera* had spoken in Spanish and Christina had heard not her actual voice, but a voice inside her mind, and she could tell that she wasn't the same person she had been before the birth. With the birth of Francisco, her life had become much larger. For the first time, she understood what it was to love someone with your whole being. Nothing else would ever be as important to her as taking care of her son.

"I'm ready now," she said to the old woman who nodded and went into the village to tell everyone that la Virgen would make an appearance as soon as the father had had a chance to hold his son.

Stefan stood in the mouth of the cave, the bright afternoon light behind him, letting his eyes adjust to the shadows. Christina was sitting on the wool blankets with her back against the rock wall, holding the baby to her breast. The midwife, whose name was Maria although everyone called her *la partera,* was squatting next to Christina. The two of them were talking in low tones that Stefan couldn't quite make out. He was surprised that Christina, almost overnight, had become fluent in Spanish while Stefan was scrambling to try to catch up, each day learning half a dozen new words and phrases. He slowly walked over to them and looked down at the baby, eyes squinched, tiny hand resting on the breast while his mouth was working to lap up the drops of milk gathering on the nipple.

As Stefan pondered the mystery of his son's origins, he began to feel distant and confused. The idea that this child came from the union of their marriage seemed too large for him to comprehend. The midwife must have recognized his discomfort; after all, he was not the first new father to feel overwhelmed at the fact that a new life had arisen in front of his very eyes. The old woman reached over and held out her hands, and Christina handed the baby, who had finished nursing, to the woman.

"*Aquí está tu hijo,*" she said, handing the infant to Stefan.

Here is your son, Stefan thought. The words echoing in his mind as he held the small sleeping boy in his arms. *Here is your son. Here is your son. Here is your son.*

Jesse and Mikey pulled their truck in front of the old shack in the mountains where an old man with a long white beard was splitting wood. As they stopped the truck, a pack of coydogs ran to the truck barking and snarling, but at a sharp word from the old man, they backed away, watching the two young men warily.

"Hey, Abe," Jesse said, climbing out of the truck.

"Hey Sonny Boy," the old man replied. "I been expecting you."

"Really?" Jesse said glancing at Mikey who shrugged. "How'd you know we were coming?"

"Your buddy Xavi told me," Abe replied, nodding toward the cabin door. "Come on in and we'll talk."

Inside, Jesse and Mikey sat at the table, and Abe poured coffee for them. "Xavi was here?" Mikey asked.

"Yeah, he come through here yesterday," Abe said, scratching his cheek at the top of his beard. "He says the war is starting up again, and you could use my help."

"That's right. You and your coydogs are the best scouts in the world," Jesse said, watching Abe reach to a top shelf and pull out a pistol, rack the magazine and lay it down carefully in front of him.

"Xavi give me this Walther. Said I might need it." The old man looked Jesse in the eye. Do we have a waiver yet?"

"Not yet. Maria and the Sisters have a waiver, but Maria's application for the rest of us hasn't been approved yet."

"Last year, she made me go into the Otay Bridge battle unarmed."

"But we won, didn't we?" Mikey pointed out.

"Yeah," Abe said. "The darndest thing I ever saw. We won by letting them beat us."

"Well, it won't be so easy this time," Jesse said.

After Patrick had stirred up the African American congregations in Los Angeles, he and Birdie moved up the coast to the Bay area. They hit a few churches, then they started working the drag shows. In church, Patrick had played Aretha, a towering spiritual figure who led by song, appealing to people's faith and hope. But in the drag shows, Patrick put on his blonde Marilyn wig and sang torch songs in a wispy voice. The audience quickly noticed he had made a few subtle changes turning the lyrics to be about Jesus, rather than a lost lover. He gave brilliant performances, lifting people's loneliness into a yearning for God.

Birdie always stood in an aisle at the front of the room, scanning the audience for possible attackers. There were never any problems in the churches, but in a San Francisco club, she spotted a man with an angry face reach under his coat. With three long fast strides, she was tackling him, snatching a pistol from his hand. After the security guards dragged the man out of the room and the excitement died down, Patrick nodded to the piano player and they went on with the show.

Birdie was not surprised by the people who hated Patrick. Not everyone thought of his presence as a gift, as she did. There were nuts out there, she knew, who would find the popularity of a transvestite singing about Jesus an abomination, an insult to God. Patrick was a beautiful young man, and the characters he created on stage lifted the hearts of many, but there are those who find beauty threatening. Birdie had to stay always alert, especially when Patrick was on stage or in a crowd. She understood now that protecting Patrick was the reason she'd been brought back to the mortal plane.

Alex looked at Tristram sitting next to him outside the lecture hall at St. Anthony University—the first stop on Alex's speaking tour. Tristram's blonde hair fell in a long forelock across his face, and he was constantly tossing the hair to the side with a practiced gesture to keep it out of his eyes. The gesture called attention not only to his lustrous hair, but also to his bright green eyes which were always moving, alert to everything around him. He was the best student Alex had ever had, able to grasp the subtleties of theology and apply them to politics and social justice in ways that surprised even Alex who'd been thinking about these subjects since before Tristram was born. Gorgeous and gifted, Tristram was everything Alex could want in a friend and lover. There were issues of course, but they were outside of their relationship. Breaking the celibacy requirement of priests didn't bother him; he was well aware that the requirement went back to the early Middle Ages when the church leadership was concerned that family dynasties were being established in the church. As for the ban on homosexuality, Paul's letters make it clear that he was something of a bigot; much of the misguided policies of the church have been derived from taking his letters to the early churches more seriously than they should be taken.

Like most 21st century Catholic clergy, Alex believed that the scripture is not a fixed document, but rather an evolving piece of literature, and what was believed in the past about God's will for humans should inform our current beliefs, but not bind them. The scientific discoveries of the last five hundred years, for example, reveal a universe that is much more complex and subtle than anything the medieval church fathers could have imagined. For example, the Big Bang Theory, after careful study and debate, had been accepted as compatible with church doctrine, and in Alex's opinion, the paradoxes of quantum theory showed that the essence of the universe, as well as the Mind that created it, is essentially unknowable by the tiny minds of humans. So, Alex reasoned, the social contract between humans also must evolve. Church fathers once regarded the Crusades as a noble Christian endeavor and the Inquisition as a valid means of confronting evil. Just as we've given up the idea that our parishioners should be boiled in oil to save their souls, so (and here Alex laughed at his own sophistry) we must give up our prejudices against gays and lesbians. Alex paused in his rhetorical revery long enough to be amused by his false analogy, an obvious logical fallacy he would never have allowed his students to get away with. *Let's face it,* Alex muttered to himself, *you desire this beautiful boy and loving him is not hurting anyone, so you allow yourself this indulgence.* The problem, he knew, lay not in his homosexuality but in the lies he told to hide it.

"You should move up to the stage, Alex," Tristram said, checking the time on his phone. "I'll come with you and make sure there's a glass of water and adequate lighting so you can see your notes on the lectern."

Alex nodded and smiled at Tristram, grateful for the young man's attention to detail. How many times in the past had he started a lecture only to have to pause to ask for water? As they walked toward the stage, he glanced around the auditorium. Every seat was filled, and people were standing in the aisles or sitting on the steps in front of the lectern. A video camera was at the back of the room and another in the right aisle. A dozen people had their phones aimed at him as he climbed the steps to the stage. Tristram had said that the lecture would appear in social media, reaching potentially millions, but Alex knew little of this kind of thing.

As he took his place at the lectern, he was aware of the broad brightly lit screen behind him with the words "What Does God Require of Us? A lecture by Professor Alejandro Beltran, STL, PhD" and the logo of St Anthony University.

"What Does God Require of Us?" Alex began, looking over his shoulder at the white screen. "It sounds like the beginning of a college syllabus, doesn't it?" He was relieved that a chuckle spread through the audience. He could tell the audience was on his side. "And the analogy fits to a certain degree. The spiritual life involves life-long study, not just of holy texts, but other subjects as well. If we notice the design of a flower, then we are learning something about God's will. If we learn about the dance the honeybee does to inform her hive-mates of the location of a field of flowers, then we start to understand the purpose of art in our lives. And if we study the ways bees serve their society, cooperating in providing for their young, then we gain insight into how our own society works, or should work. But of course, we are more than honeybees, aren't we? We have free will and self-awareness. So, we must learn not only about flowers, bees, and hives, we must also learn about ourselves. This awareness of the world and ourselves is the first requirement God makes of us.

"Micah 6:8 says that we've been told what God requires of us: *Only to do justice and to love goodness, and to walk humbly with your God.*"

Alex slowly repeated the phrase *to do justice* and paused.

"Ladies and gentlemen, believers in Christ and believers in other gods or in no gods, here is the crux of what we must do…"

In the remainder of the hour, Alex outlined the injustices in the world and how, in America with its official rhetoric of freedom and equality, these injustices are unacceptable. Destruction of the natural world which is God's wonderful gift to us; war on other nations; inequality of wealth; racism, especially the structural racism which institutionalizes inequality; abuse of women; and neglect of children are sins not just against the people who directly suffer from these injustices, but they are sins against ourselves, our own sense of goodness. "We cannot," he claimed, "love goodness and walk humbly with God, however we might define 'God' as long as we tolerate these sins."

Alex closed his homily, as he thought of this lecture, by quoting the prayer of St. Francis:

Lord make Me an instrument of Your peace
Where there is hatred let me sow love.
Where there is injury, pardon.
Where there is doubt, faith.
Where there is despair, hope.
Where there is darkness, light.
Where there is sadness joy.
O Divine master grant that I may
Not so much seek to be consoled as to console
To be understood, as to understand.
To be loved. as to love
For it's in giving that we receive
And it's in pardoning that we are pardoned
And it's in dying that we are born…
To eternal life.

The audience gave Alex a standing ovation, and a number of people came up to ask for his autograph afterward. Alex was pleased with the reception, but he wanted an objective critique because there were more events on the calendar.

"What did you think?" he asked Tristram when they were alone in a coffee shop nearby.

"It was good," Tristram said. When Alex signaled with his hands that he wanted to hear more, Alex added softly, "But you were hitting softballs."

"What do you mean?"

"Come on, Alex, *Micah* 6:8 and the prayer of St. Francis? I learned those for my first communion, didn't you?" Tristram said, letting his frustration with his friend and mentor show. "You're going to have to dig deeper, say things no one has ever said before."

Alex nodded reluctantly. "What else?"

"It was an easy audience, you know."

"Yeah, my home university where I'm a tenured professor. My students, colleagues and friends in the audience…"

"The next one is going be harder, and the one after that even harder."

"You think that maybe when Maria set up this tour, she let me start with a friendly audience to give me confidence, and then she ratcheted up the difficulty with each event?"

Tristram nodded, then he looked down at the table, "Speaking of Maria…"

Alex took his friend off the hook by answering the unasked question, "She knows about us."

"Really? Did you tell her?"

"No. She sussed it out by herself. She's very smart."

"And she's okay with our… relationship?"

"She said she's okay with it," Alex said, leaving the question only half-answered.

Tristram looked around the room, avoiding Alex's eyes. And Alex, who'd come late in life to love, began to see that nothing about love, or war for that matter, was simple.

Stefan entered the cave where his wife lay propped up on pillows, nursing his son Francisco Estevan. Christina looked up and smiled. Stefan sat down next to them, and when the baby was finished nursing, the mother handed the child to the father and said, "This is your son, Stefan."

Stefan looked down at the child's face, and he asked himself the question every father, whether he wishes to or not, has to ask, whether he wants to or not. *Is this my child?* Francisco looked nothing like him and nothing like Stefan's parents, as far as he could remember, and for that matter nothing like his red-haired milk-skinned Irish American wife. Stefan put aside the question, knowing he would have to wrestle with it later, and felt the surge of ancient hormones flood through him. He knew he would do anything for this child.

Stefan walked across the cornfield to the old brick church which stood among the houses like a stone in the middle of a pond. Eduardo and the old priest Father McCormick sat with him in the sacristy.

"What are your plans, *mi amigo*?" Eduardo asked.

Stefan shrugged, "I don't really know. Maria said we should hide here with the Yaqui until the war is over. She seems to think we're in danger. I'm very grateful that you've taken us in."

Out of respect for the fact they were in a holy place, Eduardo had taken off his baseball cap and was holding it in his hand. Stefan was surprised to see that his friend's hair was white and the same length all around his head, as if his wife had put a bowl on his head and cut away all the white hair that showed.

Father McCormick was wearing a white cotton cassock, traditionally worn in tropical climates, with a black rabat, twin rectangles descended from his collar which Stefan knew from his reading hadn't been worn since the nineteenth century. The priest must have inherited this cassock from his predecessors who had passed it down from one parish priest to the next.

"Of course, my son," Father McCormick said, reassuringly. "We are glad to provide sanctuary for you and your family."

Eduardo cleared his throat. "Stefan, you said yesterday that you wanted to work. You didn't want to accept charity?"

Stefan nodded. "Of course, give me a hoe and I'll start working in the fields right away."

Eduardo and Father McCormick tried to restrain their laughter, and Stefan tried not to feel offended.

"My son," the priest said. "The people here have been working in the fields since they were children. With all respect, you wouldn't last a day in the hot sun. However, we could use your help with something else. I've been trying to tutor the children in basic reading and mathematics, but I have other duties, so I would very much appreciate your taking over their schooling."

"Of course, I'd be glad to, but you need to know I've never taught before, and I had only two years of college before I joined the army."

"Two years of college is far more schooling than any of my other parishioners here, so you seem well-qualified to me."

"Father, there's something else you need to know about me…" Stefan said quietly, feeling that he should acknowledge the elephant in the living room of his past.

"Is this about your prison term?" Father McCormick asked.

"Yes," Stefan said, surprised. He looked from the priest to his friend and they both were looking at him kindly. "How did you know?"

"José told me. He thought I should know before we agreed to take you in," the priest said, looking at Stefan with kind eyes. "We have all committed sins, my son. Perhaps when we are alone, you'd like to confess yours, pay penance and then we needn't discuss this issue again?"

Stefan nodded. "I'd like to do that, Father."

Maria was standing in the courtyard of *El Presidio* watching Genevieve and Marta ratchet bipod mounts on the motorcycle sidecars. Marta who had been a helicopter mechanic in Iraq was explaining the armaments to Maria.

"The M30s don't have a heavy recoil, so they usually don't require a mount, but we'll be firing from a moving position, possibly over rough terrain, so the mount will help to aim and fire the weapon. We don't want live fire spraying over the field randomly."

Genevieve nodded, then turned to Maria, "I assume the waivers for Xavi and the others came through?"

Maria nodded. "Birdie was able to convince her boss Rafe that things are getting desperate down here. We can't fight these bastards with our bare hands anymore. The stakes are too high."

Genevieve and Marta looked at each other solemnly. They'd both been in firefights and seen friends die. There was no high-fiving or shouts of excitement over the fact that they would have to spill blood soon. When Marta had left the military, she'd felt relief that she'd never have to kill a human being again, now here she was about to go into a firefight with her own countrymen.

"Maria," Marta asked. "We're going to need air support. I'm not certified, but I do know how to fly a chopper if you need me to."

"Marta, you're right. We do need air support, but I don't need to tell you how vulnerable helicopters are to ground fire. We're going to be using hummingbirds for air support, and wasps as skirmishers."

Marta thought, *Hummingbirds? Wasps?* But she didn't say anything, understanding that this was a very different kind of war than the one she'd served in. She looked at the wooden pine boxes, which she'd seen double as coffins in Iraq, and counted two extra boxes. "What's in the other coffins?" she asked.

Maria looked startled, then saw where Marta was looking. "Oh," she said, "those are two heavy machine guns which will be mounted on pickup trucks."

Marta nodded. "You want the tripods mounted in the bed of the trucks or on trailers?"

"On the beds of the trucks. Zenobia will drive one and Adelaide will drive the other. Inez will operate one of the weapons and José the other."

"José is trained in the use of a .50 caliber Browning?" Marta had trouble imagining José, the gentlest man she'd ever met, mowing down the enemy at long distance.

Maria didn't answer, but looked away, smiling. These women would be very surprised to find out what José knew how to do. He was gentle enough to rock a baby to sleep and fierce enough to kill a demon with his bare hands. Looking past the poplars that lined the road, she saw a plume of dust moving quickly toward them. As the vehicle drew closer, she could see it was a red low-slung sports car. The driver was gunning it recklessly over the potholes. Fast, reckless, headed this way. *Xavi*, she thought, with a combination of relief and resentment. They certainly needed him, but he was always such a pain in the ass.

Xavi raced into the gate of the convent, fish-tailed to a stop ten feet in front of the women, spewing gravel in their direction. He emerged from the car, stretched his arms, and said, "Hey Maria, great to see you. I just came back to collect on that blowjob you promised me."

"You are the most infuriating being in all creation, Xavi," she said, both amused and disgusted.

"I know. I know," he replied, smiling at her. "A guy's gotta keep up his reputation, right?" He glanced at the Browning that Genevieve and Marta were carefully lifting from one of the pine coffins and said, "I see you guys are getting ready to party."

Chapter 13

Stefan woke up in the cave with an uneasy feeling. He turned over and saw Christina holding Francisco in her arms as he nursed. His wife was looking at him with narrow eyes. "What?" he asked, worried he'd done something wrong.

"Are you jealous of Francisco?" she asked.

"What? No, of course not. He's just a baby. Why would I feel jealous?"

"I've read that some fathers are jealous of the attention their wives give to the baby."

"Christina, no. That's not true at all. I love our son. I think he's perfect. I think you are doing exactly what you are supposed to do, paying attention to the baby. I'm a grown man. I don't need constant attention. He does." He looked at his wife with what he hoped was a calm reassuring gaze. She turned her attention back to the baby who'd had his fill of milk and was now dozing off. "Where is this coming from, Christina?"

She paused a few moments, then said in a soft voice, "I don't know. I guess I'm feeling extremely protective of Francisco right now." She looked up at him. "You've been a great father, Stefan. I couldn't ask for a better partner than you. Do you miss the time we used to have together?"

He wondered how to answer the question without triggering the latent fears she obviously had toward him, then answered carefully, "Yes, of course, Christina. I love you and I treasure the year we have had together, but our lives have changed." He gestured at the cave. "Who would have guessed we'd be living in a cave?"

She laughed. "Well, you were living in a cave under the freeway when I first met you."

"Yeah, and it was only slightly smaller than your apartment. This cave feels like a mansion to me."

She laughed again. He'd always loved her loud inappropriate laugh. Surprisingly, it didn't wake the baby who probably had gotten used to it when he was in the womb.

"Stefan…" Christina said, hesitantly.

"Yes, darling?"

"I'm sorry if I sounded suspicious of your feelings toward Francisco. My hormones are raging right now, and I get strange feelings."

"Not to worry. Just keep in mind that I love you and I will do literally anything to protect you and Francisco."

"I know you will. Now, you better get to work. It's your first day at your new job."

"I don't know how many students are going to show up, but even if no one shows up, Father McCormick may have a few things for me to do."

Stefan got dressed. Eduardo had given him a pair of canvas sandals to wear, saying they were much more comfortable than the old leather army boots Stefan had brought with him. Funny, he'd expected that the Yaqui would be wearing white cotton shirts and pants like the campesinos in old Hollywood movies. Instead, the men and women dressed in faded jeans and t-shirts with the logos of American universities; as he walked across the cornfield, people wearing shirts that said Harvard, UCLA, and Texas Tech looked up from their hoeing and waved to him. Arriving at the wooden building behind the church, he went inside to examine the classroom.

A blackboard stretched across the front of the room with pieces of chalk of varying lengths and colors resting in the trough at its front. A battered teacher's desk which must have been quite elegant in its day sat in front of the blackboard. Stefan walked past the orderly rows of a dozen small desks, noticing initials carved in a few of them. He sat down in the teacher's chair at the desk and looked through the drawers where he found boxes of chalk in a rainbow of colors, a few pencils and ballpoint pens and a stack of elementary writing tablets with the lines laid out to indicate the height of small and capital letters. From his pocket, he took the small Spanish-English dictionary José had given him and laid it on the table. He knew that he'd be learning Spanish from the children at the same time he was teaching them to read, write, and do arithmetic. He folded his hands on the desk, bowed his head and asked for help in his new job.

After a few minutes, Father McCormick showed up, holding the hand of a boy of about six.

"This is Miguel," the good father said. "He wants to start school today." When Stefan looked out the door to see whether other children were coming, Father McCormick said, "There will be other children coming to school once the parents get to know you. Miguel is Eduardo's grandson."

"Buenos días, Miguel. Me llamó Señor Jozsef."

"¿Puede decir señor Jozsef?" Father McCormick asked the boy.

"*Señor Chosef,*" the boy answered.

"*Muy bien. Ahora siéntese por favor.*" The priest indicated one of the desks on the front row, and the boy obediently walked over and sat down.

"Well," Father McCormick said, "I'll leave you to it. The boy has no book learning at all. His parents can't read or write, so you'll have to start from scratch with him. About mid-day send him home. People have their main meal at noon." The priest turned away, then turned to face Stefan again. "One other thing, Stefan. Be kind to the boy. The Yaqui, unlike the barbaric gringos to the north, do not strike their children. Their philosophy is that life is hard enough without causing pain to children."

"Of course, Father," Stefan answered, having a brief flashback to the times he was beaten by foster parents.

After the priest left, Stefan went to the front of the classroom, picked up a long piece of blue chalk and drew on the blackboard a capital letter A, as well as the lower-case version. He pronounced the name of the letter and asked the boy to repeat the name several times. He traced the shape with his index finger and let the boy study the shape for a moment. Then Stefan gave Miguel a pad and a pencil. He showed the boy how to hold the pencil and then let him draw the first letter of the alphabet between the lines. Thus, they began.

Chapter 14

About fifteen miles north of the Mexican border, in a small mountain range on the eastern reaches of the Tohono O'Odham Nation Reservation, there is a geologic formation known in this part of the world as a *ciénega*. Although the climate is very dry, a small amount of precipitation falls each year on the mountains and seeps underground until it comes to a granite shelf that slopes to the valley below, and there the water collects in the shallow soil. With steep mountains on four sides, the wide valley forms a bowl that traps the water. A gravel road runs through the length of the valley, exiting over high passes on the north and south. On either side of the gravel road, the soil is saturated with water. There are ponds disguised by reeds and cattails scattered through the valley, and in a few of the higher places, stands of cottonwoods and cypresses raise their arms to the blazing blue sky.

Huitzilopochtli hovered next to a cottonwood on the south end of the valley. Maria had told him that according to her intelligence a large convoy of militia would be coming down this road later today. The militia intended to intercept a group of several hundred Central Americans who had crossed the border intending to settle in the United States. Normally immigrants illegally crossing the border formed groups of no more than a dozen or so, customarily led by a *coyote*, the freelance smugglers who brought human beings and drugs north, and guns and money south, but in this case, the immigrants had formed a larger group, led by one of their own, and they hoped by moving quickly north their large numbers ensured that at least some of them would evade capture. The ICE border patrol had no jurisdiction on the reservation, so they had encouraged militia which had no official status to intercept the immigrants on the reservation. The Tohono O'Odham leadership had declared themselves neutral on the issue but had warned ICE that vigilantes would not be tolerated on their land. Afraid their boundaries would be violated over their protests, the native Americans had secretly sent a message to Maria that this valley was a perfect place for an ambush.

And indeed, Huitzi thought, it is perfect terrain for an airborne army of birds and insects. The vehicles of the militia would drive single file down the gravel road, not realizing that the grassy plain that stretched to the mountains on either side was a spongy wetland. When the convoy was attacked, they would almost certainly leave the road and try to form either a circle or a wedge to defend themselves. Their heavy vehicles would sink in the spongy soil, and when the men got out of their vehicles, their boots would sink into the soil as well. The general stationed José and the Sisters of the Piston on the road at the north and south ends of the valley, their heavy Brownings and lighter AKs would stop any attempt the militia men might make to escape. The only question Huitzi had is how many of the enemy should be killed, as opposed to wounded? He had sent a message to Maria asking her this very question. He didn't want to disrupt her overall strategy.

He watched as his ten thousand hummingbirds took position two hundred meters to the east of the road, and General Zaberi's one million wasps took position the same distance to the west. José had thoughtfully placed pails of sugar water close to the positions, so the birds and wasps wouldn't become exhausted by hunger.

And now they waited.

As the hours passed in the hot desert sun, Huitzi became worried that Maria's intelligence had been faulty. She had expressed the highest confidence in the source, but she never shared what the sources were, so he had no way of verifying the information she gave him. In early afternoon, one of his aides arrived with a message that Maria had sent the rules of engagement. They should engage the enemy without waiting for provocation; they had a waiver to kill both humans and demons; they should kill as many demons as they could; but humans should be maimed or wounded, killing them only when necessary. Huitzi was glad to have clarity. He would just as soon kill all the humans as well as all the demons, but he understood that rules of engagement were heavily influenced by politics, so he would accept the limitations as they came down through the chain of command.

One of his aides landed next to Huitzi and reported breathlessly, "Emperor, the enemy force had been spotted in the north moving down the road toward the valley."

"Tell our lieutenants as well as the wasps to be ready to attack," Huitzi ordered.

At first, the tactic worked perfectly. After the enemy vehicles had entered the valley, the sisters moved their motorcycles and the pickup truck with a Browning mounted in the back from their hiding place behind a large jumble of rocks. They took position at the valley's entrance, closing it off. There would be no escape for the enemy now. But then, when the enemy caravan came into view, Huitzi heard a familiar droning coming from beyond the mountain, and before he saw the biplane, he knew what it was and what its presence meant.

"CALL A RETREAT!" he shouted, and immediately hundreds of hummers rose in the air, flying in the pre-arranged pattern that signaled that all hummers and wasps should fly away from the road and toward the mountains. No sooner had they started the retreat, then the biplane appeared over the western ridge and descended quickly into the valley, and once over the valley floor, let loose a steady stream of nicotinoid, a gray fog that settled on the valley floor killing all the small fauna.

"ATTACK THE CONVOY AT THE NORTH END OF THE VALLEY!" Huitzi shouted, and the signal corps rose again and signaled the hummers and wasps to fly north toward the enemy convoy which was now parked in a line near the north entrance.

As the biplane flew toward the command position where Huitzi and his staff were, he realized they were in danger. "COMMAND STAFF, RISE TO ONE HUNDRED FEET!" he shouted, and he and his staff and retainers rose as one body and let the biplane spewing its cloud of poison to pass beneath them.

"ORDER THE SISTERS IN THE NORTH POSITION TO BEGIN FIRING AT THE CONVOY!" One of his aides flew at top speed to the north end of the valley. Huitzi watched the biplane bank and turn, then it headed back into the center of the valley, this time letting loose the poisonous fog over the slope where the wasps had retreated. Huitzi knew he could not save them. Wasps could not fly high enough to get above the fog. There was only one way to stop the biplane. A hummer of extraordinary strength and speed would have to intercept the plane in midair.

In a split second, Huitzi estimated the path and speed of the biplane and waited until it was passing directly below him. He heard the long bursts of the Browning mounted on the back of José's truck firing, as well as the short bursts of the AKs, and knew the sisters would make short work of the humans in the convoy. At exactly the right moment, he dropped down to the biplane, matching its speed exactly. The head of the pilot was a few feet below him. Huitzi landed on the pilot's head and quickly swung his needle-like beak into the right eye of the man, then into the left eye. As the pilot tried to grab Huitzi, he leaped into the air and slowed down, letting the plane fly off over the desert with a blind pilot and watched the plane crash against the far slope of the mountain. He was confident that the hummers had already left that slope and swarmed to the north end of the valley. The automatic weapons fire had ceased, and he knew the hummers would finish off any wounded demons.

Huitzi's army of birds and insects had won with the help of José and the Sisters killing all the demons and maiming all the humans who'd entered the valley, but the cost had been high.

As the adjutant landed beside him, Huitzi ordered. "Report!"

"Sir, the poison gas killed thousands of our allies, the wasps."

"None escaped?"

"Unknown, sir. General Zaberi and his staff survived, but most of the wasps were hit by the cloud of poison."

"What about our hummers, Lieutenant?"

"It appears that casualties of our forces were minimal. They were able to rise above the cloud of poison when you ordered them to, sir."

"Bring detailed reports of casualties to me as soon as possible, Lieutenant. And get a message to General Zaberi that he and I need to confer."

Huitzi thought about how the engagement had gone wrong. The enemy had obviously known that this valley was a trap set for them, and they knew they would be attacked by wasps although they obviously had not expected to face automatic weapons fire. Someone, undoubtedly a human, had tipped them off. He had to report to Maria that one of her beloved Sisters was a spy for the enemy.

Chapter 15

On his second day as a teacher, Stefan had four students, so he guessed that Miguel had given him good reviews. This morning, Miguel and three of his cousins, Mateo, Santiago, and Gabriela were waiting at the schoolhouse door when he showed up. He had planned to teach the letter B today, but once he saw he had new students, he changed his plan and began class by drawing the letter A on the board and calling on Miguel to identify it. Then he told them a story about *la abeja*—the bee—and he transformed the letter A into a rudimentary honeybee which the children were well familiar with since there was an aviary next to the vegetable garden. Then he wrote the word *abeja* on the board, underlining the first letter. Then he handed each child a notebook and wrote his or her first name on the cover. Not having ever seen their written names before, they were amazed and proud. These were *their* notebooks. He had them copy the letter A on the first page, and below it draw a bee. Then he held up Miguel's drawing because he said, Miguel had mastered this letter the day before. Miguel gleamed with pride that he was ahead of his cousins in learning to write.

At noon, Stefan told them to ask their parents if they could come every morning except Sunday. They solemnly looked at him with their large brown eyes and nodded. Then he sent them home for lunch.

Pleased with how the class was going, Stefan walked over to Eduardo's house where Concepción had prepared a large meal for him. Concepción never spoke to Stefan, just placing the platters of food in front of him with her eyes downcast, but Eduardo loved to talk and listen and talk some more.

"José arrived in his truck late last night," Eduardo said. "He's asleep now but when he wakes up, he will probably come to your cave to visit you and see the baby." Eduardo asked Stefan about his progress at school and about his four grandchildren who were now Stefan's students.

"It's just the second day, so we've barely gotten started, but the children are sweet and obedient. They want to learn." Stefan looked at his new friend and felt a surge of gratitude at the generosity that he and the other Yaqui people had shown to Christina, Francisco and him. "May I ask a question, Eduardo?"

"Of course, my friend."

"I'm not quite sure why Maria has sent us here, or how long we are supposed to stay."

Eduardo looked down and gave a small shrug. "I do not have the answers to your questions. I apologize. Perhaps you can ask José when you see him later?"

Stefan had the sense that Eduardo knew more than he was letting on, but he wanted José to be the one to explain everything to Stefan.

Later that afternoon, José stopped by to see the baby. "What a strong handsome boy," he said, smiling broadly. After admiring the baby and speaking to *La Patera* in quick Spanish Stefan couldn't follow, José glanced at Stefan and said, "Let's take a walk, my friend."

They walked silently around the edge of the cornfield, stopping in a shady glade far from the houses. José sat on a boulder and gestured for Stefan to sit beside him. Dharma, who had followed them, lay contented in the grass at Stefan's feet, and he was pleased at how well she had adapted to canine life here. Eduardo had told him that the pack had chased down a fawn the day before, so the dogs were resting today as they digested the meat and gnawed the bones.

"Eduardo said that you might have a few questions for me. If I can answer them, I will."

The bile of resentment which Stefan had kept tamped down suddenly surged up, "Is Francisco my son?"

José looked at him with an expression that Stefan thought was disgust.

"Of course, he's your son. Why do you ask?"

"I'm sorry, but the kid doesn't look Hungarian or Irish. He looks… I don't know… Spanish or something."

"What does Christina say?"

"I haven't asked her. But she seems worried that I'm jealous of the baby."

"Are you?"

"No." Stefan looked off in the distance. The sky was a dark blue. The corn stalks quivered in the wind. Everyone was taking siesta, so the field was empty. This was, he suddenly realized, a very beautiful place. "I guess I'm just scared. I've never been responsible for anyone else before."

"Good, you should be a little scared. Fatherhood is a scary thing at first, and our sick little minds try to find an excuse to run away. It takes courage to stand strong and accept responsibility for your family. The fear will come and go for the rest of your life, so just accept it and concentrate on doing the next right thing. As for Christina… It's best that you don't bring up this issue with her. Stop insulting her by questioning whether Francisco is yours. This is your crap, and you need to deal with it. Christina has her own pre-occupations—uncertainties about being a mother, about bringing a child into this fucked-up world. She needs you to be one hundred percent on her side. Your need to be reassured is a distraction she doesn't need right now."

José looked off into the distance slowly shaking his head. "Sometimes men get confused when their partners give birth. The men somehow think it's all about them, whether they can be a good father, and that uncertainty translates into doubting whether they're lovable or whether they've been tricked into taking on responsibilities they're afraid of." José turned to Stefan and said, "Son, it's time to get over yourself and pay attention to your family."

"Sorry. I shouldn't have said anything."

"Oh, it's okay you said it to me. Just don't say it to your wife or anyone else."

"What about the other people here? Won't they notice that the kid looks nothing like me?"

José laughed. "No one here has ever seen an Anglo baby. They don't know what one looks like. As far they're concerned, all white babies look like Francisco. And besides, no baby looks like its father, or its mother either. Babies look like chipmunks."

The two men laughed and sat in silence for a while, then José said, "Have I ever told you how I met Maria?"

Stefan shook his head.

"I was a young man working as a carpenter in Nazareth. And one day, I'm putting up the roof beams of a house when I hear screaming and yelling coming from down the street. I look over and there's a young girl, no more than fourteen, obviously pregnant, who's being beaten by a man. I mean he's really going at her with a leather strap, and a woman, perhaps the girl's mother, is trying to stop him. There's a crowd gathering, and I see people picking up stones, and this is getting bad. If the man doesn't beat her to death, then the crowd is going to stone her. So, I grabbed my largest mallet and ran over there. In those days I was young, strong, and hot-tempered. I didn't know what this girl had done other than get pregnant, but I wasn't going to stand by and watch this crowd kill her. By then, the girl was lying on the ground trying to cover her belly with her arms to protect her baby, and the man was whipping her on the head, but she didn't try to protect herself, only her unborn child. As the man lifted the strap to strike her again, I gave him a shove, and he fell down. He got back up, angry, but when he saw a hairy bear of a man standing over him holding a large mallet, he lost his nerve and backed away. I stood over the girl, looked around at the crowd, my neighbors who knew me as a man who could handle himself in a fight, and they backed off. Once I was sure the girl was safe, I helped her stand up and walked her back to my house."

"And you married her," Stefan said, admiringly.

"Yes, I married her. And when Jesse was born, I treated him as my own son."

"Didn't you ever wonder…?"

"Of course, I wondered how she got pregnant, but I never asked. A girl that young was probably raped. Who am I to blame a girl who was forced? And later, after Jesse was executed, the scribes wrote that Maria had been a virgin who was impregnated by a beam of light."

José laughed. "I don't know about a beam of light, but I do know that I married a beautiful girl who became the best wife a man has ever had. And she gave me a strong son who became a damn good carpenter and a wise rabbi. Knocking down Maria's father before he beat her to death was the best thing I ever did." José looked at his young friend. "Let me ask you something, son. Do you love your wife?"

"Yes."

"Do you trust her?"

Stefan hesitated, then answered, "Yes."

"Will you try your best to be a good father to the boy?"

"Yes."

"Then what's the problem? Men have little to do with the birth of babies, but we have a lot to do with protecting and providing for our families. Do your job, son, and let your wife do hers."

Stefan shifted his weight from side to side and looked down at the ground. "I guess I have low self-esteem. It's hard for me to believe that Christina actually loves me."

José looked at his young friend sympathetically, then said softly, "Stefan, self-esteem comes from doing things you can be proud of. If you meet your responsibilities as a man, you'll grow into self-respect which is much more important than self-esteem."

José let Stefan think about his responsibilities for a few moments, then asked, "Did you have another question?"

"Actually, I do.... I'm not sure what is going on."

"What do you mean?"

"Why are we here on Yaqui land? How long are we going to be here?"

José was silent for a few moments, then he spoke slowly, "I'm not sure about the big picture. Maria is always moving so fast that by the time I think I understand what's going on, the situation has changed. But I'll tell you what I think I know, but you have to understand that Maria is the one to ask, not me."

Stefan nodded gratefully, and José said, "There seems to be a three-way war starting. A year ago, The Old Man sent Jesse and Xavi to earth with the intention of destroying it, but Jesse had second thoughts when he realized that not every human should be killed. So, he convinced Xavi and Maria to help him save the world, but The Old Man still wants Xavi to follow through on the job."

"How does Xavi feel about it?"

"Xavi's hard to read. Sometimes he seems to have deep feelings of love, especially for Jesse, but most of the time, he's just a hell-raiser. My guess is that he still plans to burn the place down, but he's holding off out of respect for Jesse."

"So that's one side of the triangle? God's plan to start the apocalypse. What's the second side?"

"The second side is Jesse and Maria's great love for humans. They believe the species has tremendous potential to grow out of our hatred and violence and become truly spiritual beings. So, Jesse and Maria are trying to stop the apocalypse and give humans more time to reach our potential."

"And the third side in this war?"

"Lucifer is trying to stop the apocalypse because he wants to increase his influence over humans. He has a strong foothold already. You don't have to look any further than the last couple hundred years to see his power in human affairs. The Armenian Genocide, Pol Pot's genocide, The Holocaust, the Rape of Nanking, the bombings of Hiroshima and Nagasaki, the American Indian Wars, The Middle Passage, slavery ... I mean the influence of evil in human affairs is obvious, no? There are those who claim that Lucifer has already won."

"So, Lucifer wants to stop the apocalypse because he feels he is winning, so why knock over the board?"

"Exactly."

"And how does my family—Christina, Francisco, and me—fit into this three-way war?"

"Don't you know?" José asked, surprised.

Stefan thought for a moment. "Maria has us hiding here in the Yaqui homeland. There are no computers or internet connections here, and only a few telephones. People here live close to the earth, much the way they've lived for thousands of years."

"Think about it, Stefan. What happens to this place if The Old Man gets his way and civilization, as well as most of humanity, is destroyed?"

"I would imagine that the Yaqui Way would be a sustainable culture, able to survive the collapse of civilization as we know it."

"That's right. And what happens if Maria wins, and humankind is ready to evolve to a higher state of consciousness?"

"Then, Yaqui Wisdom would be a good model for other cultures to follow? Live close to the earth, respect nature, love your family?"

"Bingo. And what happens to this place if Lucifer wins, and civilization continues with war and oppression?"

"Then the Yaqui homeland would be an island of sanity in an ocean of madness."

Stefan quietly absorbed the enormity of the ideas José had led him to.

"You said that Xavi is the agent of God's plan to destroy the earth? Is Xavi working alone? I mean how can one entity stand up against the vast forces that Maria and Lucifer can bring to bear?"

"Xavi is the Destroyer of Worlds. He needs no other."

"You're friends with Xavi, right?" Stefan remembered seeing José and Xavi together at the convent.

"Yes, we're friendly," José conceded. "But I'm always careful around Xavi. He's very temperamental and can turn violent without warning."

Stefan shifted uncomfortably, still not understanding his place in these vast designs. A year ago, he'd been living under a bridge and eating out of garbage cans, and now José was telling him that he was part of cosmic changes. He reached down and scratched Dharma behind the ears. She looked up at him with adoring eyes. He wondered how much of these huge transformations she was aware of. He'd known for a long time that Dharma was wiser than he was.

"But why us?" Stefan asked José. "Why did Maria choose my family to come here and hide in safety? There are billions of families who are in danger now."

José looked at him without saying anything, letting Stefan work it out for himself.

"It's Francisco, isn't it?" Stefan asked, beginning to understand. "My son is destined for great things, so Maria wants to keep him safe until he's ready."

José nodded. "Whether humanity is destroyed by Xavi until only a few survive, or whether it is corrupted by evil through Lucifer's machinations, or whether it emerges into a new age of enlightenment as Maria wishes, there will be a need for wisdom and vision."

Stefan looked beyond the shade to the rows of corn, each one on a small hillock, turning their palms up to the bright sun like supplicants. He was slowly coming to terms with the enormity of the task ahead of him. For the first time in his life, he knew his purpose on earth. He was here to protect Christina and Francisco and to learn from the Yaqui.

Chapter 16

"Who is this guy I'm supposed to debate?" Alex asked, as he got dressed in their hotel room. "His name is Winston Schuler," Tristram answered, glancing at the notes he'd gleaned from the internet. "Originally a biology professor, he's made a name for himself as sort of a professional atheist. His argument usually runs in the direction of religion is based on superstitions that science has proven false. How can we still take seriously the ancient folktales of a desert people who made up stories to reassure themselves? Blah blah blah…"

"So, the tv producers are basically promoting a fight between a theologian and an atheist?"

Tristram laughed. "I guess they are. Everyone's going to be disappointed if the two of you agree with each other, or even like each other."

At the public television station, the host Alice Norris, a woman with spectacles on a chain around her neck and the distracted air of a librarian, introduced herself to Alex and Tristram, and then introduced them to Professor Schuler. Tristram disappeared into the shadows off-camera, and Alex settled himself into a chair opposite the professor.

After a lengthy introduction recounting the twentieth century's "crisis of faith" and the twenty first century's "renaissance of traditional religion" in America, she listed the credentials and publications of the two guests, holding up their latest books. Ms Norris then turned to the guest on her right and asked,

"Professor Schuler, why are so many Americans returning to traditional religion?"

"People are afraid," the thin middle-aged man answered, pushing up his horn-rimmed glasses. "We live in a violent chaotic world where things seem beyond human understanding or control. Climate change is causing forests to burst into flames and consume entire towns. Floods engulf coastal cities. Viral plagues are sweeping around the world killing millions of people. On 9/11, we watched office workers leap from burning towers. Broadcast news and the Internet bring war, famine, and disaster into our homes as never before. The world seems dangerous and unpredictable, and religion gives us a sense that there's a meaning and purpose to it all."

"Professor Beltran," Ms Norris said, turning to Alex. "People turn to religion because they're afraid of the large-scale dangers that our society faces?"

"I completely agree with what Professor Schuler said," Alex conceded. "Belief in God is a way of making sense of a dangerous world. But I would add that the reasons people turn to religion do not negate the validity of those beliefs. Moreover, the very problems that Professor Schuler has referred to have their solutions in the teachings of religion. Climate change, for example, is the direct result of people's lack of respect for nature. We have abused God's creation, neglected to care for His gift to us. Pope Francis in his encyclical on the environment made it clear that as people of faith we should take care of the earth. Not to do so is paramount to committing a sin."

"Committing ourselves to taking care of the earth is a matter of common sense," the biology professor retorted. "Our species will quite possibly become extinct unless we stop heating the earth. We don't need to accept superstition to save ourselves from extinction."

"I disagree, Professor," Alex replied. "The problem is not just bad practices or a wasteful way of life. The problem lies deeper than this. We, as a culture and as a species, have failed to embrace a set of values that will ensure that we treat the natural world, as well as other humans, in a way that respects their right to exist and to thrive. This is a moral problem, not a scientific one."

"Well, if the problem is a moral one, then religion has failed us, hasn't it, Father? The Abrahamic religions have appointed themselves as the arbiters and in some cases the enforcers of morality. So, if it is a moral failing that we're destroying the world, then we should change our morals, which means finding new teachers of morality."

"Again, referring to the pope's encyclical, he says Christians have misinterpreted Scripture and must forcefully reject the notion that because we were created in God's image and given dominion over the earth justifies destroying nature. We have a culture that puts the desires of the consumer over the needs of the world, and the greed of the rich over the needs of the poor. In other words, being environmentally and socially responsible is a necessary part of being a person of faith."

Ms. Norris shifted her position, peering at Alex over her half-moon librarian glasses. "Professor Beltran, the moral issues of the Catholic church go beyond Pope Francis's commendable stand on the environment, don't they? For example, what about the Church's stand on women clergy? And what about abortion?"

Alex felt a surge of resentment that the moderator had entered the fray. The tone of her interjection made it clear what her position was on these issues, and he felt it was unfair for him to have to debate two people on live television, but he let go of his resentment and took up the valid questions she had raised. "The ordination of women is an issue that is under discussion and debate in the church leadership. My own opinion is that women should be ordained. There is nothing in Jesus's teachings that would prohibit the recognition of women as leaders, and in fact most people who identify as catholic are women. On a practical level, it would solve the problem with a worldwide shortage of priests. As for abortion, it is seen by almost everyone as a serious moral issue; however, in my opinion, any law that attempts to ban it is not only largely unenforceable, but it fails to consider individual circumstances; therefore, I think that the Church should be very careful in taking absolutist stands."

"Aren't you going to get into trouble with your Church by expressing opinions contrary to its doctrine?" Schuler asked with a sneer.

Alex shook his head. "No, as I said these two issues—the ordination of women and the practice of abortion—are under debate in the Catholic Church. As are other issues, such as the death penalty, the availability of divorce, the involvement by the church in political issues… The church is very old and very large, so it changes slowly, but it does change."

"The Church, your church, has committed so many ghastly crimes in its history. The Crusades, the Inquisition, the collaboration with the Nazis in Germany, the rape and abuse of children… Giordano Bruno, a 16th century astronomer and Dominican friar, was burned at the stake for his cosmological theories. How can you actually believe that Christianity is a force for good?"

"Congratulations, professor," Alex said, sadly. "This is the first valid point that you've made today. The list of serious crimes committed in the name of God, sometimes even by clergy, is long and troubling. And this is not just a problem in the Catholic Church, but in the Protestant, Jewish, and Muslim communities as well. The short explanation for this shocking fact is that churches are basically just groups of people who have come together for their own reasons, and not all those people have noble intentions. If child abuse is a problem in a society, as it is in America, then America's churches will have that problem as well. If fanaticism is a problem in a society, as it was in Europe in the 1930s, then the churches will also have that problem. But there is a more subtle issue at stake here, and that is the nature of love."

"Love, professor?" Ms. Norris asked. "I thought we were talking about hate."

"Yes, we are talking about hate. And about love. Thomas Aquinas, who thought about the relationship between God and man more perceptively than perhaps anyone who has lived, said evil has its origins in one of two ways. There are those who do nothing, refusing to take a stand when faced with a moral choice. These are people who do not love enough to care. And this is the case with the current environmental crisis. People, particularly Westerners, simply don't care enough about God's creation to commit to change their habits or attitudes. It's easier, in their view, to drive than walk. They refuse to respect and admire Creation and are content to participate in its destruction. This is a passive act of evil.

"And then there are those who love too much, and this excess of passion leads them to do the wrong thing. It is possible to love the teachings of the Church too much, and this leads to fanaticism. The young men who hijacked the planes on 9/11 believed that they were doing God's will. They crashed into the twin towers with prayers on their lips. What they did was, of course, evil. They killed thousands of innocent people. But Christianity has had more than its share of fanatics as well. The Inquisition was carried out by men with prayers on their lips. As were The Crusades, and the Salem Witch Trials. The Jews who carry out the bombings in Gaza, The Hindu who assassinated Gandhi… The list of fanatics who have done evil acts is endless. These fanatics don't lack faith. They lack wisdom."

Professor Schuler and Ms. Norris were silent as they absorbed the implications of what Alex had said, then Schuler, obviously thinking he'd won the debate, asked, "Father, isn't what you just said a very strong argument against religion?"

"No," Alex answered. "It's an argument against the misuses of religion. Religious faith is a powerful force, perhaps the most powerful that humankind has ever possessed, and therefore religion must be taken seriously and used wisely, lest it destroy us."

"Well, how'd I do?" Alex asked as he removed his coat and tie in the hotel room.

"You did well," Tristram said. "Your ideas were sophisticated, but also accessible to laypeople. I like the way you conceded the one good point that Professor Jackass made, then turned it in an interesting direction."

"But..." Alex prodded.

"I'm afraid you may have offended some people..."

"Really?" Alex tried to remember what he might have said that could have been offensive.

"That business of comparing Israeli pilots to the witch hunters of Salem..." Tristram said, gently.

"Oh that. Well, it's true. Israeli policies in Gaza are vicious."

"Perhaps, but the word 'Jews' was probably not helpful to your argument."

"Right..." Alex thought about it. "What's next on the schedule?"

Tristram thumbed through the pages on his clipboard. "Maria has scheduled you for a lecture at a college in Iowa."

"What's the topic?"

"Angels."

"How is your teaching going?" Christina was sitting up, the baby nursing at her breast.

"Fine. The children are eager to learn. They seem different than the children I remember in California."

"Different how?"

"Calmer. More present. Less distracted and fidgety."

"American children are fed a diet of sugar and computer games nowadays," Christina said, remembering the children she'd seen as a therapist before she worked at the VA hospital.

"I'm sure that's part of the difference. Also, the Yaqui children have more stability in their lives and more..." Stefan searched for the right word.

"More what?"

"More love, I guess you'd say. Their mothers and fathers spend a lot of time with them, and their grandmothers and grandfathers, uncles and aunts, cousins are all around, and people here seem to actually *like* children."

"Do you think all that attention makes them spoiled?"

"No, not at all. The children are told what is expected of them. And also, the children have jobs to do."

"You mean chores?"

"Meaningful work. When the children go home at noon, there's a family meal, then everyone goes into the field to work, or they feed the chickens, or they help build a shed. The older girls take care of babies, and the older boys help the men build stone walls."

"Aren't they allowed to play?"

"Yeah, the people take frequent breaks from work, and while the adults are sitting and talking, the children are playing tag or jumping rope."

"You like it here, don't you Stefan?"

"I really do. The people are gentle and kind, not only to the children but to each other. When I was living on the street, I saw so much cruelty and violence. Living here seems like paradise."

"*La Patera* says that by tomorrow my stitches will have healed enough, so I can leave the cave and take a walk. She says I need to get to know the other women." Christina looked away from the entrance of the cave to the darkness that led into the chamber below. "She says that in the old days before the priests came, this cave was considered a sacred place. Women used to come here to give birth, boys and girls were initiated into adulthood, and people would spend time here when they were troubled or grieving."

"A magical place?"

"I guess." Christina looked at her husband, this good man, this poet who'd been to prison and suffered, her partner who would do anything for her and Francisco. "I've been having strange dreams, Stefan."

"Strange in what way? What are the dreams about?"

"They're about Francisco and who he is and what he's going to be when he's grown."

"Okay, I'll bite. Who is Francisco and what is he going to be when he's grown?"

"Please don't make fun of me, Stefan. This is serious. We are in a very weird circumstance. We don't know how long we're going to be living here with the Yaqui, so thinking about his future is important."

"You're right, darling. Sorry for my flippant tone. How do you see Francisco's future?"

"Thank you. In my dream, Francisco grows up to be a great teacher. The Yaqui come to respect him a great deal, then he sets out beyond the land of the Yaqui to carry his message of universal peace and love, but he encounters soldiers who arrest him and take him to their president. After a long dialogue, the president becomes frightened by the power of the message Francisco brings, so the president/king condemns him to death. Then Francisco is rescued by his Yaqui friends, and they hide in the mountains. But the message he brought has already started spreading among the nations of the world...."

"Then what happens?"

"I don't know. I woke up."

"Maybe the dream will continue when you go to sleep tonight?

"Maybe, but I don't think so. My feeling is that I've been allowed to see that part of the future I need to see."

"And what is the future you needed to see?" Stefan asked, not sure where this conversation was going, but seeing that his wife had made a vital decision.

"We need to raise Francisco here, among the Yaquis. We shouldn't take him back to California. His destiny, and ours, lies here."

Patrick and Birdie moved up the west coast, performing in larger and larger venues. And each time Patrick performed, there was a crowd of protestors outside, and then a local TV station in Seattle did a news story about him, and the crowds became unmanageable, milling in the street outside the clubs and churches. Birdie was worried. There were far too many people for her to anticipate every possible attack. Trying to narrow the field in order to make surveillance possible, she decided the profile of a possible attacker would be someone much like the man with a gun she'd stopped in San Francisco: a middle-aged white man with anger in his eyes.

So, the attack in Boise caught her completely by surprise. As Patrick came out of a church with Birdie beside him scrutinizing every white man who faced them, a teenage girl in the crowd screamed "Blasphemer!" and raised a pistol and fired. Birdie leaped at the girl, grabbing the weapon and knocking her down. The crowd melted around her, people backing away from the crime. Birdie glanced at Patrick who was holding his hand to the side of his head, blood trickling between his fingers.

As it happened, the bullet only nicked Patrick's ear. He was taken to the emergency room where an intern put a bandage on him and hurried off.

Patrick looked up at Birdie and said, tears coming into his eyes, "Momma, why do people hate me? I've never done anything to them. I just wear pretty clothes and sing."

"Dear boy," she said. "Dear, dear boy…" She stroked his head and said softly, "They're afraid of you because you are beautiful and true. You are bringing words of faith to people who would never listen to a preacher. You are preparing them for the coming of the Lord."

She vowed never to let a stranger get close to him again.

After José left the Yaqui, he drove to El Presidio and reported to Maria what had happened in the Battle of the Marshy Valley, as they were starting to call it. His report corresponded with what she had heard from Inez. José could see his wife needed to think about their overall strategy, so he left her alone in her office, sitting at her desk, staring at a map of the western United States.

Maria did not understand how things had gone so wrong, but she knew what Huitzi's conclusion was. He'd sent her a message saying there was a traitor in her camp. And she had to admit, it did appear to be the case. The band of vigilantes had been expecting an attack at that time and place, and they knew it would be led by hummers and wasps. The biplane with the nicotinoid fog had been waiting nearby until the wasps were airborne and their position could be seen. If the enemy had been forewarned, then there must be a spy in the ranks of the sisters. But how is that possible? Maria went over the roster: Theodora, Adelaide, Genevieve, Zenobia, Inez, Delphina... She'd known these women for years. Betrayal by any of them was unthinkable. Then Maria thought of Marta, the novice. She'd been with the sisters for only a year. Although Marta was certainly the weak link, it was difficult to imagine that she'd purposely betray them.

Maria went back to the basic facts as José had relayed them. Given that this was the second engagement with Huitzi's forces, the enemy would have assumed that hummers and wasps would have been the main force they were facing. A biplane with pesticide would have been easily obtainable in one of the farming communities close to the border. So, the question remained: how did the enemy know the time and location of the ambush?

Maria stuck her head out of her office door. "Marta? Could you come in here please?"

When Marta was sitting in the hard narrow chair that made everyone who sat in it feel as if they'd been called to the principal's office, Maria asked, "Marta, do you have your phone with you?"

Marta used her prosthesis to lift her phone out of her front pocket. She handed it to Maria who glanced at the screen and said, "Do you always keep it turned on?"

Marta nodded. "I turn it off only at night."

"Did you have it with you yesterday at the battle?"

Marta's face quickly changed from curiosity to awareness to embarrassment to outright shame. "Oh my god, Maria. I wasn't thinking. Do you think the vigilantes tracked my phone? Is that why they seemed to be waiting for us?"

Maria looked at the young Latina without giving her any indication of emotion or judgement.

"Oh, Maria, I'm so sorry. There were casualties on our side?"

"I haven't gotten a count from Huitzi yet, but José guesses that thousands of wasps and at least two hummingbirds were killed." She let the numbers sink in, then said. "They were our allies, Marta."

Marta looked at the floor. A tear rolled off her cheek and hit the wooden floor.

"I'm grateful that none of the sisters was injured," Maria said. "Nor was José. But your carelessness put them at risk, Marta. You're a veteran of the war in Iraq. Did you make this mistake over there?"

Marta shook her head, avoiding Maria's eyes.

"You've gotten sloppy, Marta. And your sloppiness cost lives."

Maria let Marta stew in her own guilt for a long minute, then said, "Dismissed."

Now Maria needed to deal with Huitzi. She hoped that she could keep the hummers and wasps on their side. Huitzi and Zaberi could withdraw their forces any time or even change sides.

A few days after the birth of Francisco, Christina was feeling strong enough to leave the cave and walk through the cornfield where people worked every day except Sunday. As she followed the well-worn path through the rows between the mounds with Francisco in her arms, women looked up at the two of them and smiled from beneath broad-brimmed straw hats. On the other side of the field, she came to a row of small houses. She stopped in front of one, wondering whether she should knock on the door, but as she was considering this, a woman came out of the house and walked toward her. She was wearing a cotton print dress of blue and orange flowers. Her black braids were wound on the top of her head. And her broad brown face was pleasant. She stood in front of Christina, politely looking at the ground. Christina didn't know what the etiquette of this situation might be, but she thought perhaps since she was the visitor, she should speak first.

"*Buenos dias*," she said.

"*Buenos dias*," the woman answered.

"*Me llamo Christina*," she said, remembering the first day of her college Spanish class.

The woman nodded. "*Concepción*," she said and pointed to herself. She then stepped to the side and made a sweeping gesture toward the front door of the house. Christina thought it was the most gracious invitation she'd ever encountered.

Chapter 17

"So, I'm basically your bodyguard in this little *tête-à-tête* with Huitzi?" Xavi asked with only a hint of an ironic sneer on his lips. Maria was driving José's pickup truck. Xavi had always liked this area of the world because it had scorpions, Gila monsters and huge rattlesnakes. He liked the way Gila monsters grabbed hold of you and wouldn't let go, grinding their teeth into your skin, letting their poisonous saliva seep into your blood stream. Even if you cut off its head, a Gila will not let go. *Now that's a true warrior species*, he thought.

"Yes," Maria answered. "I need your protection, Xavi. Thank you for coming along." She hated having to depend on Xavi for anything, but she knew that Huitzi blamed her for the loss of his troops in the Battle of the *ciénega*, and Huitzi could be unpredictable when provoked.

"I thought he was your son?"

"He is."

"He would kill his own mother?" Xavi asked.

"He killed four hundred of his brothers and sisters shortly after he was born, so yes, he would kill his own mother if he thought his honor demanded it."

"You know I don't like the guy, right? And he doesn't like me."

"Yes, I gathered that you two would love to kill each other, but I must ask you, Xavi, don't pick a fight with him, okay? We need him and his warriors, so don't fight him just because he pisses you off. And if it does come down to a fight, I don't want you to kill him, okay?"

"Does he know that I'm not immortal, but like him I can be killed only by another god? Does he know he can kill me, and I can kill him?"

"I'm sure he realizes you can be killed, Xavi, but he won't try unless his honor demands it. For him, everything is about honor. He would rather die than be dishonored."

"So, the rules of engagement are that my role is strictly to protect you, and I don't fight him except if it's necessary. And if I fight him, I shouldn't kill him or incapacitate him because we need him to fight the forces of darkness?"

"That's right, Xavi. Thank you."

"If I'm a good boy and you are pleased with my work, then later out of gratitude, you might…" He leered suggestively at Maria's breasts.

"Xavi, let me be clear once again. You and I are never, never, never going to hook up. Got it?"

"Well, that's what you say now, but sometime in the future, you might suddenly change your mind and succumb to my charms."

Maria rolled her eyes. "Xavi, you really don't know the meaning of the word no, do you?"

"No."

"Wait a minute," Maria said, peering at the landscape. "This looks like the road."

She turned onto a narrow dirt road that led through the desert. After a mile of stirring up fine red dust that somehow seeped into the cabin of the truck causing them to sneeze, she pulled into a wide glade. A single cottonwood tree rose above the desert, and Maria realized there must be an underground water source because cottonwoods need a lot of water.

Huitzi perched on a high branch, his feathers shining blue and green in the sunlight. Xavi looked around, knowing Huitzi wouldn't come alone. His bodyguards were almost certainly hidden in the dry brush that surrounded them. Of course, Maria was immortal, but the body she now inhabited was not, so if Huitzi or his hummers were to kill or injure her, then their current mission would suffer a critical setback. Xavi was all business now. He bent his knees in a slight crouch. He analyzed Huitzi's position, his eyes, the tilt of his wings, listening carefully for any movement in the brush. Xavi realized how vulnerable Maria was. The whole arrangement smelled like an ambush to him.

"You have a traitor in your midst," Huitzi said.

"No, we do not. A mistake was made. It won't happen again," Maria answered.

"She needs to be punished."

"Who needs to be punished?"

"The one you call Marta. She betrayed us. Lives were lost."

Maria was startled to hear Marta's name. *How did Huitzi know it was Marta who carried her phone into the battle? He must have a spy in the convent. A hummingbird in the rafters perhaps? And why was Huitzi letting me know that he knew? Was this a red herring to lead me in the wrong direction? In any case, it's clear that Huitzi doesn't trust me.*

"If you don't have the stomach to kill the traitor, then give her to me, and I will deal with her," Huitzi said.

"No, I'm not giving anyone to you."

Maria was aware that Huitzi no longer thought of her as an ally, and in his world, if you weren't an ally, then you were either an enemy or collateral damage. She slowly took a step backward, and as she did, Huitzi dived from his perch and flew straight at her eyes at top speed. But Xavi was even quicker than a hummer. He put his hand in front of Maria's face, so the needle-like beak punctured the palm of his hand and Xavi closed his fingers over the bird, planning to crush it, but then a hundred hummers were attacking him from all sides, slashing his skin and going for his face. As he batted them away with both hands, he shouted, "Run!"

Maria turned and ran as fast as she could, lifting her hands to her face to protect herself from three hummers pursuing her. She opened the door of the truck and jumped in, closing the door behind her just in time to keep her assailants away. As the truck started rolling, she turned the wheel hard right crashing through the brush toward the cottonwood tree where Xavi was warding off the hummers. Blood was pouring from the back of his hand where Huitzi's beak protruded. She pulled the truck beside Xavi and reached over and opened the passenger door.

"Xavi, get in!"

Xavi, noticing the truck for the first time, dived into the cab and slammed the door behind him, still holding Huitzi in his bloody hand.

As Maria revved the engine and pulled onto the highway, Xavi yelled, "What should I do with Huitzi?"

"Throw him out the window!" Maria answered, pressing the accelerator pedal to the floor.

Xavi cranked open the window with his left hand and stuck his right hand out the window. When he opened his fingers, Huitzi looked at him with murder in his tiny eyes. Xavi extracted Huitzi's beak from the flesh of his palm and threw the God of War tumbling into the air. Maria watched in the rear-view mirror as Huitzi regained his equilibrium and hovered over the blacktop, watching the truck speed away.

Xavi winced, holding his injured hand. Blood was dripping from the wound and falling on his thigh. "Damn, that hurts. I forget how fragile these mortal bodies are."

A dozen miles down the highway with no sign of hummers, Maria pulled to the side of the road and took a close look at Xavi's hand. The puncture went clear through, ripping a one-inch hole on the back of the hand. In the glove compartment, she found José's first aid kit, washed the wound with hydrogen peroxide, and applied Neosporin and a bandage and wrapped Xavi's entire hand in gauze.

"Let's get you back to the convent. Sister Delphina needs

to look at that stab wound. We don't want to lose you to infection, Xavi."

What a disaster, she thought. *We've lost Huitzi our most important ally, and Xavi our most powerful warrior is wounded. Xavi will heal. The question is: will Huitzi continue to fight against Lucifer's forces, or will those two become allies?*

Chapter 18

When Maria and Xavi got back to the convent, she was surprised to see Jesse, Mikey and Abe sitting in the common room talking with Zenobia. "Sister," she said to her, "Could you find Delphina and tell her we have a casualty?" She helped Xavi, who was feeling faint, to a chair and sat beside him. Delphina, carrying her black bag, came hurrying from the women's sleeping quarters and sat in the chair next to Xavi. She gently unwrapped the gauze and looked at the stab wound. The bleeding had stopped, but the ragged edges of the wound looked ugly.

Maria signaled to Jesse, Mikey and Abe to follow her back to her office where she gave the old man a hug and said, "Abe, it's nice to see you. We haven't talked since the preparations for the battle at the Otay Bridge last year. I heard that you and your coydogs saved the day."

"Well," the old man said, maneuvering his tobacco wad from one cheek to the other. "The coydogs were the real heroes. All I did was drive them there in the truck. They did the rest."

"And you two," Maria said, giving a hug to Jesse and Mikey. "Thanks for bringing Abe here. Did you get the migrant children settled with the Adventists?"

"Oh sure, Mrs. Nazarene," Mikey said. "The farmers were glad to see them, and I think they'll treat the immigrants well."

"And you know that Christina and Stefan have had their baby boy whom they named Francisco, and they're living with the Yaqui now?"

"No, I didn't know, Mother," Jesse said. "Do you think they'll be safe there?"

"For the time being they're safe," Maria answered. "José is there now, and if they need anything, he'll let us know."

"Mother, what's happening in the war?"

"There have been some new developments, Jesse," Maria answered carefully. "We need to have a meeting so I can explain to everyone what's going on."

"Well, it's funny you should bring up angels, Mr. Leslie," Alex said sitting in an overstuffed chair in front of a cardboard flat with an image of a shelf of books. The set was meant to convey the illusion that he and the moderator, a professor named Sheldon Leslie, were having a conversation in the library of a spacious estate when they were actually in a television studio in Des Moines, Iowa. Alex didn't mind. He liked the fact that the professor was genuinely interested in conversation, rather than trying to debunk Alex's ideas. "Let me paraphrase St. Thomas Aquinas who argues that the perfection of the universe requires the existence of intellectual creatures like God Himself, and so he loves human beings into existence. That is, He gives us corporeal bodies so we can live in the world He has created."

"So, you're saying that God creates by making His love emanant?"

"Exactly. According to Aquinas, existence of things flows from His will. However, Aquinas posits that angels are not physical creatures, but rather they are creatures of pure intellect."

"How do we know that angels actually exist, Professor Beltran?"

"Sacred Scripture speaks definitively about the existence of angels, so their existence belongs to Sacred Doctrine, but whether they exist in realty or merely in theory, one can draw conclusions about the nature of the angelic hosts. Angels are pure spirit, that is, non-corporeal forms; in other words, they have no physical bodies."

"Let's back up for a moment, Professor Beltran," Professor Leslie said, waving his pipe around which irritated Alex slightly since there was no tobacco in the pipe. The pipe was merely a prop, like the flat behind them with a picture of books rather than the fact of books. Alex smiled slightly, thinking that it was appropriate that they were talking about the appearance of angels as opposed to the fact of angels on a set with the appearance of a pipe-smoker in his library when in fact the pipe smoker and the library were illusions created to present a context for their discussion. Alex caught himself before he went down the rabbit hole of the illusions and delusions that television created.

"Professor Beltran, exactly what are angels according to Catholic theology? Are they the souls of dead people?"

"According to Aquinas, no. Angels are not dead people, they are beings created by God to manifest certain ideals."

"Meaning…?"

"Meaning that angels exist because God wishes them to exist, just as we exist because God wishes us to exist. But angels and humans are different kinds of beings," Alex said.

"Because we have corporeal bodies and angels do not?"

"It's not quite that simple. Aquinas believes that angels are completely immaterial creatures; however, he also notes we know from Scripture that angels sometimes assume bodies. For example, in Genesis 19:1 two angels visit Lot in the evening when he is sitting at the gate of the city of Sodom. Lot immediately recognizes them as angels and bows his face down to the ground in reverence. He then has a conversation with them about where they will stay for the night. Later in the evening the angels eat a meal with Lot. Clearly, they have physical bodies, and yet Lot knows they're angels."

"So sometimes we can see angels and interact with them as if they are human?"

"Yes. According to the Old Testament, angels can take human form and move among the world of men and women."

"So, Professor Beltran, for all I know you are an angel?"

Alex laughed. "No, no, I'm certainly not an angel, but I've met people whom I suspected were angels, or at least they had angelic qualities. The 13th century theologian St. Bonaventure believed that angels were composed of matter and form like everything else in the universe except God, who is made of pure spirit. So according to Catholic theology and tradition, angels could be walking around among us looking exactly like people."

"So, let me see if I understand what you are saying, Professor Beltran. Angels exist as pure spirit, but they can transform themselves into physical bodies and move about among us, and we may or may not recognize them as angels when they are among us."

"That's a pretty good summary of St. Thomas Aquinas's ideas on the subject."

"And why would angels take corporeal form and move among us? Do they have a purpose when they are here?"

"Yes. When angels appear among people, it is always for a specific purpose. The apostle Peter was comforted and reassured by angels during a storm at sea. Daniel fights his way through enemy forces with the help of the archangel Michael. Angels are often portrayed as warriors. In Acts 12:23, we discover that angels were involved in the death of Herod; and in 2 Kings 19:35, they help the Israelites slaughter the Assyrian army. But the main purpose of angels is to deliver messages from God; in fact, the word angel literally means "messenger." Most of the mentions of angels in both the Old and New Testaments have them conveying the word of God to humankind, be it a warning, a commandment, or a rejoicing."

"Professor Beltran, you said earlier that you see evidence of angels among us today. In your view, why are they here?"

"We live in a perilous time. Great changes are occurring in the natural world caused in large part by our disrespect for creation. Pope Francis has made it clear that we have a responsibility to honor and protect the natural world, which is God's gift to us. In the Holy Father's view, we have a grave misunderstanding of the gift he has given to us. Nature has not been made available to us so that we can pillage it, but rather so we can honor and protect it, and we should take from nature only what we need and no more."

"What is our responsibility in this time as people of faith? In other words, what are the angels among us saying?"

"As men and women of faith we have a responsibility to treat other people with dignity and respect. For example, right now, we have tens of thousands of refugees at our southern border who have fled their native lands because of war, corrupt governments, and environmental destruction. We must welcome these refugees into our country and treat them as honored guests, not as enemies."

"The angels are telling us to change our immigration policy? Perhaps the angels should run for Congress..." Professor Leslie was almost smirking as he said this.

"You're making the application of moral principles to public policy sound absurd," Alex said, trying not to sound angry. "But it's not absurd at all. The great evils of our time are racism, xenophobia, homophobia, militarism, misogyny, cruelty, greed, selfishness... These are clearly sins that carry over into the laws and customs of our nation. Changing our public policies to reflect simple decency would be a very good start in saving the world."

When Alex and Tristram were outside the television studio, Alex asked, "What did you think?"

"You did well," Tristram replied. "You were able to explain some pretty difficult theological concepts and use them to argue for changes in public policy. Nicely done."

Alex smiled and nodded. He was increasingly depending on Tristram's advice during this tour.

"There is a problem though, Alex."

"What is it?"

"You've been getting death threats."

Chapter 19

Everyone had gathered in the common room. The six Sisters of the Piston—Theodora, Delphina, Genevieve, Zenobia, Inez, and Adelaide—sat on two couches facing the front of the room. Marta, the novice, sat in a chair next to Adelaide. Xavi sat in a chair to the side, cradling his bandaged hand. Jesse and Mikey were standing at the back of the room, looking curiously at Maria, wondering what was going on. José, who had returned from the Yaqui homeland an hour before, stood next to the window. On his right hand, he wore a heavy leather glove that reached up to his elbow. A large brown and white hawk perched on his forearm, a hood covering its head.

"Okay, let's get started, everybody. There are some urgent developments that are happening that you need to know about." Maria glanced around the room at the beautiful faces looking at her, trusting her. She felt a terrible fear she had let them down, making mistakes that may get them killed. "First, you need to know that General Huitzi no longer trusts us or thinks of us as his allies. He and his hummers attacked Xavi and me yesterday when we went to have a parley."

"What caused him to turn on you?" Jesse asked, knowing everyone in the room had the same question.

"He blames us, with some justification, for the slaughter of wasps and hummers at the battle the other day." Maria noticed that Marta was looking at the floor, ashamed.

"You mean we screwed up?" José asked.

"Yes, we screwed up," Maria admitted.

"It was my fault," Marta said, lifting her head to look around at her friends. "I brought my phone to the battle, and they must have tracked it. The vigilantes knew where we were, and they were ready to attack the wasps and hummers."

Maria said, "Thank you, Marta, for taking responsibility. But there's nothing we can do about mistakes we made in the past; we have to push forward without General Huitzi's help."

"Do you think that Huitzi will turn the wasps against us as well?" asked Sister Inez, the former CIA field operative.

"I think we have to assume that the wasps, who suffered most of the casualties in the battle, will believe Huitzi when he tells them that our mistake cost the lives of their comrades," Maria answered. "General Zaberi will almost certainly withdraw his forces."

"Where do we stand now?" Mikey asked from the back of the room.

"Before I get into tactics, I want to point out to you that José has borrowed Sebastiano, a red-tail hawk, from a Yaqui friend. Sebastiano has searched the interior and exterior of the convent and found a hummer living beneath the eaves of this building. He promptly killed the bird and brought it back to José who let Sebastiano eat the little spy. We believe that General Huitzi has been aware of our plans all along, but Sebastiano will make sure no hummer comes within a hundred meters of this compound again. Yes, Sister Delphina, you have a question?"

"How is Christina? Has she had her baby?" asked Delphina, the doctor.

"Yes, Christina gave birth to a healthy boy she named Francisco, after our most beloved of saints. The two of them, as well as Stefan, are safe in the Yaqui homeland. Stefan has taken on the job of schoolteacher for the Yaqui children, and the three of them are getting settled. José reports that they are planning to stay in the Yaqui homeland and raise their son there. I believe this is a wise decision on their part. Yes, Sister Theodora, you have a question?"

"How is Father Alex and his friend Tristram? Where are they now?" asked Theodora, the attorney.

"Alex and Tristram are touring North America. Alex is giving lectures and interviews on college campuses and on television and radio. We want the faithful to understand what is at stake and what their responsibilities are."

"And what are their responsibilities?" Sister Zenobia who was both a schoolteacher and an explosives expert.

"Their responsibilities are to prepare themselves morally for the end of the world as they know it."

"I thought we were trying to prevent the end of the world?" Jesse said, puzzled.

"I'm fairly certain that we've lost that battle," Maria said and waited for the idea to sink in. "Without the alliance with the hummers and the wasps, it's unlikely we can prevent Lucifer from winning the war for America. Once America is firmly in the hands of the Evil One, he will be able to spread his darkness around the world, toppling governments, creating havoc, causing wars, spreading hate and lies. I'm afraid that the world will go into a dark age."

The room was completely quiet. Finally, Sister Adelaide, the scholar and visionary, raised her hand. "Is there nothing we can do to prevent The Evil One from taking over the earth?"

Maria looked at Xavi and asked, "You work for the Old Man, what will he do if we lose the battle with evil?"

Marta looked puzzled and turned to Adelaide next to her and whispered behind her hand, "Who's the Old Man?"

"God the Father," Adelaide whispered.

Xavi shrugged. "I can't speak for the Old Man, but my guess is that he can't afford to let his brother Lucifer take complete control of the earth."

"So, what will he do?"

Xavi didn't answer, but just stared at Maria.

"He'll tell you to destroy the earth to keep it from falling into Lucifer's hands?" Maria asked, already knowing the answer.

Again, Xavi shrugged. "Like I said, I can't speak for the Old Man. But remember, last year he sent Jesse and me to earth to destroy it, but his plan at that time was that we would destroy one city at a time until these stupid humans got the message. I thought it was a bad plan and I told him so at the time, but hey, I'm just the help, he doesn't have to listen to me."

"If he orders you to destroy the entire world, will you do it? Are there some people you will protect?" Jesse asked, looking at his friend.

"It's really not up to me. The Old Man has been in charge for a long time. If you want special dispensation for specific individuals, you'll have to take up the issue with him."

Jesse and Maria looked at each other, communicating without words. It was clear what needed to be done. Jesse, Xavi and Mikey needed to meet with the Old Man.

After the meeting in the common room, Marta came to Maria's office in tears. Maria took the young woman into her arms and let her sob on her shoulder. Marta's face was glistening with tears and her cheek was scratched from her prosthesis. The poor young woman kept forgetting that she had the prosthesis and trying to wipe her tears away with her left hand.

"There, there…" Maria said. "It's alright."

"What do you mean it's alright?" Marta said. "The world is ending and it's my fault. How can it be alright?"

"You made a mistake, Marta. Anyone could have forgotten to leave their phone behind."

"Is the world actually ending?" Marta looked in her mentor's eyes, hoping she'd misunderstood.

"I'm afraid so, but the good news is that there's another world beyond this one, my dear."

"How can you know that's true?"

"Trust me, Marta, I know."

"Will I be sent to hell?"

"No, people are not sent to hell for forgetting to turn off their phones," Maria almost laughed, but the young woman was genuinely worried, so Maria decided to take her concerns seriously.

"So, we're all going to die?"

"Oh, yes, of course. Dying was always the part of the plan. Every living thing dies. Well, almost every living thing. There are mushrooms that live in Idaho that don't seem to die, they just keep growing… I've always wondered if they made a special deal with Lucifer… Well, anyway, you and every other human will die."

"Soon? Will the sisters and I die soon?"

"I don't know. The future is not fixed. It keeps changing. Every time you do something or think something, you change the trajectory of life. The future doesn't actually exist except as an idea."

"Will I go to heaven?"

"I imagine so, but it's not up to me."

"But I killed people in Iraq, and I worked on helicopters which killed a lot of people."

"Just live your life as best you can. Try to be a good person today. That's all anyone can do."

Maria watched the young woman walk away, wiping away her tears. *I hope she doesn't accidentally stab her eye out with her prosthesis*, she thought.

Next, she called Jesse and Xavi into her office.

Chapter 20

After a week as schoolmaster, Stefan showed up at Eduardo's house at midday and was happy to see José's truck parked in front. He knocked on the front door and hesitantly went inside to see the two men sitting in *el porto* talking quietly. Both men nodded at Stefan in greeting and Eduardo gestured to a chair.

"José says that Maria is expecting an attack on the Yaqui homeland soon," Eduardo said quietly, as if he were talking about the weather.

"You're not surprised by this?" Stefan asked.

"No, we've known all along this might happen," Eduardo said. "José made the risks clear when he asked us to take you in as our guest."

"And you still took us in?" Stefan felt a surge of gratitude.

"Of course," Eduardo said, raising his chin. "The Yaqui do not turn away from our duty just because it may be dangerous."

"Thank you," Stefan said, then he asked the questions which begged to be asked. "Who is attacking us, and what do they want?" He hated the fact that his voice had become a hoarse whisper.

"The forces of Lucifer have somehow learned that you and Christina are here."

"And why would they be interested in Christina and me?" Stefan asked, dreading to hear the answer.

"They are not interested in you. They want to kill or kidnap Francisco," José said, looking Stefan in the eye. "You know that he is the Chosen One." It was not a question.

Stefan nodded slowly. "What can we do?"

José nodded to his truck. "I want to show you something."

They went out to José's truck, and he opened the tailgate. Inside were pine boxes that Stefan recognized from his days in Iraq. José opened one of the boxes and took out an AR-15 semi-automatic rifle, which closely resembled the M-16 service rifle Stefan had carried in Iraq. Stefan examined the rifle and José handed him a canvas bag of cartridges. Any reservations about taking life that Stefan had felt since leaving Iraq evaporated as his instinct to protect his wife and son took over. He slung the cartridge bag over his shoulder.

"Thank you, José."

Stefan called Dharma who emerged from beneath the porch and followed him across the cornfield to the cave where Christina and the baby were hidden.

As Stefan got closer to the cave, he suddenly noticed the total silence in the air. No birdsong. No voices. No sounds coming from the cave. Something was not right. He and Dharma ran the last fifty yards to the cave, and Stefan saw a woman lying sprawled in the middle of the cave. Dharma sniffed the woman and looked up at him. His heart almost stopped. He turned her over. It was Maria, *la patera*. He put his finger to the side of her throat. No pulse. He scanned the cave while Dharma quickly sniffed the floor and ran outside following a trail. Christina was gone and so was Francisco. He looked around the cave twice more, thinking that perhaps they were hiding. Panicked, he ran into the sunlight and checked behind rocks and bushes. A hundred yards away, men and women in their broad straw hats were hoeing the field. The sky was so bright, it hurt his eyes. He felt stunned.

He sprinted across the field, holding his rifle, shouting at people "Have you seen my wife and baby?" They shook their heads and looked at him, puzzled.

"Did any stranger go into the cave?" Again, they shook their heads. He turned and ran across the cornfield to Eduardo's house. Perhaps Christina and Francisco were hiding in one of the houses? But deep in his gut, he knew they were gone.

Then he heard Dharma barking urgently. Stefan ran back across the cornfield and saw the dog standing in front of the trail that ran up the hillside behind the cave and off into the dry scrubland. Stefan followed her as she ran up the trail, stopping every now and then and looking back at him. Dharma led him to a dirt road empty of cars. Stefan's worst fears were confirmed. His wife and son had been kidnapped.

Two men had rushed into the cave catching Christina and *la partera* completely by surprise. When *la partera* had stood up, holding up her hand as if to tell them they were not allowed in the cave because it was a sacred space, one of the men had punched the old woman in the stomach and then in the face, knocking her down.

The other man stood over Christina where she sat on blankets next to the rock wall, and said to her in English, "Stand up." As she stood, holding her baby close, he had picked her up and carried them into the sunlight.

There were people in the cornfield working, but they didn't turn to look at what was happening at the cave. It was as if a spell had fallen over the landscape.

Christina took a breath to scream, but the man said, "If you make a sound, I will hurt your baby." She caught her breath and said nothing, allowing herself to be carried up the path behind the cave through the cedar and prickly pear and away from the Yaqui village.

The man carried her and Francisco as if they weighed no more than kittens. The other man walked ahead of them, a revolver in his hand which he pointed forward, ready to kill anyone he saw. They came to a dirt road where a black suburban was parked by the roadside. At the wheel was a man with slicked back black hair and long Elvis sideburns. Christina, holding

Francisco tightly to her chest, was placed in center of the back seat with the two kidnappers sitting on either side making escape impossible. They drove off on squealing tires, heading north away from the Yaqui homeland.

Chapter 21

Jesse and Xavi took the Cobra, though Maria had instructed Jesse to drive because Xavi was too reckless, and he was essentially one-handed after the attack by Huitzi. Mikey was the best driver of the three, but Maria decided that she may need Mikey if the convent had to be defended, so just Jesse and Xavi drove north. She was hoping that Xavi, who was good friends with the Old Man, might make it easier for Jesse to be in the same space with his father. She knew that Jesse had unresolved problems with his father, but she hoped the two of them could put all that old business behind them and concentrate on the issue at hand.

Xavi, of course, hated the deliberate, careful way that Jesse drove at a fast but reasonable pace, slowing down for curves and passing other vehicles cautiously, but Jesse ignored Xavi's *kvetching*. They went through the border checkpoint without incident, crossed the Otay Bridge where the battle had taken place the year before, made good time through the desert east of San Diego, and arrived in the evening at the resort where the Old Man kept an office.

Summer was the off-season, so the Old Man had booked the entire resort for himself and his staff. Maria had called her ex-husband's office and told him the two boys needed to meet with him. She made it clear that the situation with his brother Luke had gotten out of hand, and the Old Man needed to intervene or else all Hell—literally—was going to break loose.

Jesse and Xavi checked in and went up to their suite, the

same one they'd stayed in the year before. Jesse remembered that meeting, the last time he'd talked with his dad, and winced because it hadn't gone well. In fact, it had ended disastrously with Jesse throwing a glass figurine of an angel at the Old Man. If he hadn't ducked, it would have cracked his skull. Jesse vowed that this time he would control his temper. The two boys bathed, Xavi in the large master bath which included a sauna and full-body warm air dryer, and Jesse taking a modest shower. After he was clean and dry, Jesse went into the living room area and sat on the couch. He thought about looking in a mirror, but he knew it was unnecessary because his appearance was what he had willed it to be. He was a thin, handsome young man of medium height with short hair and a well-trimmed beard although he was always surprised that in his earthly incarnations, he tended to have a thin frame, brown skin and a narrow but pleasant face. He often passed as Latino, but if asked, he said he was a Jewish Palestinian, which was of course his best-known incarnation. He was dressed in clothes appropriate for a stay in a resort: white chinos, flowered shirt, and gray canvas deck shoes. He believed in the importance of blending in.

Xavi, on the other hand, came out of the bathroom wearing a shirt of silk and gold foil, a floor length skirt of goat leather embossed with silver, and satin slippers that curled upward and featured tasseled toes. He had a red silk scarf around his neck, and he carried a large purse embroidered with a battle scene. At his belt, a mother of pearl scabbard held a jeweled dagger.

"What are you wearing, Xavi?"

Xavi looked surprised. "I'm dressed as Ajatasatru. Today is his birthday."

"Who?"

"Ajatasatru, the great Haryanka warrior king of Magadha." Seeing Jesse's puzzled face, Xavi said exasperated, "Don't tell me you don't know who Ajatasatru was."

"Sorry," Jesse said, concerned that he'd insulted his friend.

"How come I know everything about your western culture,

but you know nothing about my Indian culture?" Xavi shook his head in disgust. "We really need more multi-cultural education on the celestial sphere. Just a few weeks ago, one of the angels asked me how many of my wives I'd burned."

"You're right, Xavi. Maybe we can bring up multiculturism to my dad when we talk to him this evening."

"Well, anyway, Ajatasatru, son of Bimbi Sara, was a great warrior king who conquered all of what today is northern India. He was a contemporary of Mahavira, Gautama Buddha, Zarathustra, and Socrates. Very important in Indian history."

"Got it. I'll remember him from now on. So, you're dressed as this guy Ajatasatru, and you're going to the meeting with the Old Man in this… costume?"

"Oh, for samsara's sake, Jesse. It's not a costume."

"Sorry, Xavi, I think you look great. Let's go to dinner."

Jesse and Xavi were the only guests in the dining room. The waiter, who looked only a few years older than the boys, not surprisingly remembered Xavi. The year before the boys had been in the restaurant and the waiter had recommended the sirloin. Xavi had exploded at him, threatening to eat his grandmother. Later, Xavi had felt bad about the incident and gave the waiter a huge bundle of cash as a tip.

This time, the waiter was careful to recommend only vegetarian dishes to the two boys, and Xavi smiled in gratitude. Jesse ordered a White Cabernet Sauvignon from Wilson Creek Winery to go with dinner, and the waiter served the expensive wine with aplomb.

"You know the California vineyards are bursting into flames these days? We lost 27 vineyards in the Napa Valley alone in the last year." Jesse said. "I figure we better drink the wine while it still flows." He looked sadly at the bottle on the table. "There are so many beautiful things in this world."

"I know what you mean," Xavi said. "I was in Las Vegas a week ago. What a fabulous place. I love playing roulette. And the show girls! This one redhead had the longest legs I've ever seen!"

"Xavi, I think you've missed my point..." Jesse began, but then dropped it, knowing he and Xavi were so different, his friend would never understand the deep grief he felt over the ecological disaster that was unfolding.

Jesse and Xavi were waiting in the Old Man's office, done up in nineteenth century titan of industry style with oak paneling and brass fixtures, when the Old Man himself walked in. Much to Jesse's surprise, he was dressed as an ancient Indian Emperor. He was wearing even more gold and silk than Xavi was, and instead of a jeweled dagger, he had a full-length sword at his side. Jesse thought all that was missing was an elephant to carry him in.

"*Namaste*," the old man said in an informal greeting, his palms joined together in *Anjali mudra.*

"Pranama," Xavi answered in the most polite and honorific greeting reserved for spiritual teachers, his palms also joined together although one of his hands was bandaged.

Jesse tried not to roll his eyes. He knew that Xavi took these traditions very seriously, but the Old Man was manipulating him. The Old Man hadn't gotten to be the Old Man for nothing. Xavi was eating it up, smiling and feeling good about his boss. Xavi glanced at Jesse as if to say, *See, this is how it's done. Why can't you be more like your Old Man?*

"I see you're honoring Ajatasatru today, Xavi. How appropriate!" The Old Man sat behind the oak desk and leaned back, looking up into the air. Did you know that I helped Ajatasatru defeat his grandfather Chetaka in the Great War?"

"No, sir, I did not know," Xavi said respectfully. "How did that come to pass?"

"Well, as you know the war started because Ajatasatru's queen wanted her husband's two brothers to give her a beautiful necklace and a large elephant. The brothers refused because they'd inherited the valuable items from their father. Fearing reprisal, the two brothers fled to the republic of Vaishali where their grandfather Chetaka ruled. War broke out with tens of thousands of horses, elephants, chariots, and infantrymen on each side. King Chetaka was an expert archer and each day he fired one arrow. Each arrow killed one of Ajatasatru's generals. As Ajatasatru was moving towards defeat, he practiced penance for three days and offered prayers to me, and so I protected him from the merciless arrows of Chetaka and helped him win the war. Among other gifts, I gave Ajatasatru a huge chariot with spiked maces on each side which moved through the battlefield crushing whole ranks of soldiers…."

Xavi shifted uncomfortably. "Was that you, sir? I heard that it was my sister Indra who helped Ajatasatru win the war…"

"Yes, well, Indra got all the credit, of course." The Old Man cleared his throat and added, hastily, "but the huge chariot was based on my idea…"

"Of course, sir," Xavi said, then quickly changed the subject to the problem at hand. "The reason we're here is to work out a strategy so that your brother Luke doesn't end up with all the world to himself. Left unchecked, he would pervert this civilization into a playground for his demons and a concentration camp for the humans. No one wants this, right?"

For the first time since the Old Man had entered the office, he looked at his son and shook his head slowly, showing his disappointment. "This mess would not have occurred if you had done as I instructed you to do last year. You had one simple task. Burn down one city. If the humans had gotten the message, then we could have stopped there and let these arrogant little apes clean up their act. I needed them to respect what the Lord Their God has created. Stop poisoning creation. I mean… do you know how long it took me to invent a porpoise? Or an eagle? Even a nematode requires centuries of planning." Here, the Old Man shifted his gaze from Jesse to Xavi. "Why in my name did you not do as I instructed?"

"Yessir," Xavi said, trying to sound contrite. "Jesse and I

made a mistake. We thought that we could find a few humans with good character, and we could save them, and then get on with the burning of The City of Angels."

"The plan was to destroy one city as a warning, then if the humans didn't change their ways, we'd destroy more. Instead, you started a war with my brother!" The Old Man shouted, hitting the desk with his fist.

"Yessir," Xavi conceded. "As I said, we made a mistake, but the fact is that without your help we are not going to be able to control this situation."

Jesse's silence and his level stare was beginning to make both his father and his friend uncomfortable. The Old Man met his stare and asked, "Jesse, what's your take on this mess?"

Jesse took a deep breath, put aside his resentment, and focused on what he needed from his father. "Whatever mistakes have or have not been made, we are in a situation in which there are few options. We need your help."

"What about Huitzi? I thought he and his hummers had joined up with you."

Xavi shook his head and held up his bandaged hand.

"Huitzi did that to you? I take it that you can't count on him as an ally any longer? What about the wasps? Have they turned against you as well?"

"We're not sure yet, but our alliance with the wasps was never very strong, so I'm guessing that the Queen of the Wasps has withdrawn her forces and will make peace with the winner when the war is over," Xavi said.

"So Huitzi has also probably made a deal with Luke…" The Old Man who had always been a master strategist was starting to be interested in the problem they'd posed. "He must have promised them their ancestral lands would be unmolested if they turned against you."

"It appears that way, sir," Xavi said.

"And where's my brother now? Is he holed up in that fortress of a mansion he has outside the City of Angels?"

"Yes, we believe he's holding Christina and Francisco there as prisoners."

"Who?"

"The prophesized Mother and Child," Jesse answered, surprised that his father didn't know about the prophecy.

"Oh, them. I know nothing about the mother and child. That's one of your mother's projects. I've got nothing to do with it." The Old Man made an unconscious gesture of washing his hands, then caught himself and lowered his hands to his side. "Okay, give me a rundown of your assets."

"Well, we have Maria and José, of course," Xavi said.

The Old Man shrugged. "Maria is a good leader and strategist. So that's a start." Jesse noticed that he hadn't mentioned José. There had always been bad feelings between them because, Jesse believed, José had treated Maria and Jesse much better than the Old Man had.

"We have Evangelina Peregrine."

The Old Man smiled. "That's Birdie's newest incarnation, right? I hear she's a kickass martial artist. The real deal. An Amazon of Vengeance."

"Yessir. And we have the Sisters of the Piston."

"Good fighters and guerilla warriors. Are they still riding around on those hogs?"

"Yessir, they are. They are the coolest warriors I know."

"Well, the Sisters can take on the demons and that ragtag group of racists, vigilantes and crazies who follow Luke." He turned to his son. "Aren't they the ones who crucified you last year?"

Jesse didn't answer. All three of them knew that Luke and his rightwing crazies would never have crucified Jesse unless The Old Man had sanctioned it.

"We have Jesse, of course. Christina and her baby. We also have Stefan Jozsef."

"The poet? How did he get involved in this?"

"It's a long story, sir, but he's married to Christina."

"Is the poet a warrior?"

"He's been trained as an infantryman and as a medic, sir."

"Hmmm, some of the best warriors I've known have been poets. Don't underestimate him."

"We won't, sir. And now that his wife and son have been taken by Luke, he's highly motivated. And we have Abraham the Patriarch who brings with him a pack of about thirty coydogs."

"Abe? I haven't seen him in ages. How is he doing?" The Old Man seemed genuinely interested in his old friend.

"He's a bit addled at times," Xavi said. "I wonder if he's aging more quickly now that he lives on the mortal plane."

"As you know," the Old Man said. "Abe and I go way back. He helped me get started in building a male-centered religion. Before it was all about female power with Gaia in charge of everything and Maria playing with the animals as if they were her toys. Abe and I rebranded the whole religious enterprise. Male priests. The sky as the seat of power. Controls over the forms of ritual and prayer. No more broad-hipped fertility goddesses. Instead, the spear and the spire became the focus of prayer…"

"Yessir, I'm grateful to you, sir," Xavi said.

Jesse was getting tired of Xavi being so sycophantic toward the Old Man. Of course, it was necessary to play to his ego if they were going to win him over to their cause, but Xavi was going overboard. As for the Old Man claiming to have invented porpoises, eagles, and nematodes, it was all bullshit. It was well-known, even by humans, that the species evolved over millions of years, long before Abraham started calling a desert whirlwind the *One and True God*, not allowing anyone in his tribe to worship other gods. It was, of course, an attempt by the patriarch to consolidate his own power in the tribe by nullifying the power of the priestesses, witches and midwives who had ruled the desert tribes for generations. Little did Abe realize that by vesting all power in one jealous male god, he was destroying thousands of years of traditional female wisdom and creating a religion that would eventually control everything, even the very wombs of women.

“Well, I see why you’re worried. You have excellent warriors, but far too few.” The Old Man narrowed his eyes and looked at Xavi. “You left someone out.”

“I serve at your command,” Xavi said, bowing his head slightly. “However, I have an injury which may put me at a disadvantage if I’m forced to fight Luke.” He held up his bandaged hand. “We really do need your help, sir, if we are going to keep your brother from taking over the earth, especially now that he has the prophesized Mother and Child.”

“All right,” the old man said, waving his hand dismissively. “Let me think about this and I’ll get back to you.”

“With all due respect, Sir, things are happening quickly.”

“I understand.”

As the two boys left, the Old Man looked at his son walking away. The boy had said very little in the meeting, but his resentment against his father was palpable. *How did things become so broken between us*, the Old Man wondered, turning to look out the window at the desert stretching out to the blue mountains in the distance. *Why does he hate me so much?*

Chapter 22

Tristram noticed that Alex was distracted all morning, thinking no doubt about the topic of the debate he would have that day with another theologian on the nature of the soul. As an expert on the philosophy of Thomas Aquinas, Alex had argued in one of his articles that to Aquinas humans were basically animals with souls, and in this way, different than other animals. The body is corruptible, that is, subject to change and decay, but the soul is incorruptible and permanent. The body of a human, unlike that of a horse or a spider, is subject to the reasoning ability of the mind; therefore, the good we do in the world is not the result of our instincts, as are the acts of eating, having sex, having friends, caring for our children, but rather are the result of humans having knowledge of the difference between good and evil. Even if humans and animals commit the same acts, humans bring reason to the acts and therefore are morally responsible for what they do. As for the soul, once it breaks free of the body it will always grieve for the body it left behind. In other words, we survive our deaths but are damaged by them. Our souls merge with God, but also remain distinct.

In the taxi on the way to the lecture hall, Tristram could see Alex moving his lips, practicing the language of his argument. Tristram had learned to leave his lover alone during these moments. It was part of Alex's genius that he could come out with perfectly formed sentences on arcane subjects while seeming to have invented the ideas on the spot. Right now,

Tristram wished that Alex was not so absentminded. They'd received threatening phone calls a number of times, as well as letters that promised retribution in this life and the next. Tristram didn't understand how self-professed Christians could feel that Alex was committing sacrilege when all he was doing was summarizing and interpreting Christian theologians. Alex had quoted passages from Aquinas and other theologians that early term abortion, that is before the quickening, is not a sin because the soul has not yet entered the embryo. This one statement from Alex, which was Aquinas' position Alex was merely paraphrasing, had generated hundreds of complaints from viewers when he had stated it on public television. How could Christians be upset at Alex for restating something that had been part of Church law for centuries?

Whatever the Church's position on abortion nowadays, Tristram thought, the issue had attracted an army of outright crazies who bombed abortion clinics, murdered health care providers, and harassed people like Alex who were merely stating well-established historical positions. These nuts were very big on saving fetuses but despised the idea of helping children. Tristram felt himself fuming as the taxi pulled up in front of the college lecture hall where the debate would take place. A sizable crowd had gathered waving signs spouting slogans such as ABORTION=MURDER and BELTRAN KILLS BABIES and ABORT ABORTIONISTS. The people were red-faced with anger as they shouted at Alex who calmly got out of the car and, with Tristram beside him and policemen in front and back of them, calmly walked into the building.

The debate went well. Alex's opponent was an elderly Baptist pastor who argued, essentially, that if we love Jesus then we should be rightwing conservatives. Referring to the 613 commandments in the Old Testament, as well as the 1,050 commandments in the New Testament, most of them from the apostle Paul, the pastor focused on individual sin, such as adultery and larceny, as the source of our distance from God, so, he reasoned, we should support law-and-order politicians. It follows, he said that undocumented workers, having broken the law by coming to this country illegally, should be punished for their actions and deported. Similarly, America had a responsibility to battle the forces of godlessness by ruthlessly searching out terrorists in foreign countries. Women should be subject to the rule of men. Children should be physically punished so they will learn the consequences of sin. And most of all, abortion should be illegal. The government's sole purpose, according to the pastor, was to uphold the ten commandments. The only counter to this sinful world is repentance and salvation by accepting Jesus Christ into our hearts.

Alex, for his part, began by gently ridiculing the idea of over 1,600 commandments from God: "If we were to try to follow all of these commandments, we wouldn't be able to do anything at all. And many of these commandments contradict each other or simply do not apply to today's world. Some of the commandments are patently absurd. Deuteronomy 25:11 states that when two men are fighting and the wife of one of them joins the fight and takes the other man by the balls, then the man whose balls have been grabbed should cut off her hand, and not pity her. Seriously? This passage gives us advice on how to fight dirty? Leviticus 15:19 tells men not to sit in the same spot where a woman sat when she was menstruating because she's unclean. "Clearly, we cannot follow many of the rules and commandments in the Bible, and the reason is that the Bible was written by men, and perhaps by women, who lived in a tribal society that had a very different sense of the universe. As society changes, and as our understanding of the universe grows, so must our understanding of God and morality change and grow. Even some of the Ten Commandments are not applicable to today's world. The first commandment is "Thou shalt Not Have Any Gods Before Me." This is the logic of the Taliban, not of the kind of open and tolerant society that most of us want to live in. Jesus, in *Mark 10:20*, realizing perhaps that the bureaucracy of religion had managed to make morality so complicated that no one knew what to do, reduces the commandments to six: *Do not kill, Do not commit adultery, Do not steal, Do not bear false witness, Do not defraud, Honor thy father and mother.* If we follow these six rules, then we are living a good life. Notice that Jesus does not say anything about worshipping Him or another being.

"As for following the law of the land... keep in mind that Jesus welcomed everyone, even foreigners, even thieves, even prostitutes to his side. He was a dark-skinned, Jewish, working man who was executed for the crime of sedition and nailed to a cross between two common thieves. To be good Christians, or indeed good people of any faith, we should practice Christ's radical love and inclusion of marginalized people.

"As for the issue of abortion... there are dozens of people outside this building right now who are willing to do anything to stop women from having abortions. St. Thomas Aquinas, probably the wisest person to ever study the Word of God, wrote that abortion in the early stages, that is, before the quickening, is not a sin because the fetus does not yet have a soul. And these people outside the building, who are so sure of their position, believe that they know better than Aquinas when the soul appears in the fetus? How is it that they know more than the wisest of Christian philosophers?

"And Aquinas goes even further, reasoning that we know the world through our bodies, and the soul enlivens the body. If a body is not able to live separately from the mother, then does it exist as a separate being with a soul? Aquinas would say *no*: the fetus in the first months after gestation is not a separate being and therefore does not have a soul of its own. It is part of the mother's body until it is viable outside the womb."

When the debate was over, Alex walked over to the Pastor and shook his hand, and the pastor politely shook hands. *This is how it should be* Alex thought. *We should discuss and debate moral issues with tolerance for the other side. Demonizing those we disagree with is not healthy or helpful.*

Alex and Tristram walked out the door with a policeman ahead of them and one behind. Suddenly, there was a scuffle to the right of them, and Tristram turned in time to see a pistol emerging from the crowd and pointing at Alex. Tristram leaped in front of the pistol, trying to grab it, but the gun went off. The bullet hit him in the chest, and he fell back into Alex's arms while a policeman wrestled the assassin to the ground.

Maria was sitting in a chair in Alex's hotel room watching Alex pace back and forth across the carpet. He shook his head, muttering *no, no, no.* Maria went into the bathroom and brought him a cup of water which he swallowed in one gulp. Then he sat on the edge of the bed with his face in his hands and sobbed. She felt his grief growing and filling every fiber in his being.

Alex looked up at Maria who was hovering over him, helpless. "Maria, could you please leave? I'd like to be alone," he said.

Out of respect for Alex's desire to experience his pain in private without worrying about how he appears to others, Maria left the room, and Alex was able to think about grief and what it says about the mystery of love. *If I actually believe that a better life awaits us after death, then why would I grieve for my friend?* Alex asked himself. *Shouldn't I be happy that my friend has graduated to the next phase of existence? Perhaps Tristram is in heaven, sitting in a patio of perpetual morning, sipping fresh-squeezed mango juice and listening to the Goldberg Variations by Bach. But instead of being happy for my friend's release from the pain of this life, I am experiencing an agony of grief that's barely begun.* Alex knew that for the rest of his life, despite his Christian faith, he would feel a deep sadness over the death of his friend.

Grief, Alex thought, *is pain caused by the recognition of separateness. When we love someone and they love us in turn, we think of our two selves as one. Our separateness has disappeared, and we cannot imagine a life without that person. We may think of the union as sacred, something ordained by a higher power. The strongest union between two people is that of mother and child, and the death of a child scars the mother for life. The connection between father and child or between siblings or between friends or lovers is also a sacred bond, and we experience pain and loss when the union is sundered. People often speak of the end of a marriage as feeling like one's heart has been torn from their chest or as if a limb has been hacked off. These similes are not exaggerations; the pain of grief is manifested in the body.*

In the case of Christians who profess to believe in an afterlife, these primordial feelings may seem to contradict theology, Alex suddenly realized, *but this doubleness is not a contradiction at all. The two experiences exist simultaneously. The idea of an afterlife does not change the experience of grief because one exists in the mind while the other is a lived experience.*

In the case of Alex, his belief in the sacredness of scripture exists inside his belief in a larger truth which he has explored through his studies of science. For example, measurements of the rate at which the universe is expanding have led to the theory that approximately 14 billion years ago everything we know—trees, houses, chairs, dogs, books, truth, light, and even galaxies—was locked into a small space the size of a Shetland pony; and then, for some reason we'll never know, everything was released in an explosion we call the Big Bang and ever since then, the universe has existed as an expanding orb.

An absurd notion, right? And yet, this is what mathematics and physics tells us is true.

The more humans learn about the basic structure of reality, the more mysterious it appears. For example, physicists tell us that atoms are made up of mostly empty space; the distance between the nucleus and the outermost electrons is proportionate to the distance from the sun to Pluto; and the distance between atoms is proportionate to the distance between stars. In other words, reality, as we know it, is made up almost entirely of empty space. The human body, as well as everything else, is not a solid thing, but rather a location where particles are vibrating at the speed of light in a vast emptiness. We are, you might say, made of the stuff of gods; that is, we don't exist at all except as Idea.

Scientists in other fields have made remarkable discoveries about the nature of reality as well. Take a look at the structure of cells, for example, the basic building block of life as we know it. Most people, if they think of cells at all, imagine them as tiny Lego blocks locked onto other Lego blocks that make up the body of a living thing, an oak tree, say, or a flounder. But actually, scientists have discovered that each cell is a miracle of specialized parts. There are microscopic cables connecting the nucleus to the walls on which machines carrying spare parts crawl. Mitochondria, separate organisms which have evolved to live inside cells, transport nutrition to the nucleus. And there are bits of mysterious organic material, some of which seems to be alive, floating in the fluid of the cell. And DNA with its billions of bits of information organized in a spiral ladder rests in the middle of it all, a time machine carrying detailed schematics for building a whole new being.

Contemporary science does not indicate that the universe is a well-designed machine which we can understand with observation and study, but rather that reality is a progression of interlocking mysteries from the infinitely small to the mind-boggling large. If someone asked a 19th century scientist whether he believed in God, he would likely have said "Of course I don't believe in God. I'm a scientist." But if you ask a 21st century scientist whether he believes in God, he'll likely say, "Of course I believe in God, I'm a scientist."

Alex, better than most of us, understands that the universe is essentially unknowable, but evidence points toward an Intelligence far greater than ours that exists in every nook and cranny we examine, and we experience the unifying Intelligence, not as something mechanical but as something ineffable which some of us choose to call Love. And how do we experience Love? Through the stories we tell each other.

Maria called José and told him what had happened.

"Would you call a meeting of the Sisters and tell them of Tristram's death?" she asked her husband.

"Of course," José said. "Although Tristram distanced himself from us, he obviously loved Alex."

"He gave his life to protect his friend," Maria responded. "His love needs to be honored."

"He'll be mourned by all of us," José said. "I'm sure the sisters will want to have some kind of memorial for him."

Maria went to the hotel restaurant and ordered food, but when it was placed in front of her, she didn't recognize what it was. Something brown and something green. She ordered a cup of coffee and drank it without tasting it. Normally, she loved to eat. She loved being human and experiencing the world, but right now all she could think about was Alex and the pain he was experiencing.

She took a walk outside through the streets of the nameless city where this evil thing had happened. She looked at the faces that passed her on the sidewalk, thinking that each of them would experience death, their own as well as their loved ones. What must it be like to be human, aware of death in a way that animals are not, and yet not aware of the infinite life of the spirit? People invented stories of gods to explain their small lives, and they invented death because it seemed inevitable. Lacking both the wisdom of gods and the faith of animals, humans must live in a world that is bounded by birth and death with no sense of what comes before or after. Maria suddenly pitied humans in a way she never had before, and now she understood why love was so essential in a mortal life.

The next morning, Maria knocked on Alex's door. The man who opened the door was not someone she recognized. Alex had always been supremely self-confident, but this man seemed on fire, his grief completely replaced by resolve. His long uncombed hair looked like a thundercloud, and his black eyes flashed like lightning. Smelling of sweat and adrenaline, he obviously had been up all night. He turned away from her, walked over to the desk where an open book lay, and he lifted it like a weapon. Not against her, certainly, but against the forces of hate and ignorance which had killed the man he loved. Alex waved the book in the air and spoke rapidly in a patois of English, Spanish, and Latin. Maria recognized it as a rough translation of a sentence that Aquinas had begun a thousand years before but never finished. Alex had for the first time in history completed the sentence, and in this way, he had discovered the true nature of death.

Maria was excited for Alex; after all, he had made a great discovery which could benefit humankind, but as his friend, she was also worried. Clearly, he had become possessed by something larger than himself. A lesser soul would become corrupted by this knowledge, especially combined with the anger at the death of his friend and lover.

No, she thought, looking more closely at him. *He's going to be alright. He's been taken over by a sense of mission. He understands now what is at stake in this battle for the soul of America. As tragic as Tristram's death is, some good is coming of it. The battle is no longer an intellectual exercise for Alex. Instead, it is a fight against evil.*

"Pardon me for asking," she said tentatively. "But what arrangements are being made for...?"

"His parents flew into town..." Alex looked at her puzzled. "What city are we in? My mind is in a fog."

"Memphis," Maria said, suddenly remembering that this was the same city where Dr. King had been assassinated. What is it about this country that its spiritual leaders keep getting assassinated?

"There's nothing we need to do?" She asked.

"No, the funeral will take place in Houston where they live," Alex answered vaguely. "I suppose I should be there for the services."

Maria had always been fascinated with the way that humans experience grief, much the same way that crows and elephants experience it. First, they are stunned, then they have rushes of feeling—anger, sadness, hilarity—then they retreat into themselves for a time, sometimes weeks, sometimes years, then they throw themselves into productive activity. But within this process, there's a lot of variation between individuals. Alex seemed to be alternating between vague absentmindedness and an overwhelming ambition to change the world. *Good*, she thought, *we can work with this.*

"Tristram would want you to continue the speaking tour, so I suggest that you go to Houston for the funeral, and then pick up your schedule again."

Alex looked at her, his brown eyes gradually changing from sadness to ferocity to resolve. "Yes," he said. "There's work to be done."

Chapter 23

Christina woke in a wide bed covered in silken sheets. She loved the feel of them against her skin, having been sleeping on woolen blankets in a cave for the last week. She looked around at the sumptuous bedroom, Persian rugs on the floor, the walls painted in a light fuchsia which softly reflected the morning light from outside. Suddenly, she panicked. *Where's Francisco? Where's my baby?* She ran to the door and tried the knob. Locked. She went to the window and pulled back the curtains. The bars on the window bisected the lovely desert morning. She paced back and forth, trying to think of a way out of this gilded cage. She ran back to the door and banged on it with her fist.

"Help!" she yelled. "I need to see my baby! Help me, please!"

The door opened and a woman dressed as a nurse came into the room, carrying Francisco. "Not to worry, Dr. O'Malley," she said, in a chirpy English accent. "I was just bathing the little tyke. Here you go," she said, handing the baby to Christina. "I imagine he's hungry by now."

"How long have I slept?" Christina asked, trying to remember how she got here. Then she remembered, she and Francisco were kidnapped! Men had killed *la partera*. She wondered where Stefan was. And who was this nurse? She seemed vaguely familiar.

"Oh, you've been asleep for about twelve hours, but not to worry, I fed the little tyke formula when you were asleep."

Christina noticed she was wearing silk pajamas. Was this

some sort of resort? She felt she had slid down the rabbit hole. Silk pajamas and barred windows didn't seem to be part of the same place. "What is this place?" she asked, opening her blouse to let Francisco nurse.

"Oh, this is the home of Mr. Luke Ferris. Perhaps you've heard of him. He's actually quite famous."

Christina did know the name. He was a rightwing radio host, a wealthy businessman who was always going on about immigrants and how they were stealing the country from patriots. She had made a point of not listening to him, turning off the radio whenever his unctuous voice came on.

"And who are you?" she asked the chirpy English nurse.

"Me? Oh, don't mind me, Dr. O'Malley. My name is Paula, but everyone calls me Polly," she gave a broad smile.

The woman seemed increasingly familiar to Christina. Perhaps she'd worked at the Veteran's Hospital where Christina was a therapist? "What's your last name, Polly?"

"Thackwaite," the woman said. "My name is Polly Thackwaite."

Christina thought, *what an unusual name, I'm sure I've heard it before. But where?*

"Would you like to get dressed for dinner? It is served at six p.m. sharp," Polly said.

"I'd prefer to stay here with Francisco," Christina said. "Could you please bring some food to my room?"

"Oh, I'm sure Mr. Ferris wouldn't mind your bringing the baby to dinner, Dr. O'Malley. In fact, he would probably insist on it."

"And why would he insist on it?" Christina asked, feeling her suspicion rising in her chest. *I don't trust this woman one bit,* she thought.

"Everyone likes a baby, don't we?"

"Polly, who is Mr. Ferris? Is he the owner of this place?"

"Mr. Luke Ferris is my employer. He owns this property, which is his personal residence. He is a successful businessman and, as he puts it, he dabbles in politics."

"And he dabbles in kidnapping women and children as well?"

Polly didn't seem to have heard her, or perhaps she'd been instructed to ignore any untoward remarks about how Christina came to be here, wherever *here* is.

"Polly, where are we?"

"I don't rightly know, Dr. O'Malley," Polly said absent-mindedly as she was folding the blankets and putting them on the end of the bed.

"How can you not know? Are you a prisoner here?"

"Not exactly. But I am serving a sentence."

"Serving a sentence? This place is some kind of prison?"

"No, as I said, it is Mr. Ferris's personal residence."

"Isn't Luke Ferris the guy on rightwing radio who is always talking about immigrants and how they are destroying America?"

"I think that is perhaps an oversimplification of his views."

Great, Christina thought, *my baby and I have been kidnapped by a rightwing nut who wants to think of us as his guests. I need to find a way out of here.* She decided to play along with this elaborate dance until she saw a chance to escape. She needed to keep Francisco with her always, so when the opportunity came to escape, she could take it.

"Polly, Francisco and I need to bathe, but I have nothing suitable to wear to dinner."

"No worries there, Dr. O'Malley, Mr. Ferris had a dinner dress made for you. It's in the closet whenever you'd like to try it on. Also, there are underthings in the top drawer of the dresser."

"Mr. Ferris had underthings purchased for me? How did he know my size?"

Polly smiled indulgently, "Mr. Ferris knows all about you, Dr. O'Malley. He's been studying you for years."

A chill went up Christina's spine. *Who the fuck are these people, and what do they want with me and my baby?*

A tall handsome man with salt-and-pepper hair, wearing a white dinner jacket, black slacks, and a black bowtie, was sitting in the library where faint violin music could be heard in the background. He rose to greet Christina who carried Francisco in her arms. He extended his hand, but she ignored it.

"Christina, I'm so glad you could join me," he said.

"Girl's gotta eat," she said glancing around at the magnificent white and gold library. It had three large globes on brass stands in a row down the center of the room. The walls were made up of rows of leather-bound books. There was a balcony that made up the second floor where more books sat on shelves. Above the top row of books, paintings of old bearded white men who looked like Renaissance philosophers looked toward the ceiling where a dozen winged angels flew through billowing clouds. In a brilliant *trompe l'oeil*, one of the angels seemed to be descending by a rope into the room.

"An impressive room, isn't it?" asked the handsome man. "It is an exact replica of the Admont Abbey Library in Austria, built in 1776. It is often referred to as the most beautiful building in the world."

"Yes, it is certainly beautiful," Christina conceded. "Mr. Ferris, why have you brought me here?"

"My, you certainly get to the point quickly, don't you?" Luke turned and gestured toward the doorway where Christina could see a richly appointed dining table. "I will explain everything to you over dinner."

Although there was a bassinet next to her chair, Christina continued to hold Francisco close to her as she sat at the table. Without apologizing or asking permission, she unbuttoned the top of her silk blouse and let Francisco nurse.

"A lovely sight," Luke said admiring her. "If I were an artist, this is how I would paint you. Mother and Infant."

"Now that we have established that you're not an artist, Mr. Ferris." Christina said as the first course was served. "Please tell me, what are you? I mean other than a kidnapper of women and children." She felt like she was starving, so she lowered her silver spoon into a light bone broth. Slightly salty. Perfect to start one's juices flowing.

"Please, Christina, call me Luke. I'd like to be your friend. As for me, I'm merely a businessman who's made a little money," he said, waving his hand dismissively at the sumptuous room where they sat. Christina noticed that the dining room was decorated in cream and blue, an interesting contrast to the white, black and gold of the library.

"I apologize if my men made it seem you were being kidnapped. They were instructed to invite you and Francisco here."

"Your men murdered *la patera* in front of me!"

"Yes, very unfortunate. I guarantee that the perpetrators of that crime will face justice." Luke said. "Oh good, the next course is being served. I think you will love this dish."

Christina watched a servant place half a cup of lightly steamed vegetables on her plate, then spoon a cream sauce over it. She tasted it. Absolutely delicious. She hadn't eaten since breakfast the previous day. More dishes followed. Roasted potatoes in clarified butter. A slice of rare roast beef with a trickle of blood coming from its center. English pudding with a meat gravy covering it. And finally, a maple flan for dessert. Through the meal, sparkling water was served. Luke apologized for not serving wine, glancing at the baby. He was the perfect host, encouraging Christina to talk about the baby, her career as a therapist, the difficulty of working in a healthcare system, and finally, her real passion, working as a counselor to the homeless. Despite her fear and distrust, Christina found herself talking openly with this charming man who seemed more interested in her opinions and experiences than anyone she'd ever met. As they were finishing dessert, Christina realized that Luke seemed to know everything about her, and yet he'd never mentioned her husband, Stefan.

With a start, she realized she was being seduced.

Chapter 24

In the courtyard of the *El Presidio,* Maria reviewed the caravan. She would be driving the black van loaded with supplies with Jesse in the seat beside her, followed by a line of the Sisters of the Holy Piston on their Fat Boys. Each Harley had a sidecar. Stefan carrying his semi-automatic rifle and his canvas kit climbed into the sidecar beside Theodora while Mikey climbed into Delphina's sidecar. Bringing up the rear was José in his pickup with Xavi in the seat beside him. A canvas tarp covered the bed of the truck, and beneath the tarp were ammunition and heavy armaments.

When a dozen armed Yaqui men showed up, José climbed down from the truck, walked over and spoke softly and respectfully to them in Spanish. From what Stefan could hear, José was telling them that this battle was the first of many, and Maria wanted to hold the brave Yaqui in reserve to guard la Virgen and the Chosen One once they returned. Stefan was glad to see that José opened the truck door for Dharma allowing her to jump in. Maria had asked José to drop off Xavi a few miles from Luke's residence, so he could intercept the hummers, delaying them from joining the main battle. She was planning to catch Luke by surprise at his personal residence and was reasonably certain that she and the sisters could handle the rescue of Christina and the baby without Xavi's help if he could keep the hummers away. Maria lifted her right arm and brought it down, signaling the caravan to follow her, and they rumbled down the road to the north.

Sitting beside Maria, Stefan was amazed by how quickly his life was changing. The last week of teaching children in the schoolhouse, eating Concepción's homemade tortillas, talking with Eduardo in the evenings, and sleeping with his wife and son were the happiest of his life. He didn't know whether he'd return, nor did he know where Maria was leading them, but he knew life would never be the same again. Dharma put her head on his knee, and he absent-mindedly stroked her ear. The only thing Stefan knew for certain was that he and Dharma would willingly give their lives for Christina and Francisco.

A few hours later, the caravan of vehicles, a van, five Harleys, and a pickup truck, was waiting in line at the border. It was noon and the sun blazed down. As they inched forward toward the INS guards, Stefan took off the helmet Maria insisted he wear and put on the baseball cap Eduardo had given him. Stefan tried to keep his voice calm as he asked Maria, "Okay, we haven't had time to talk yet, but we're going to be in line for a while here. Can you tell me what is going on? Who took my wife and son? Where are they now? Why did they take them? What are we going to do about it? In short, what the fuck is going on?" He voice had grown more intense as he went along.

Maria looked around, and when she was sure no one could hear their conversation, she said, "Stefan, you've been aware since you were visited last year by Xavi in your little cave beneath the Ventura Freeway that you are, shall we say, at the vortex of huge changes that are happening, right?" When Stefan nodded, she continued, "Although I didn't know it at the time, by joining us, you became the catalyst of a chain of events that led us here. "

"Are you saying that I caused my wife and son to be kidnapped?" Stefan hated the panic he heard in his voice.

"No, no, not at all. You were the *catalyst* which is not the same thing as the *cause*. The conditions were right for you to provide the spark for world-changing events."

"Maria, I don't care about world-changing events. I just want to find my wife and son and if I need to, kill the bastards who took them."

"Well, we know where they are."

"Why didn't you say so? Where are they? Are they safe?"

"Christina and Francisco are safe, and they are being held in a residential complex owned by a corporation controlled by Luke Ferris."

"Luke Ferris? You mean the right-wing radio host and corporate CEO who finances rightwing political candidates? What would that rich wingnut want with Christina and Francisco?"

"I'm not sure what Luke's plans are, but there's something you need to know about Francisco."

"Okay, tell me," Stefan said, turning his head to the side to look at the lines of cars.

"Stefan," she began. "José told me about the doubts you're having. It's perfectly natural for a man faced with the miracle of birth to become confused. Let me assure you that Francisco is your son. The differences in physical appearance between the two of you are slight and superficial. Also, you need to be aware that your role in his development will be profound. You must provide him with a model of what it is to be a good man, the way that José did for Jesse. You and Christina will teach him to be kind, aware, honest, and hardworking. Got it?"

"Got it," Stefan said, feeling slightly ashamed for doubting the integrity of his wife. "Now tell me the celestial stuff."

"Francisco is a very special baby. By this, I don't mean it in the usual sense that every baby is special or in the helping profession lingo that he has special needs. I mean that he is special in the sense that if you and Christina can protect him and raise him, then he will become a man who changes the course of human development." She paused, letting Stefan absorb the enormity of what she'd said.

"How will he change human development?" Stefan asked slowly.

"I don't know, but I know that he is the Chosen One, the child we've been waiting for."

"The Chosen One? What does that mean?"

"Remember Chapter 12 of the *Book of Revelation*? The Woman, the dragon and the child?"

"Sorry, Maria, my Bible skills are a little rusty. Refresh my memory."

Maria glanced at the line of cars ahead of them which was barely moving. "Okay, in *Revelation* 12, John sees the vision of a woman about to give birth and a devouring dragon waiting to pounce. Who are this woman and child? What is the dragon and why does he want to devour the baby?"

"You're saying that Christina is the woman and Francisco is the baby, but who is the dragon? Is it Xavi? Or how about Huitzi?"

"No, no. The dragon is Luke Ferris."

"My wife and son are in the hands of a dragon?"

"Well, yes and no. Luke can change himself into any form he chooses. He could be a dragon, but he is far more dangerous as a wealthy man with a political agenda. Luke wants Francisco because he represents the future. Luke wants to control the world of humans and the best way to do it is by controlling its leaders."

"I don't understand. I thought Luke Ferris is just a rich talk show host and corporate CEO asshole."

"Stefan, Luke Ferris is Lucifer."

"My wife and son have been kidnapped by Satan?" Stefan asked incredulously.

"Yes. One of Satan's many forms."

Stefan sat in the front seat of the truck, Dharma resting her head in his lap, and looked at the line of cars ahead of them inching toward the U.S. border.

"Wait a minute, Maria, the *Book of Revelation* is a prophecy, right? Are we bound to its predictions?"

"Oh, by no means. *Revelation* is a poem, or rather a dream of Jesse's which he dictated to John of Patmos almost two thousand years ago. The dream is a highly imagistic narrative of what would happen when he, Jesse, returns to the earth. But I have to say that so far, it's been pretty accurate. For example, *Revelation* says that the woman flees to the wilderness to a place prepared by God where she and her child are nourished. And indeed, the Jesuits prepared the Yaqui homeland. Although the priests were cruel at times, the last hundred years, it's been a peaceful place where people live a simple life. It is a perfect place for you and your family to hide."

"But Luke found us there and kidnapped Christina and Francisco, and here we are."

Maria nodded her head in agreement. "Yes, here we are." She gestured toward the border guards. "The line is starting to move. We should be across the border soon."

"What else does the *Book of Revelation* predict?" Stefan asked.

"It predicts that a war will break out, and the Archangel Michael and his angels fight with the dragon and his angels, and the dragon is cast out, and his angels are cast out, and they go to live on the earth."

"Wait, didn't that already happen? Jesse told me that last year when Reverend Sheffield was leading the migrants across the Otay Bridge, there was a parallel battle in heaven."

"That's right, there was, but the battle ended in a draw."

"So, there's going to have to be another battle?"

"It appears that way."

"What does *Revelation* say comes next?"

"It says that when the dragon saw that he had been cast to the earth, he persecuted the woman, but the woman was given two wings of a great eagle to escape the dragon who spews water from his mouth causing her to be carried away by a flood, but the earth helps the woman by opening its mouth and swallowing the flood and so the woman escapes and returns to her place in the wilderness. And the dragon is enraged with the woman, so he makes war on the rest of her offspring, who keep the commandments of God."

“What the hell does that mean?” Stefan felt a rage rising inside him that he and his family had gotten caught up in this mythological catastrophe.

“I don’t know what it all means or how it’s going to turn out, Stefan. At this point, I’m just winging it. Anything could happen,” Maria replied, rolling down her window and showing her American passport to the INS agent.

Chapter 25

Alex showed up at the lecture hall in Chicago escorted by armed guards. The police were holding back an angry crowd. He walked past a tripod which had a headshot of him looking intently into the camera, his clerical collar clearly visible. Beneath the photograph was his name and the title of his lecture: *Is Evangelical Christianity the greatest threat to human existence today?*

After a lengthy introduction by one of his friends, a Benedictine known for his gentle manner, Alex walked to the lectern and began talking about the crimes by self-professed Christians to accomplish fascist political ends. The bombings of abortion clinics, the harassment of women seeking health treatment, the attacks on people worshipping at synagogues and mosques, the burnings of African American churches, the vandalism of Jewish cemeteries, the mass slaughter of Jews at Shabbat in Pittsburgh. "And these are attacks that occurred in the United States in the last few years. If we include the assassinations and bombings that have occurred in the last fifty years, the list becomes incomprehensibly long. And this is not a problem confined to this county. Croatia, South Africa, Germany, Canada, Norway, and France have also seen right-wing Christian nationalists committing terrible crimes against people who have done nothing wrong, nothing illegal, but happened to be in a place that was targeted. These so-called Christians are racist, authoritarian, homophobic, xenophobic, and misogynistic. They are, in short, doing everything they can to undercut the work to which Our

Lord Jesus Christ devoted his short life on Earth. And the evangelical leaders who encourage these acts of violence are not Christians in any meaningful sense. They profess to be Catholic or Protestant, but they are neither—"

At this point, there was an explosion in the room and Alex was knocked against the wall behind him. The last thing he saw was the auditorium ceiling which seemed to be opening to the night sky...

"The outer perimeter is being guarded by Loud Boys who've dug foxholes every fifty feet." Sister Inez, the former CIA operative, said to Maria as they sat in the van. "They've also stationed a few dozen of their men near the front entrance to the mansion, probably intending to use them to support and reinforce the foxholes that are under attack. The Loud Boys are irregulars armed with AR15s, hunting rifles, shotguns, and pistols. They don't seem to have any artillery or heavy machine guns. So, they outnumber us, but we have superior arms and training. We should be able to break through their line without a problem."

"What's the best way to break through the perimeter?" Maria asked.

"Sister Zenobia and I discussed the possibility of having a small decoy force stage a diversionary attack on the east side, drawing the reinforcements in that direction. Then our main force attacks on the west side, breaking through the line of fox holes and charging the back gate of the complex. There's a loading dock there and a metal door with an electronic security system we can easily hack. This will enable us to enter the maze of buildings from the rear which they probably are not expecting."

"Whom should we send as the decoy force?"

"Abe and his coy dogs would be effective, I think," Sister Inez answered. "The coydogs can sneak up on the foxholes without being detected. Abe has thirty coydogs and one kelpie, so if five or six of them dive into each fox hole and start attacking the men, biting their right hands, and going for their throats, the men will abandon their positions, climb out of the fox holes, and run in all directions. This activity will create a great deal of noise, drawing the reinforcements to that sector. Once the reinforcements have moved to the east, we will throw grenades in the foxholes on the west, take those positions and use them to provide cover for the squad that will attack the loading gate at the back of the residential complex."

"Okay," Maria said, "Let's pull over at the next parking lot and quickly brief everyone on their missions. We'll need three teams: the diversionary squad of Abe and his coydogs, a perimeter team to take the western foxholes and hold the ground, and an assault team to hack the loading dock gate, enter the complex, find Christina and the baby, and extract them. I need you to decide who will be on which team. It's going to have to be a quick briefing because I want us to attack Luke's compound before dawn."

Just then, Sister Adelaide, their communications officer, knocked on the window of the van and Maria lowered the glass. "There's something you want to know," Adelaide said, holding up her phone. She pushed a button and Maria watched a news report about a bomb explosion at a college auditorium in Chicago. A visiting professor who was a Jesuit priest from Houston was killed. Several others were injured. The newscaster brought up the possibility that the bomb had been planted by anti-abortion activists, but the police were not commenting on the investigation.

Alex woke in a hospital room lying on a bed wearing nothing but a thin hospital gown. Wires and tubes connected him to machines beside the bed. A female doctor, two male nurses and a technician stood around the bed, staring at him. The doctor looked at her watch and said, "Time of death

18:41." One of the nurses wrote this down on his chart. The technician turned off the machines, and quickly detached the wires and tubes from Alex's body. All four of them looked sadly down at him for a moment, then left the room.

Alex noticed Tristram standing in the doorway, smiling. He walked over to the bed and took Alex by the hand. Alex rose and walked with Tristram out of the room, through the corridor, down the stairs and out the door. It was a beautiful summer night in the city, and Tristram seemed the happiest Alex had ever seen him.

At the end of the street was a building that looked like one of the train stations from a hundred years before. Alex and Tristram walked through the revolving door which was made of polished brass. Inside was a large room with marble floors and a ceiling that portrayed angels peering over the sides of clouds, looking down at the people, thousands of them walking toward a blue light in the distance. They walked with the crowd for a while, then Alex saw that the blue light was the sky, and as each person came to the edge, he or she stepped off into the air and was lifted, as if by a gentle breeze, into distant heaven.

Birdie saw the report of the bomb explosion in Chicago that had killed Alex, and she immediately canceled Patrick's entire performance schedule and made plans to return to *El Presidio*.

When he got back to the hotel room, she told him of the deaths of their friends, Patrick was shocked. "Why would anyone kill Alex? He was such a beautiful man."

"I don't know, sweetie. We live in a world full of evil, that's all I can say. I've canceled your tour."

"What?" Patrick responded. "Don't do that. People need us to speak out now more than ever. We can't let the demons win. We just can't."

"It's too dangerous, Baby. I can't protect you from bombs."

"I don't care. I'm doing what I was born to do. I have to keep carrying the message."

"You want me to contact the venues and tell them that you'll be performing after all?"

"Oh, yes, please do, Mama."

Birdie liked it when he called her *mama.*

Patrick looked out the window. Evening light was slanting across the buildings causing the streets to be in deep shadow. "What city is this? I'm losing track."

"Dallas. You're doing a performance at a club on Greenville Avenue tonight."

"Dallas," Patrick said quietly. "I've been working on a new song. I'm going to try it out for the first time tonight."

"That's wonderful. I didn't know you were writing."

"Oh yes, I'm always writing." Patrick tapped his head. "I hear the song in my mind, and I practice it until I've got it right."

"Marilyn's going to sing it?"

"Oh, yes, it's perfect for her. It's an anti-war song called "Gentlemen Prefer Bombs."

Chapter 26

Christina had a bitter taste on her tongue, and she wondered whether Luke had drugged her. She guessed he had because he kept looking at her breasts in a creepy way, and drugging a woman was the easiest way to rape her.

"Would you excuse me," she said. "Where is..." She batted her eyelashes bashfully, as if she were too shy to use the word *toilet*.

"Oh, of course, my dear," Luke said, smiling and standing up. "Polly, would you please show Christina the way to the facilities?"

Christina hadn't realized that Polly was standing behind her against the wall. The older woman bowed her head slightly and gestured toward the door. "Please follow me, Dr. O'Malley."

Carrying Francisco, Christina followed the older woman down the hall to a bathroom which was decorated sumptuously, but she was no longer impressed by Luke's wealth. Clearly, he was a son-of-a-bitch who drugs women and rapes them. Laying Francisco gently on the bathmat, she leaned over the toilet and stuck her fore finger deep into her throat, and all the rich food, along with the rape drug it was laced with, came abruptly out of her, and splashed in the toilet bowl. She rinsed her mouth with water from the faucet and looked around the bathroom, her mind racing. There was a window, but it was too small for her to crawl through holding the baby.

She opened the drawers beneath the sink, hoping to find a weapon. She found a brand-new toothbrush, still wrapped in plastic. She remembered Stefan telling her that toothbrushes were not allowed in Leavenworth because they could easily be turned into weapons. She tore open the package and examined it. There was no time to sharpen it, but maybe if she could break off the round tip of the handle to make a sharp spike? Holding Francisco against her side with her left hand, she used her right hand to place the end of the toothbrush between the handle and the water faucet. Taking the bristled end firmly in her right hand, she used her full weight to push the toothbrush until the end broke off, leaving a jagged tip.

She rummaged through the other drawers and found a matching mirror and hairbrush with silver frames and handles, heavy enough to use as clubs. She thought about breaking the mirror and using a glass shard as a weapon but was afraid she'd lose the element of surprise if she made a lot of noise. Next, she used her scarf to make a sling to hold Francisco, swaddling him tightly, so he wouldn't fall out when she ran. She slid the broken toothbrush into a fold of the swaddling. This freed both of her hands to hold the silver handled mirror and hairbrush.

She stood in front of the bathroom door, steeling herself for what she was about to do. She thought briefly about a self-defense class she'd taken in college taught by a woman who had studied… something from the far east. On the last day of class, her teacher said *Remember, a woman's legs are much stronger than a man's arms. A man's most vulnerable spot is his kneecap. Next go for the groin. And if you're too close for the knees and groin, go for the eyes. If you have a blade, go for his throat.*

Then she remembered talking with Stefan about this moment which somehow, they both knew was coming, a time when she would have to fight the devil by herself on his turf. Her husband asked, "What is the most dangerous being in the universe?"

She had shrugged. She hated riddles.

"A mother defending her child. Christina, I pity the demon who takes you on."

Christina was ready. She opened the door.

Xavi was stationed at the mouth of the narrow valley at the east end of a plain where Luke's mansion sat like a jewel in a bowl of dust. Xavi could hear them coming, the hummers. He guessed that Luke had sent a call to Huitzi for reinforcements, and the warrior god had sent a company, approximately a thousand warriors, to Luke's aid. Xavi knew that Huitzi was too smart to risk coming himself. A company of his best fighters was enough to show significant support for Luke without putting his army or himself in possible jeopardy. He didn't hear any wasps, so he felt confident that they had returned to their cave in central Texas.

The brush was thick here, so the hummers couldn't fly through it without being slowed down. And they couldn't fly over it without being visible for miles around, so they would follow the dirt road through this pass, moving quickly in a narrow column, hoping not to be detected. Once the hummers were through the pass, they could spread out and their charge would be unstoppable. Xavi needed to stop them here. He and Huitzi were evenly matched and could injure or even kill each other, but normal mortal hummers like the ones that were approaching were no problem for Xavi.

He hid behind a large boulder, listening to the humming sound of their wings grow closer. Hummers could move at one hundred miles per hour for short distances, but for a long trip across the desert, they were probably traveling at half that speed with frequent stops for water from tanks and streams. Timing his actions perfectly, Xavi waited until the lead hummers were ten seconds away, and he stepped onto the road and held up his palms facing the oncoming force of birds. His hands made a double helix of energy that the first hummers crashed into, bursting into flame. Caught by surprise the ones behind tried to stop, causing a pile up that pushed the front ones into the energy field. The birds were catching fire and going up like roman candles, turning night into day. Some of the sergeants quickly grasped the fact that Xavi was the center of the force field, so they led their birds in a wild attack against him, but the force was strongest from his palms and the poor birds were attacking the field at its strongest point. Some of the birds escaped the fate of their brothers by flying up into the night, beyond the energy field; at which point they turned and fled the way they'd come. It was disaster for the hummers, half of them dead in the first few moments of the battle, the remainder in full rout.

When the battlefield was quiet, Xavi walked among the dead and the wounded, putting out of their misery the birds whose feathers were scorched so badly they couldn't fly, and encouraging the flying wounded to go back to their general with a message. *Shiva Destroyer of Worlds is waiting for Huitzilopochtli God of War.*

Dharma loved being part of the tribe of coydogs. After their initial distrust the year before, they'd accepted her fully into the pack. She knew that the bravery she'd shown at the battle of the Otay Bridge had helped to gain their respect, as well as her complete obedience of Abraham the Patriarch who was the master of this tribe.

Abe had divided his tribe into five squads and led them quietly through the brush to the edge of the clearing that marked the kill zone in front of the foxholes occupied by Loud Boys. The coydogs were downwind and could smell the bodies of the Loud Boys, and Dharma and the coydogs knew many of the Loud Boys were not human, but demons disguised as humans. Dharma guessed about half the Loud Boys had come up from Hell with Luke. Abe, who had lived among the coydogs for hundreds of years, spoke their language, and he'd explained that their role was to create a diversion, so the strike force could blast into the mansion complex and save the woman Christina and her baby who were being held as prisoners. Dharma was proud to serve with these canines who had years of experience in their guerrilla war against real estate developers in the hills east of Los Angeles.

At a signal from Abe, the coydogs moved in their groups of six toward the foxholes. Making use of shadows, rockpiles and natural depressions, they were able to get within ten feet of the Loud Boys who were not expecting an attack. When Abe barked GO! all the canines leaped into the fox holes, biting, clawing, screaming, barking, and howling, creating as much noise and panic as they could. The human Loud Boys quickly climbed out of the fox holes and ran for safety with the guards at the front door of the mansion. The demons in the foxholes, however, kept their wits and tried to shoot the coydogs before their right hands were mangled and their throats torn open. Once all the fox holes had been taken, Abe gave a whistle and the coydogs leaped out of the holes and scurried back to the shrub where they would be invisible to the guards running toward the fox holes where demons lay dead or dying.

Dharma heard explosions on the other side of the compound, and she knew the assault on Satan was underway.

Chapter 27

Christina came out of the bathroom holding the silver mirror and hairbrush. Polly was waiting in the hall, her arms crossed, and her lips pressed tightly together in anger. Christina bowed her head as if embarrassed by how long she'd been in the bathroom which seemed to put Polly at ease a little bit. Keeping the mirror behind her back, Christina held up the hairbrush in her left hand and said, "This is so beautiful, I've never seen anything like it. Do you think Luke would let me take it back to my room?"

When Polly turned her head slightly to look at the hairbrush, Christina swung the mirror around and hit the woman on the side of the head, catching her completely by surprise. Stunned, she looked at Christina and lifted her hand to the place where blood was starting to come out. Christina hit her with the hairbrush on the other side of the head, and Polly went down. Christina had never hit anyone before in her entire life, and she was a little surprised and ashamed that she enjoyed the solid feel of hitting Polly's skull.

So far, she hadn't felt any effects from the date rape drug. The only thing she'd consumed in the last twenty-four hours was dinner, but the food seemed to have slowed down the absorption of the drug. She tried to remember the charts she'd been required to memorize in grad school that showed how long it took the body to absorb pharmaceuticals. She guessed she had approximately half an hour before she started to feel the effects, and perhaps forty-five minutes before she passed out.

She looked at Francisco in her arms. *Damn Luke Ferris!* Whatever she digested, she passed on to the baby. It takes a special kind of evil to give a nursing woman a date rape drug.

She turned and ran down the hallway from the dining room where she'd left Luke in the middle of dessert. She felt a little dizzy, no doubt from the drug her body was absorbing, so she was hoping to make it out of the complex and into the surrounding desert without being detected, but she was very aware that she had no idea where the exit doors were, and she was afraid she would pass out before she and Francisco had escaped.

At the end of the hall, she had to decide whether to turn right and go through a door or to turn left and follow the hall past large windows that looked onto a foliage garden. And suddenly coming from nowhere it seemed, Luke's chauffer Elvis wearing a white sequined suit appeared in front of her, blocking her path. Since she couldn't turn back without taking the chance of running into Luke who was no doubt aware she was on the run, she covered Francisco with one arm protecting him, and charged Elvis wielding the heavy silver mirror.

"Come on, Darlin', this way!" Elvis turned and opened a door for her. She hesitated, remembering he was the driver who helped kidnap her.

Elvis said, "You a hard-headed woman and you think I'm nothing but a hound dog but trusting me is the only chance you got. We gotta get out of this heartbreak hotel." And opened the door a little wider.

Christina thought, *well, if you can't trust Elvis, who can you trust?* And carrying her baby, she went through the door and found herself in a garage with half a dozen expensive-looking cars.

She heard gunfire and explosions coming from outside.

As the coydogs were snarling and howling and biting, and men and demons were screaming, Abe fired his AR15 at the ground and for good measure threw a grenade off into the woods. All this racket caused the men stationed at the front door to take position to guard their east flank and the men in the foxholes to look toward the noise as well. This distraction gave Zenobia and Inez the chance to throw grenades in two of the fox holes, and the two strike teams tumbled into the foxholes. Marta, whose prosthetic provided an effective brace to hold her sniper's rifle, carefully took out each of the 1000-watt searchlights around the complex.

"SECOND TEAM, FOLLOW ME," Inez shouted.

The extraction team, consisting of Inez, Jesse, Zenobia, Theodora, and Stefan ran through the darkness toward the garage door in the back of the complex, leaving Maria, Delphina, and Genevieve in the foxhole firing at the Loud Boys stationed at the front door.

At the garage door, Zenobia checked to see whether the heavy steel door was locked, then placed small packages of plastique on the right, left and top of the door.

"FIRE IN THE HOLE!!!" she yelled, and everyone dived for cover.

Elvis opened the rear door of a black limousine and held it open for Christina.

"Why are you helping me?" she asked as she hurried toward the open door.

"I'm actually working for Maria, darlin'. I volunteered to keep an eye on Luke and report to her what he's up to." He glanced at the door they'd come through. "Believe me, Miss, I'm all shook up. It ain't no good he's up to."

"I thought you were dead," she said, but when she saw the hurt look on Elvis's face, she regretted her offhand remark.

"A little less conversation, please," Elvis said in his cavernous voice. "It's now or never."

Christina, holding Francisco, slid into the back seat of the limo, and Elvis hurried around to sit in the driver's seat. "Let's shake, rattle, and roll!" he rumbled as the car roared. He reached over to press the button on the dashboard that would have opened the metal garage door when there was an explosion, and the heavy door burst from its hinges and hit the back of the limo.

When Christina regained consciousness, there was a ringing in her ears. She looked down at Francisco and he seemed to be screaming, terrified, but she couldn't hear him. Elvis was slumped over the steering wheel, passed out. She suddenly realized that Luke was sitting beside her, smiling. He reached over to take the baby out of her arms. A surge of primal fear rushed through her body. She grabbed the broken toothbrush out of the folds of swaddling, and swinging her arm as hard as she could, jabbed the jagged point of the broken toothbrush in Luke's eye, sinking the shaft four inches into his brain.

If he'd been mortal, it would have killed him. Instead, he reached up, felt the toothbrush protruding from his eye, and said, "Damn, that hurt."

As he turned his head so his good eye could look at her, Christina saw the raw hatred in his face. Luke reached toward Francisco, and Christina thought *Oh, no no no. He's not going to hurt my baby*, and she tensed her body to attack him with her fingernails.

Before she could leap, all six doors of the limo sprung open, and six automatic weapons muzzles appeared, all pointed at Luke. Stefan shoved the barrel of his rifle into Luke's mouth and pulled the trigger without a moment's hesitation. Luke's head exploded, and bits of bone, brain, and blood coated the back window of the car.

From far away, Christina could hear her husband's voice. "Christina, it's me, Stefan. Are you hurt? Is Francisco hurt?"

She could hear the baby crying. She was helped from the car. *Stefan, my dear Stefan has come for Francisco and me with the sisters. Of course, they have. Of course they have.*

Maria, Genevieve, and Marta were pinned down in a foxhole with Luke's demons firing and advancing on them.

"I'm out of grenades. How many do you have?" Maria shouted over the noise of automatic weapons.

"None," Genevieve said. "I'm out of grenades and I have only half a clip for my rifle."

"I have only a few rounds left," Marta said.

"Choose your shots carefully, ladies," Maria said. "We don't want to run out of ammo when we're pinned down."

There was an explosion at the back of the residence, and Maria guessed it was the second team blowing off the door of the garage. Then silence.

Maria waited. Still no sound. Then she heard a man scream in terror. Then howling from what... the coydogs? No, these were the howls of wolves. Then more men screaming. A single gunshot. Then another man screaming. And another. Then she heard a deep panting and growling.

"Momma!" Maria gasped.

"What?" Genevieve asked, puzzled.

"IT'S MY MOTHER. SHE'S HERE!" Maria yelled and stuck her head above the edge of the foxhole. She saw the dark profile of a large tiger moving almost invisibly through the shadows. A wolf was dragging down a screaming man. A hawk screeched from above.

"Gaia?" Genevieve asked, incredulously. "She Herself is here?"

"Yep," Maria said smiling. "She Herself. And she's brought her wolves and her raptors."

"I don't hear anything now," Marta said. "Did Gaia and her minions leave?"

"It sounds like they killed or frightened off all the demons and Loud Boys," Maria said. "The second team should have a clear escape path now. Let's retreat to the woods and wait for them."

"What about him?" Christina asked, nodding at Elvis slumped over the steering wheel of the limo. "He was one of the good guys, wasn't he?"

"Yes," Jesse said. "He was one of us. Don't worry about Elvis. There will always be a special place in heaven for the King. It was only my uncle Luke's hubris that allowed him to think that Elvis had penance to pay in Hell. Luke couldn't pass up the chance to possess a prize like Elvis. Ever since he died, Elvis has been here acting as part of a second front, spying for Maria."

Francisco was calming down, nursing in his mother's arms while she sat in the back seat of the Suburban. The other sisters climbed in, Theodora at the wheel, Inez riding shotgun, and Stefan and Zenobia on either side of Christina, the better to protect her. "Isn't Jesse coming?" Christina asked, noticing that he was leaning over Luke's body in the back seat of the limo.

"No," Inez said. "Jesse needs to talk with Luke. Perhaps they can work out terms of a peace treaty."

"Talk with Luke?" Christina asked incredulously. Weird things were coming at her too quickly to be able to absorb them all. "Isn't Luke dead? I mean, I saw Stefan blow his head apart."

Zenobia looked at her, puzzled. "You cannot kill Satan, Christina. All you can do is slow him down."

Christina felt her stomach churning from all the stress. As she started to retch, Zenobia held a small bag like the ones on airplanes under her chin. Christina threw up several times. "Thank you," she said. "I didn't want to throw up on my baby."

"It would have been okay if you had," Zenobia said, her broad black face radiating kindness. "Babies can be bathed very easily. A little vomit doesn't hurt them." She wiped the corners of Christina's mouth, then handed her a flask. "Rinse your mouth, dear. Get that nasty taste of the devil out. I hope he didn't kiss you."

"No, he didn't. Why? Would that have killed me?"

"Oh, no, the kiss of the devil will not kill you, it will just make you wish you were dead. It's like having your soul dipped in shit and set on fire." She looked out the window at the garage wall. "I was once kissed by the devil."

Christina looked at this beautiful black woman, her curls cut close to the scalp, her regal nose that looked like it belonged to an Ethiopian princess, and then she looked around the inside of the vehicle at Elvis, Stefan, Birdie, Theodora, Zenobia, and Inez—these gifted and passionate people who had risked their lives to come to her aid. And now, in a moment of clarity, she understood what had happened in the last few weeks. The devil had kidnapped her and Francisco because they represented humankind's best hope, and these heroes had come to protect not only Francisco, but the future itself. At last, she understood what they meant when they called her baby *the Chosen One.*

Theodora said, "Here, everyone, better put these things on. It's going to get really loud in here."

Theodora turned around in her seat and handed each of the women a pair of noise canceling headphones. She even had a tiny pair for Francisco. "Where'd you get the baby muffs?" Zenobia asked.

"Maria gave them to me," Theodora said, turning around and pushing the button that opened the second set of garage doors. The Suburban peeled out of the garage, the sisters with the muzzles of their rifles flashing, shooting in the air, not to hit any of their friends.

Chapter 28

Jesse lifted his uncle from the limo. It always surprised him how light gods are when the bodies they inhabit are dying. He carried Luke through the door into the hall where Polly, the nurse who had killed over forty of her patients, backed away from Jesse, her eyes wide in recognition, turned and ran in the opposite direction. The other servants, seeing the Son of God carrying the shattered body of their Evil Master, hid in the recesses of the mansion, knowing they would soon be returning to their cells in Hell.

Jesse took his uncle up the wide stairs to his sleeping quarters and laid him on a bed. In the normal course of things, Luke's body would die, and his essence would return to Hell, but Jesse didn't have time for this process, so he decided to save Luke's body now, so they could discuss the terms of an armistice.

First, he pulled the broken toothbrush from Luke's eye. Jesse was impressed with Christina's courage, but of course, she had an advantage. Not even Satan himself can withstand the fury of a mother protecting her baby. Gaia Herself inhabits the mother's soul at that moment.

Next, Jesse took the shattered head in his hands and molded it back into its proper shape, healing the broken vessels and crushed cells, suturing and cauterizing and soothing the shocked tissues, and finally restoring the memories and encouraging the mind to speak again. Finally, after half an hour, his uncle opened his eyes and said, "What in holy hell happened?"

"You got beat up by a girl, Uncle Luke," Jesse said, laughing.

It wasn't the first time a mortal had fought with a god, but it was the first time a mortal had won.

"Oh, yeah. That bitch Christina. Oh, does my head hurt," he said sitting up and holding the side of his head.

"It should. You actually died and I brought you back."

"You brought me back? Why?"

"Because I need to talk to you, Uncle Luke."

"Now? I have the worst headache since Fat Man exploded over Nagasaki."

"Did you have something to do with atomic weapons?"

"Oh, yeah, I was the one who explained to Bobby Oppenheimer the basic principles. Well, he gave credit to Krishna. Remember *Now I am become Death, the destroyer of worlds?"*

"Isn't Shiva the destroyer of worlds?"

"Usually, but Shiva, your buddy Xavi, was vacationing with one of his consorts that day and he'd left Vishnu in charge of destruction, and Vishnu had come to Oppenheimer in his incarnation as Krishna.... I know, I know... all these Hindu Gods keep changing their forms, so it's hard to keep track, but anyway, Krishna was the one who encouraged Bobby to go ahead and use the atomic bomb, but I was the one who helped him and his team to build it. But Bobby didn't understand what he'd done. He thought he'd ended those people's lives when actually he'd just ended this phase of their existence and enabled them to move on to their next life."

"I didn't know you'd invented atomic weapons, Uncle Luke. I guess you're proud of that, huh?"

"You betcha I am. It was the largest single step humankind has ever made to wipe themselves out on this plane. But you know what?"

"What, Uncle?"

"This whole global climate warming thing is probably going to kill more people than all the wars these dumb monkeys have ever fought. With rising seas, wildfires, changing seasons. If they don't drown, they'll burn. And if they don't burn, they'll starve. Imagine the wars over food and water! I'm really looking forward to watching this. And when the destruction is over, then it will be easy for *my people to take over.*" Luke seemed to have forgotten his headache. His right eye was burning with excitement over his vision for the future.

"That's actually what I want to talk with you about, Uncle Luke."

"Oh, what do you want?" Luke turned his head, seeing his nephew for the first time since the surgery.

"I don't want you to take over the earth."

"Of course, you don't want me to take over the earth, Jesse." his uncle said, smiling indulgently. "That's what this whole fight is over... who gets to rule the earth, who gets to determine the fate of humankind. You want to teach the humans how to be better, do better. You want to teach them love and acceptance, so everybody can sit around the campfire singing "Kumbaya." Your dad, on the other hand, has given up on humans. He wants to wipe out all the people, so he can start over with a different species. But I want things to remain the way they are. All fucked up. I like war. I like plagues. I like hunger and pestilence. Disaster creates opportunity. Buy when the market is down, you know?"

Luke peered at his nephew with a shrewd look in his one good eye. Jesse knew that look. His uncle was about to make a pitch. "You know, Jesse, you and I are actually on the same side. Neither of us wants the Old Man to wipe out humans. We want them to continue building their civilization. Of course, we have different visions of the future, two different paths for humankind, you might say, but we can work out something that meets both of our goals. What do you say?"

"No, Luke, I can't agree to a partnership with you."

"Why not? It would meet both our needs. We could even divide up the population. You'd get all the goody-goodies who want to do the right thing—feed the hungry, save the whales, grow organic vegetables, install wind turbines on every roof—and I'd get all the wife-beaters, child molesters, greedy oilmen and old women who beat their grandchildren. That's fair, isn't it?"

"You know it doesn't work like that, Luke. Humans are not all good or all bad. The wife-beater might also want to save the whales, and the child molester might have a spiritual awakening in prison. It happens all the time."

"So, you want everyone to accept your message. You want the whole shebang, every human soul to follow you. You want to have the Big Tamale for yourself and leave nothing for me, your poor uncle."

Jesse tried not to laugh at his uncle's attempt to solicit pity. What Luke was proposing was a terrible idea. Good and Evil in partnership? This is what had gotten his father in trouble, trying to have it both ways. Ruining poor Job's life and then restoring it as if the boils and fevers and deaths of his children had never happened. No, no. Maria and José had taught him that you had to declare which side of the boundary you were going to occupy, then commit to it fully. There's no compromising with Evil.

Seeing he'd failed to convince his nephew, Luke shrugged. "What now? I go back to Hell and wait to see what happens on earth?"

"Something like that."

"Okay, I'll retire from the battle for now, but you know that your Old Man is going to send Xavi to destroy the world. In fact, the two of you were supposed to wreak destruction last year, but you lost your nerve and started adopting kittens and puppies instead."

Jesse noticed that Luke was barely smiling, as if he knew something that Jesse didn't. "What?" Jesse asked. "You know something, don't you? You've set something in motion, haven't you?"

"Well, I may have encouraged Huitzi to kill Xavi, but you know he doesn't have to do what I say… And without Xavi, the Old Man has no way to destroy the world. But you know, the humans are doing a pretty good job of destroying the world on their own, so Xavi's efforts may be redundant."

Jesse looked toward the door. "I have to warn Xavi."

"Oh, I'm sure that Xavi already knows that Huitzi is hunting him."

Luke's phone buzzed. Looking at the caller i.d., Luke said, "Excuse me, I have to take this… Hello, Jeb. I guess you've heard about the excitement down here. You're where? Now? Okay, come on in. I think the front door is unlocked. See you shortly." Luke put the phone aside and said to Jesse, "Your dad is here."

"Really? Why?" Jesse dreaded seeing his father.

"He says we need to talk."

When the Old Man walked into the bedroom and saw his brother sitting propped up in bed, his eyes widened. "Oh my, what happened to you? It looks like you had an argument with a chainsaw."

"It's certainly been a long evening, Jeb. You know that woman Christina? The mother of the Chosen One."

"Yes, I know who she is."

"We were having a nice dinner together. That woman can eat like a horse! And when dessert came, she excused herself to go to the bathroom, so of course I sent Polly, you know the nurse who killed so many of her patients? A very sweet woman who killed only the terminally ill. Anyway, Christina attacked her! And when I chased her out to the garage, she stabbed me with a toothbrush!" Luke pointed to his eye socket from which blood was trickling down his cheek.

"It does look ghastly, Luke," the Old Man said sympathetically. "But what happened to your head? Looks a bit like a deflated soccer ball."

"That damn poet Stefan shot me in the head!"

"So why are you still alive?"

"Oh, your son," Luke gestured vaguely at Jesse. "Decided that this is the best time to discuss the fate of the world, so he did some of his conjuring to keep me alive. It's been a very long day, Jeb. Can't you just kill me, so I can go home?"

"Not so fast, Luke," the Old Man said. "I actually agree with Jesse for once."

"Thanks, Dad," Jesse said, trying to keep the sarcasm out of his voice.

"We have to end this three-way war."

"Jeb, I've never wanted to be at war with you," Luke said in his most sincere voice, prompting Jesse to roll his eyes.

"Actually, you've been at war with me for eons, Luke," the Old Man said.

"I admit the three of us have been at cross purposes," Luke whined. "You want to destroy the world, so we can start over. Jesse wants to save the world by making everybody goody-goody, and I want to transform the world to be more to my liking. But I never wanted to fight with you, big brother. Not really."

"What are you proposing, Dad?" Jesse asked.

"I suggest that we compromise."

Jesse jaw dropped in surprise. This was something that had never happened in the history of the Universe. The Old Man had always insisted on getting his own way, and everyone else had to accept his will or be destroyed.

Luke's one good eye narrowed in suspicion. "Okay, let's hear your proposal, Jeb."

"I will order Xavi to destroy most of the world but leave a few areas unspoiled. Each of you, Luke and Jesse, can choose an area of one hundred thousand contiguous hectares that Xavi doesn't touch. You'll also choose a certain tribe or culture to stay safe in that area while the rest of the world goes up in flames."

Jesse thought quickly. He knew that if things continued as they were, his father would order Xavi to destroy everything. At least with this compromise, some people would be safe. He quickly decided whom he would choose to save. He could see that Luke was making a similar calculation.

"Dad, you know that Huitzi is stalking Xavi, right?"

"I'm aware of the situation between the two of them," the Old Man said.

"What do you think is going to happen?" Jesse asked. He knew his father was blessed with a certain amount of foresight. "Will Xavi kill Huitzi?"

"Probably not. It's not such an easy thing to kill a god," the Old Man said, glancing at his brother's badly dented head.

"But according to legend, Huitzi killed four hundred of his brothers, as well as his sister," Jesse pointed out.

"Yes, well, that was a long time ago before the pantheon was designated. It used to be that every tree, every river, every mountain was home to a god. There's been sort of a weeding out since then. There are a lot fewer gods than there used to be," the Old Man said, sighing.

"But—" Jesse suddenly had dozens of questions about theogony that had never occurred to him before, but his father waved his hand dismissively.

"This is a conversation for another time, Son," he said. "Right now, we need to move things forward before more damage is done. Luke, I'm going to kill you now, so you can get some rest. Your head must feel like a bowling ball at the end of a championship match."

Luke nodded gratefully, and Jeb touched his brother's chest with his forefinger. Luke sank slowly into the large bed, his body almost disappearing in the satin sheets.

"Jesse, I suggest you get your people ready for what's coming."

Chapter 29

Xavi chose the location carefully. He needed a place where it would look to Huitzi that he had the advantage, but there needed to be a quirk in the landscape, easy to overlook, that gave Xavi the advantage. There needed to be an escape route in case the battle wasn't going well for Xavi. He also needed for Huitzi to think that he had the element of surprise on his side.

After considering several possibilities, Xavi chose a high mountaintop east of Alamogordo and west of Carlsbad above the tree line. The open air, lack of cover and steep slope on all sides would give Huitzi the advantage in his airborne attacks, but what Huitzi probably didn't know was that halfway down the mountain was a rocky cave that led down into the earth and linked up with hundreds of miles of caves that made up the Carlsbad Caverns. In the darkness, Xavi would have the advantage because he didn't need light to see whereas Huitzi did. If he could lure Huitzi into the cavern, then seal the entrance, Huitzi would be at a severe disadvantage.

To bait the trap, he asked his friend, a mockingbird named Oscar, to repeat a conversation near a hummingbird nest. The conversation should include the information that the God of the Hummingbirds would never find Shiva the Destroyer of Worlds because Shiva had retreated to his mountaintop retreat to meditate on the tallest mountain next to the Pecos River. Xavi told Oscar not to be obvious in giving the information; instead, he should include it in a song bragging to a prospective mate about how important Oscar is that even Shiva the Destroyer holds him in respect. If hummers question him, he should hold out from telling them the source of his information as long as possible. "Make it believable," Xavi said.

Then Xavi went to the mountaintop and built a small shrine from rock and decorated it with gold and silk. It shone in the sunlight, and the sky was dark blue above in the morning and red in the evening, and the stars shone down with a billion faces at night. Xavi looked down at the river in the distance, and he went down into the cave and explored its many tunnels and chambers.

Then Lord Shiva, the Auspicious One, the Slayer of Demons, Xavi, sat on a flat rock on the mountain top, his legs crossed, a rattlesnake wrapped around his neck, the adorning crescent moon above him, the river Pecos meandering in the valley below. His chosen weapon the trident rested lightly in his hand, pointing its three spear tips, the past, the present and the future, toward the heavens. The damaru, the skull-drum, beat on its own a slow complicated rhythm which is the rhythm of existence by which the whole universe has been created and ordered. Lord Shiva is anaconistic, simultaneously existing in this world but not of this world. In this time but not of this time, Lord Shiva's third eye watches his enemy fly toward him across the sands of the desert.

Huitzi stayed close to the sandy ground, barely over the mesquite and prickly pear, not wishing to be seen except as a blur moving faster than an automobile, stopping for water and a sip of nectar every now and then, wishing to arrive at the mountaintop where he'd heard Xavi had taken up residence. Of course, he knew it was a trap. Xavi wasn't stupid like that mockingbird who'd sung about Xavi the Magnificent. Well, that bird wouldn't be singing again. Huitzi had killed it with a single stab to its blue-feathered throat. Approaching the mountaintop, he would be wary. Perhaps Xavi, the coward, would have reinforcements stationed nearby, or perhaps he'd poisoned his trident, or just possibly Jesse and his crowd would be on hand to perform magic. We shall see.

He wasn't afraid. He was Huitzilopochtli, the Sun God, God of War, God of Human Sacrifice. His priests used stone knives to cut out the hearts of a dozen victims a day to protect their people from perpetual night. He was born fully armored and ready to kill without mercy his rebellious sister Coyolxauhqui and his 400 brothers, the Centzonhuitznahuac and Centzonmimizcoa, who had conspired to kill their mother—not that their mother had been grateful. As the Nahuatl song says:

There is nothing like death in war,
nothing like the flowery death
so precious to Him who gives life:
far off I see it: my heart yearns for it!

Shiva, on the other hand, was merely a destroyer of cities and no match for a killer of gods. Huitzilopochtli would defeat Shiva as a hummingbird defeats a hawk, through speed, courage, and ferocity. He would like to maintain his form as a bird, but if he needed to transform into a human, he would attack Shiva with club, bow, and spear and protect himself with his round *chimalli* shield and his helmet made from the head of a jaguar.

José drove Christina, Stefan, and Francisco back to the Yaqui homeland, and Dharma rode in the back of the truck. Eduardo and Concepción were standing in front of their house as they pulled up.

"*Hola.* How's the flower?" Eduardo said in the traditional Yaqui greeting, opening the door and helping Christina climb out of the truck while holding the baby. Concepción went over to Christina and admired the baby. Christina realized that until now, none of the Yaqui women other than *La partera* had seen Francisco, and she vowed that she would raise Francisco to learn the Yaqui way. She understood that her son had a special destiny, but as a psychologist, she knew that he needed what every child needs: to be loved and valued within a community that lived close to the land. She was grateful to the Yaqui for what they'd done for her and her family. She would learn their language and their customs, and she knew Stefan would as well.

She followed Concepción into the kitchen and began helping her to prepare the evening meal. She watched her new friend pat the thick corn batter between her palms, shaping the tortillas in an almost unconscious motion that came so easily that Concepción barely paid attention to it, speaking to Christina in fast Spanish all the while. Although she missed more than a few words, Christina understood that Concepción was being gracious and generous, telling her that she and Stefan could stay in their house as long as they liked. Christina looked down politely and thanked Concepción for being such a true friend.

After dinner, the men went onto the cool porch to talk and greet the other men who stopped by. Christina could hear their slow deep voices talking about weather and crops. The schoolhouse roof needed repairs. The padre needed help in moving pews. Stefan's son had been born, and the men wanted to see the boy. Christina didn't wait to be asked but took Francisco out to the front porch and held him up so all the men could admire the baby. Christina, a White California feminist, was going to have to get used to a society which seemed sexist by the standards she was used to. She guessed that mothers did not breast feed in front of men, that women did all the work in the house, that men expected to be waited on by women. For the time being, she would respect these traditional roles. So, when Stefan came inside and started toward the kitchen, obviously planning to help Concepción and Christina clean up after the meal, Christina caught his eye and subtly shook her head. "This is women's work, Stefan. Go sit with the men, and when they work, you learn their skills."

Stefan was puzzled. The woman he'd been married to for over a year would never have used a phrase like *women's work*, but after a moment, he got the message. "Right," he said. "Respect the local customs and traditions. Got it." He went back outside and continued listening to the men talk, and when they got up to go look under the hood of José's truck, he went with them and listened to them discuss the carburetor even though he'd never had the slightest interest in internal combustion. Later, standing in the growing shadows, Stefan looked out over the cornfields, the tall stalks casting rows of shadows on the broad leaves of the squash, and he knew that he could count on these men to come to the schoolhouse the next day after the children had gone home, and the men would help him fix the roof to protect the classroom and the children from rain.

While the men were standing around the truck, Christina went onto the front porch and sat in the cool evening with Concepción who was repairing a straw hat, weaving dry reeds over a hole in the brim. Concepción paused, and seeing that Christina wanted to help, she took a handful of reeds from a burlap bag and placed them in front of Christina. Concepción took a reed, tapered and tubular, and with a small knife cut off both ends, then split it lengthwise down the middle, then taking the two ends of the reed in her two hands, rubbed the reed against the edge of the small table between them until the reed was flat. Then Concepción took another reed from the burlap bag and handed it to Christina who cut off the ends, split it down the middle and rubbed it until it was flat. When Concepción smiled her approval, Christina felt elation as she hadn't felt in many years. She picked up another reed and repeated the action. *I have so much to learn before I can be of use to this community, but I have an excellent teacher.*

After a while, Christina's fingers, unused to this kind of work, began to bleed, and Concepción gently put her hand over Christina's hand and shook her head. To make sure her pupil understood, Concepción moved the burlap bag of unfinished reeds off to the side, out of Christina's reach. Christina was filled with gratitude at the wisdom and kindness of this Yaqui woman.

Christina knew that there was an apocalypse coming, but she suspected that Maria and Jesse would protect these people, this place. She and Stefan would have to adapt to a traditional lifestyle in a close community that worked the land. As long as the Yaqui could tend their crops, they would have enough to eat. For clothing, most of them wore what looked like cast off North American clothes—jeans, t-shirts with college names on them, old running shoes, billed hats with company logos. Christina guessed that Catholic Charities collected donated clothes north of the border and brought them down to this area. If North America was going to burn and collapse, the Yaqui would have to return to their traditional ways, weaving cloth, tanning hides, wearing straw hats. As for water, the rudimentary plumbing system would eventually fail, and people would have to start hauling water from the nearby river. The church and the schoolhouse were constructed of lumber and aluminum siding with shingled roofs, but the houses were made in the traditional way, the walls of woven reeds and the roof of reeds coated with thick layers of mud for insulation. Most of the old crafts were still practiced in this community, so the Yaqui would have an easy adjustment to a pre-industrial existence.

She was sure there would be marauders, including well-armed former soldiers and drug traffickers who would attack the Yaqui once the government collapsed. She would bring up the subject of training the Yaqui to defend themselves. José had already delivered automatic rifles, so he evidently was aware of the challenges the Yaqui would be facing.

She and Stefan would make their home here, learning the Yaqui way, raising their son to be Yaqui. The rest of his fate, whether he fulfilled the prophecy of being a great teacher and leader, was, as the war veterans she used to counsel said, *above my paygrade*. Or as she'd heard Concepción say, *si Dios lo quiere*—if God wills it.

Maria sat in her office staring at the wall. Alex was dead. Tristram was dead. Xavi was battling Huitzi who had turned against them. Christina, Francisco, and Stefan were safe with the Yaqui, at least for the time being. José, Mikey, Jesse and the Sisters were here in the convent, sitting in the common room, waiting for her instructions. Maria had contacted Patrick and Birdie, telling them to give up their tour and make their way to the Yaqui homeland. And now, Maria finally conceded that she and Jesse had lost the battle to save humanity, and she had no idea what to do next.

Although Jesse had persuaded Luke to withdraw his forces, the Old Man was likely to order Xavi to go ahead with the demolition of the earth which had been scheduled for the previous year. Xavi wouldn't dare disobey the Old Man again.

She wondered what was the bond between the two deities. Xavi was an ancient Hindu god whom some believed ruled all the cosmos. He was responsible for both the creation and destruction of worlds. On the other hand, the Old Man, or Jeb as his brother called him, was just a desert deity, a whirlwind with a voice that somehow had come to own the earth. *How was this possible?* she wondered for the millionth time. The earth had always been Gaia, the maternal force of rejuvenation, Maria's mother. Maria thought of the White Tigress, her mother's favored form, and a warm glow came over her. How was it that the Eternal Mother had come to be subordinate to this male usurper? He certainly had a talent for domination, but could she thwart his will and save humankind which he was so intent on destroying, or more accurately, so intent on allowing them to destroy themselves?

As Huitzi flew toward the mountaintop to the west of the Pecos River, he could see Shiva. The Destroyer of Worlds was sitting cross-legged on a flat rock, his hands resting on his thighs, forefingers and thumbs barely touching each other, forming a circle where the energy could flow from his chakras and back into his body, so nothing was lost. Shiva's jeweled scimitar was in its sheathe, as was his dagger. His trisula stood beside him of its own volition, its three prongs of soul, fire, and earth both guided him and described him. He was one of the oldest of the gods, born of his own volition.

As Shiva sat on the mountaintop perfectly still, his third eye watched the approach of Huitzi, God of War and of the Sun. He knew the story that Huitzi had been born armed and in full armor, and his first act was to kill his four hundred brothers and one sister. Shiva knew that when Aztec warriors died in battle or as sacrifices to Huitzi they first became part of the sun's brilliant retinue and then after four years they went to live forever in the bodies of hummingbirds.

"Where are your brave warriors, Huitzi?" Lord Shiva shouted as he rose to face his enemy.

"I have no need for mortal help to kill you who merely destroy worlds while I murder gods."

"We shall see," Lord Shiva said, planting his bare feet on the stone, bending his knees, keeping his back straight, and taking up his scimitar and his trisula.

Huitzi, wearing his armor of feathers and sunlight, flew at Lord Shiva's face. When Shiva swung his sword, the tiny bird changed directions and nicked Lord Shiva's right eye making blood flow down the cheek of the god. As Huitzi flew away, Shiva pointed his trisula and fire came from the first prong, singeing the feathers of the Aztec god. Huitzi spun around in midflight and attacked Shiva from his right side where he was now blind. But with his third eye Shiva saw Huitzi's mind and ducked his head as the bird came close to puncture Shiva's throat and Shiva thrust his trisula again at the bird this time with the full strength of the earth, and the tip of the trisula hit Huitzi's wing, breaking it off.

Huitzi flew down the mountain to rest beside a stream and eat insects and sip the nectar of flowers for the God of War burns so much soul he must eat every hour. He rested beside the stream to let his feathers repair themselves and his wing grow back. And Lord Shiva rested as well, sitting once again on his flat rock on the mountaintop, his legs crossed, his right eye healing itself, his left eye watching the sky and his third eye watching Huitzi who was resting beside the river while he healed.

And the next day, Huitzi the God of War and of the Sun, flew up the mountain and again attacked Lord Shiva, trying to tear the skin of the feet that stood on the rock, but Lord Shiva repelled the God of War with his scimitar which was the incarnation of truth that could not be denied, and his sword sliced off the tail of the hummingbird.

And the next day and the next and the next Huitzi attacked Lord Shiva who defended himself and the Lord of War and of Sunlight repaired to the river below the mountain to heal and to refresh himself. And this battle continued for many days but only in the sunlight, Huitzi being blind and weak in the darkness of night, and Lord Shiva knew this and waited his chance.

On the fifty second day, Huitzi attacked Lord Shiva on the mountaintop, but the Destroyer of Worlds saw the sun was behind a cloud and Huitzi was not as strong as he had been before in the bright light of day. And Lord Shiva ducked under the fierce attack and rolled down the mountain, holding his weapons against his body, not to be injured by them. And he rolled to the mouth of the cave he had discovered before, and with the hummingbird right behind him, Lord Shiva rolled into the cave and down into the darkest part where the sunlight had never been. And there Shiva stopped and turned and with his third eye seeing his enemy, blind in the darkness, who had followed him hoping to kill him. And Shiva drew his jeweled dagger which Huitzi could not see in the darkness, and Shiva smote him down and the bejeweled bird who was the most beautiful, fierce, and dangerous of the gods but one, fell to the floor and lay there stunned.

And Shiva walked out of the cave and piled rocks at the

entrance, closing it off, knowing that Huitzi would awaken, heal his wounds, and weakened by darkness, work for a thousand years pecking his needle-like beak against the pile of stones and eventually would be free.

Maria sat with her companions at the dinner table and looked at each one, seeing them clearly as no one else possibly could. On her left was her beloved José, a mortal who had stood by her for two thousand years. Sitting in a chair next to him was the Dominican Sister Theodora, an attorney and black belt in Jujitsu and Kung Fu. And beside her the Carmelite Sister Adelaide, a visionary and a mystic who could visualize a computer program and hack it as easily as she could understand a holy vision. And there was Sister Genevieve, from the French order The Little Sisters of Jesus, a gifted motorcycle mechanic with a PhD in psychology. And the novice Marta, the one-handed mechanic who had come so far in the last year, losing her bitterness and learning to love her sisters and through their example, the world. And the beloved Sister Zenobia, who had such a passion for helping women and yet was also an explosives expert who came to them from Africa. And Sister Delphina, the medical doctor from the Sisters of St. Joseph. And finally, Sister Inez, the former CIA operative who had led them to victory against Satan. All these sisters, fierce warriors against evil, had served the cause well. But what she and Jesse were about to tell them would shock them to their cores. The world as they knew it was ending, and they needed to prepare for what was coming.

Jesse stood between her and Mikey, his best friend, whose Dred locks and narrow black face made him beautiful and serene in this moment. He had faced Lucifer and fought him many times, and now was prepared to defend these nuns.

"My friends," Jesse began. "Xavi, who as you know is Shiva Destroyer of Worlds, has been ordered by my father to destroy the world. My father allowed his brother Lucifer to choose a patch of the world that would escape the destruction, and he allowed me to choose another patch. The area that Lucifer chose was the Houston metroplex because he has many worshippers there, especially those hiding among the evangelicals. The area I chose was the Yaqui homeland southwest of here. We will be few in number but pure of heart. We must evacuate this convent that we call El Presidio and relocate to the homeland to save ourselves."

The nuns were silent at first, looking at each other in shock. Finally, Sister Theodora, the attorney always aware of laws and legal procedures, raised her hand.

"Are we allowed to tell other people? Our families, our sisters in our home orders?"

Maria answered, "Yes, you may tell whomever you wish, but it's unlikely they will believe you. They will think that you've lost your mind, and they will worry about you. What I suggest is that you contact those you love in the next hour, tell them how much they've meant to you, then pack your kit. We leave for the Yaqui homeland in two hours. Dismissed."

Stefan remembered that shortly after meeting Maria and coming to El Presidio a year ago, she predicted that he would write a new holy book. He had silently scoffed at the idea. Who was he, after all, but a homeless veteran who lived in a cave beneath a bridge in Ventura? True, he'd spent many years reading and studying poetry, and he'd written hundreds of poems and thousands of unfinished ones, but the hubris of him thinking he was the next great ecclesiastical writer was absurd.

But now, the world he'd known his whole life, the scurvy republic he'd served in one of many colonial wars as well as the larger world it dominated, were quickly hurtling toward demise by fire, flood, and pestilence. He remembered the ambitions he'd had about receiving acclaim for his writing. All such ambitions had become irrelevant. The Academy of American Poets with its many posturing literati, the halls of academe with its much sought-after endowed chairs, the foundations that dispensed laurels and cash to the well-connected, the *New Yorker* with its archly superior tone, the many back-scratchers, brown-nosers, and time-servers, as well as the fiercely independent editors of magazines that had such small audiences that most Americans didn't know they existed, were about to be consumed in the holy conflagration that his friend and comrade-at-arms Xavi, aka Shiva Destroyer of Worlds, was about to unleash.

Stefan, better than anyone else who would survive, knew that the new world would need its testament, its foundational epic that incorporated its history, cosmology, and morality. Stefan laughed at the idea of his being the new Homer, but he would have to do. He would write an epic describing the old world in all its glorious failings, and he would predict the new world from its rough beginnings to its shining promise. He would begin by telling stories to his students, the Yaqui children who had been entrusted to him, and then he would find a rhythm because Anna Akhmatova once said that to write a long poem first you must find a rhythm that can be sustained, and then the poem will write itself.

And Stefan wrote:

In the beginning there was the Void.
And the Void was limitless, stretching forever in all
directions in a vast sea of nothingness.
And the face of God moved across the dark water.
God neither was, nor was not. God was neither one
nor many, male nor female, young nor old.
God was the Void's awareness of itself, the
presence of the absence.
And in the Void formed a pebble, and the pebble
contained everything that was later to be.
The stars were in the pebble, and the sun and moon.

The earth was in the pebble with its air and water, its trees and animals, its soil.

The love of mothers for their children, the desires of men for women, every need, every dream, every wish was in the pebble. Sunlight, snow, rain. Clouds and lightning. Winter nights, summer days. Hunger, satiety. Everything we know, everything we do not know.

And the many gods too were in the pebble. And our misunderstandings of them. The wisdom of those who wait, the weapons of those who fight. Everything you see and everything you cannot see was in the pebble waiting to be released.

God touched the pebble and released the potential, and there was a great explosion that sent the stars flying out in every direction at the speed of light. And the stars became light. And from the light everything was formed.

And out of nothing, God became everything. And everything became God.

Chapter 30

Xavi was excited to drive his Viper again. He started by speeding through the desert of northwest Mexico to the region where the Tepehuán people live. Although he was under instructions to sweep the earth clean of humans except for the Yaqui and the Houstonians, he always liked indigenous people who'd never accepted the temptations of western civilization. They wove reeds into baskets and rope and hats, carved wood into bowls and spoons, bows and arrows. They shaped the clay of the earth into pots and ornaments, and they hunted deer, jackrabbit and coyote, using the tanned hides to make sandals.

He decided to spend a few days with these wise people before he started his appointed task. He'd visited here many times through the ages, and the shamans knew him as the "old god" and also the "fire god." They always offered to sacrifice a child to him and then eat the child as a sign of their devotion to him, but as part of the ritual, older than kindness itself, he pardoned the child and thanked the shaman and the elders for their piety. He ate corn, beans, and squash with them but declined to eat mutton or other meat, telling the shamans, as was the ritual, that animals were their brothers and sisters, and men and women should always have respect for them. The ritualistic feasting lasted three days, at the end of which Xavi, or Xiuhtecutli, as the Tepehuán people called him, announced that the time had come for him to destroy the world, but the Tepehuán would be spared because of their piety. As long as they maintained the Old Ways, they would be under his protection. He then climbed into the Viper and drove off while the shaman shook a rattle and chanted a prayer thanking him.

Xavi drove across the border past Tucson to the Colorado River where he hijacked a truck carrying pesticides and drove it into the river, poisoning the water supply for decades. He sped his Viper up I-10 to Tucson where he blew up the Salt River water works, forcing people to drink untreated water from the farmlands to the north. Many of them would sicken and die. In San Diego, he blew up a Navy munitions dump on the waterfront, which started huge fires that engulfed the city.

Los Angeles was easy. He started a small fire on a hill that overlooked the city, knowing that the flames would spread quickly through the parched hillsides and suburbs and reach the heart of the city in no time. San Francisco, he destroyed, not for the first time, with an earthquake, Seattle with a typhoon, and Anchorage with a deep freeze that would last for months. He boarded a flight full of Russians fleeing the chaos and landed in Vladivostok where he burned down the warehouses holding the food supplies, resulting in a riot that would destroy the city. He broke into a lab in Seoul, stole a vial of anthrax, and spread the infection in Peking, Shanghai, Taipei, Manilla, then onto the coastal cities of Australia. For now, he was concentrating on the major cities. Later, he would make another pass to pick up the smaller towns. He knew what he was doing. He enjoyed his work. This was necessary housecleaning, humans having become so numerous, destructive, and immoral that they needed to be drastically pruned back.

However, he took the liberty of sparing indigenous tribes who'd kept their old ways of living. Besides the Yaqui, Tepehuán, Navajo, Hopi and other native North American peoples, he spared the Yakuts, the Buryat, the Chukchi and Khakas, Yupic and Mansi of north Asia, as well as the Dayak, Iban, Murut and Bunong in Southeast Asia, the Amish and Seventh Day Adventists in North America, and the many holy men and women in their isolated monasteries and retreats. In Africa, he spared many traditional peoples, including the Bambenga, Bambuti, Batwa of the Congo basin, and in the central Sahara, he spared the Tuareg. He also sent a quick warning to deserving individual congregations such as Reverend Sheffield's in southern California. He knew that by granting these exceptions he was violating his charge to destroy the species that was destroying Creation, but he made the decision that the people who were trying to live their traditional life in harmony with nature, should not be punished for the sins of the modern world. If Xavi had to, he would defend his decision to the Old Man, but he felt it was in his discretion to decide which peoples lived and which didn't.

He also knew that his alliance with the Old Man was over. Jehovah, Jeb, YHWH, Jove, Zeus, God the Father, Elah, Odin, the Sky God who had over 650 names in the many tribes and nations of the world had had a good run these many thousands of years, but Xavi could feel the power slipping away from the Old Man. The female gods were rising again. Gaia and her daughters Maria, Houtu, Mat Zemlya, Prithvi and the Spider Grandmother were reclaiming the earth. Beside them would be his consort Kali, who oversees death, time, and change. She would be the warrior-defender of the mother-gods. The time of Jehovah and Lucifer was passing, and the male power in the future would be Jesu, his friend Jesse, the God of Loving-Kindness. In this spirit, Xavi was sparing the humans who had respected the old ways and the old goddesses. He believed it would be a new and better world.

Epilogue: Mighty Dharma

Dharma woke with a start and looked around. It was dark, and she didn't know where she was. This wasn't the cave where she lived with Stefan most of her life, or Christina's apartment where she and Stefan had settled the year before. The smells here were strongly canine, and the sounds were the deep sighs of contented dogs snuggled together. Then she remembered she was sleeping with the other dogs in the crawl space below Concepción's house. But Dharma knew something was wrong. Baby Francisco was in danger.

Dharma squirmed between the other dogs and emerged in front of the house. She sniffed the front steps, but she detected only the scent of Eduardo, Concepción, Christina, and Stefan. She listened and could hear Stefan's heavy rhythmic breath, which she knew so well, coming from the front room. She sensed Christina and Francisco peacefully sleeping beside Stefan. For the first time, she resented the rule that dogs were not allowed in the house. How could she protect her family if she were not allowed to sleep with them?

She stood alert beside the front door and looked out into the night. The moon shone down on the cornfield, each white tassel catching the light. Dharma remembered the dream that had awakened her. She trotted off into the woods behind the chapel, heading east. She would know what to do when she got where she was going.

Along the trail which led into the mountains, she came across fresh deer droppings from a doe and her fawn, laid down moments before. If she had been with her pack, they would have given chase, hoping to catch the fawn, but Dharma had more important things to do right now than to hunt deer. She lay down and rolled in the droppings, twisting and wriggling, smearing the fresh dung in her fur, especially the area under her tail. When she was satisfied that her smell was disguised, she continued trotting east toward the place up ahead she had seen in her dream.

When she came to the cliff, she scampered to the top, and settled in. From here, she could see the river and the trail that ran beside it. She waited. Eventually she saw what she was waiting for. Two large male wolves were following the river, one behind the other. Dharma could see their yellow eyes shining in the moonlight. As they passed below the cliff, they stopped and the lead one who was larger than the other, stopped and looked up in Dharma's direction. The two wolves sniffed the air, then satisfied with what they sensed, continued down the path.

Once they were out of sight down the trail, Dharma descended from the cliff and followed them. She knew she was no match for either of these large wolves, let alone both, so stealth and cunning were called for. She'd grown up on the streets of a violent city, and she'd been trained by Abraham the Patriarch in guerilla warfare, so she knew a thing or two about fighting against a superior foe. She pushed down her fear and thought about baby Francisco. She was ready to die to protect him.

She had met wolves before and gotten along with them. She knew that these two assassins were not ordinary wolves. No wolf would come into a human village to kill a baby. These were demons disguised as wolves. She followed them for a while, traveling slightly faster than they, slowly catching up to them. Eventually, she saw them up ahead, moving single file along the narrow trail. Then a plan came to her, and she knew what she was going to do.

When she was fifty yards behind the two wolves, she lengthened her stride, then switched into full cheetah mode, leaping down the trail, stretching her body faster and faster. The wolf heard her coming only moments before Dharma hit him, fangs bared, tearing the wolf's anus wide open, knocking him down, yelping in pain. Then Dharma turned and ran back the way she'd come, running as fast as she could. She knew she'd wounded the wolf badly and he'd be in no shape to continue his mission. The other wolf, realizing they'd been ambushed, gave chase, planning to kill Dharma. The wolf's long legs carried him quickly down the trail. Dharma knew he was faster than she was, but she was hoping to lead him far away from Francisco.

She could feel the big male gaining on her. In a face-to-face fight, he could easily kill her, but she was more agile. She zigzagged in tight turns, staying out of the reach of his powerful jaws. She ran down the river trail until it petered out, and she headed up the slope away from the river with him close behind. They ran through the dark woods until dawn came, streaking the treetops with light. She was panting hoarsely. She knew she couldn't run much further. When she came to a clearing, she stopped and turned. He would kill her, but she hoped to wound him, so he wouldn't be able to walk the long distance to the village. She thought of Francisco asleep beside his mother, and Christina and Stefan who would surely die protecting him.

The wolf was running quickly across the meadow toward Dharma. She could see murder in his eyes when suddenly a dark winged shape struck the wolf from above. Dharma saw a red-tailed hawk, wings stretched out longer than a man's height, rising in the sunlight, turning and coming back at the wolf who had blood running from one eye. A wolf is defenseless against an attack from the sky. The wolf looked up in terror as the hawk descended again, traveling at a frightening speed. The hawk struck again, raking her talons across the face of the wolf who yelped in pain and ran for the cover of woods. The hawk landed in the top of a pine tree, perched, standing guard in case the wolf returned.

Dharma knew that Francisco was safe. With one wolf maimed and the other half blind, they would have to abandon their mission. But she also knew that this wasn't the last time Francisco would be in danger. Nor was it the last time Gaia intervened.

About the Author

MICHAEL SIMMS is an accomplished poet, writer, editor, publisher, teacher, blogger and entrepreneur. Seven collections of his poetry, five novels, and two widely adopted poetry textbooks have been published or are under contract with publishers. He has also been the lead editor of over 100 published books, including the bestselling *Autumn House Anthology of Poetry*, now in its third edition. Simms has taught at a number of universities, including Chatham University's MFA program from 2005-2013.

www.ingramcontent.com/pod-product-compliance
Lightning Source LLC
LaVergne TN
LVHW030918080826
845145LV00013B/2954

* 9 7 8 1 9 6 3 6 9 5 4 5 8 *